Salvage  Pirates

Rabaul and the *Hakkai Maru* Treasure

Fritz Herscheid

Salvage Pirates: Rabaul and the *Hakkai Maru* Treasure

Paperback Edition first published 2020
ISBN: 978-0-6489591-0-6

E-book Edition first published 2020
ISBN: 978-0-6489591-1-3

All Rights Reserved.

Copyright @ 2020 Fritz Herscheid

i

Dedication

For my lovely wife June, who makes everything possible.

And my brother Peter, a kindred spirit for always being there when I need him.

Also by Fritz Herscheid

The Last New Guinea Salvage Pirate
Paperback edition available from Amazon .com (USA)
ISBN 9798688180503.

Kindle e-book editions are available on *Amazon*

Acknowledgements

I would like to thank Geoffrey Ainsworth for proofreading. Geoff has a quirk for spotting grammar and spelling mistakes from 100 yards. Thanks!

Foreword

This book is what I like to call a 'reality fiction', meaning that it's based on historically accurate events. However, the names of most characters have been changed to protect the innocent and not-so-innocent. Suffice to say, any resemblance to actual events, locales, or persons, living or dead, is entirely coincidental.

***

It's set in the early 1970s, when scuba diving was still in its infancy. A diver was usually taught by someone who was ex-navy or who hadn't died trying. The *US Navy Diver's Manual* was the diver's 'Bible'. Internationally recognised diving schools, such as PADI, FAUI, BSAC, together with their more onerous rules, were yet to appear in New Guinea.

Ship's navigation was still an art form, driven by sextant, chart, pencil and paper, running fixes, hourly logbook entries and chart notations, and dead-reckoning. The luxury of GPS navigation was still waiting to be invented.

Navigating the dangerous and poorly charted coastal waters of the Pacific islands necessitated a strict routine of watches for the 'officers', and usually two hours on and six hours off for the helmsman. Reliable autopilots for small ships were yet to be perfected.

Rabaul and the *Hakkai Maru* Treasure

Life on a small boat could be interesting. There was little privacy, and one had to learn to live with the idiosyncrasies of others. If someone was humping a girlfriend, everyone knew about it, and some would try to get in on the action. The daily attire aboard salvage vessels was very casual, usually Speedos for the guys, and bikinis for the girls.

Buying powerful but volatile nitroglycerine-based explosives was never a problem, and licences to use them easy to obtain. Every small ship and this is especially true of salvage vessels, had an arsenal of weaponry. Ex-army .303s were popular, and powerful. Surplus WW2 ammunition was cheap and readily available. They were also easily converted into pistols and modified for use underwater, mainly for protection against sharks. No licence was required for any rifle.

It's also a time when men worked hard, long hours and played even harder, a time when the man was the hunter and women the hunted. Australian women were now slowly starting to embrace the contraceptive pill, and with their newfound sexual freedom, many were eager to be hunted. Pinching a woman on the bum was not yet considered to be sexual harassment.

No one gave a second thought to anyone walking street carrying a rifle or going into the local to buy ammunition or dynamite. No – just hitchhike.

We relished the freedom of riding motorbikes without helmets. Gun paranoia and the hypocrisy of Women's Liberation movements were all still in their infancy. Simon and Garfunkle ruled the airwaves with 'Bridge Over Troubled Waters', and we enjoyed the Beatles with 'Let it be'. It was a more straightforward, less-regulated and complicated world. I think, in many ways a better, more exciting world.

Fritz Herscheid

Table of Contents

Introduction

The Hakkai Maru

The Hakkai Maru and her sister ship, Myoko Maru, were built by Tama Zosensho K.K., at Tamano, Japan for Itaya Goyo Shosen K.K. Tokyo. She (or 'He,' as the Japanese say) had a gross tonnage of 5,124 GRT, a length of 422 ft, a beam of 58 ft, and a draft of 27.2 ft fully loaded. Her fuel capacity was 1,298 tons. She was a modern diesel-motor vessel of 855 N. P. H., which drove a single propeller giving her a cruising speed of 14 kn and was capable of a maximum speed of 16.5 kn. The Hakkai had a working radius of 25,000 nautical miles at 14 kn. In March 1941 she was taken over by the Japanese navy and converted to a Navy repair and salvage vessel. She was also fitted with a large foundry and refinery in the forward hold. The prime purpose of this was the smelting of plundered, precious metals.

The Crew of The *MV Scorpion*

Skipper

Simon Jaeger's family migrated to Australia from Germany in the early 1950s when he was just six years old. He was schooled and grew up in Australia. Starting life in a new country at such a young age had its challenges. In time, anything that may have been European was thrashed out of him as he slowly acquired all the usual Australian habits and mannerisms, both good and bad. The one thing that didn't change was his blond hair and blue eyes.

As a teenager, he was part of the first group in Australia to take up the martial arts of karate. This discipline and his neighbourhood mates helped to build his self-esteem and shape his character.

From his first tentative forays into the ocean waters spearfishing, he fell in love with the underwater world. Scuba diving naturally followed, and it was ultimately the warm waters of Rabaul, with its magnificent and largely untouched deep shipwrecks in the harbour, that sealed his future.

The Skipper's Guest

Julie McVey, '**Blondie**' to her friends, was a real stunner in every way. She was exceptionally beautiful and had an amazing personality. In the physical sense, she was perfect. Her looks were stunning, she had full, round breasts, a tiny waist, gorgeous legs, and straight, long blond hair. She had poise and in every sense was a sophisticated and sexy young lady – every man's dream woman.

She had no specific role on the boat except to enjoy herself, and above all, keep the skipper happy. She was not entitled to a share of the salvage profits, so on that score, there was no jealousy from the crew. They all agreed, she was a pleasure to have on board and brought some excitement, beauty, and class to the boat.

Engineer

Tony Thomas, our Pommy ship's engineer and diver, he was the oldest of the White crew, skinny as a rake, pockmarked face, and a two- or three-pack-a-day smoker. He was the classic Pom in every sense of the word.

He was also the most unlikely member of the crew; he was married and faithful to his wife. He was not one to go skinny dipping with the crew, a very strait-laced guy. But he was an expert diesel mechanic and small-ship engineer. He certainly knew his way around an engine room.

He was not the most fearless of divers. If he had to do anything, he thought was dangerous, you could hear him muttering right until his head disappeared below the surface. I can bet he was still at it underwater. His carrying-on was a constant source of amusement.

However, we gave him credit for his willingness to carry out any task put before him, despite his fears. It seems that overcoming adversity is a strong Pommy trait. Maybe that's why they won the war!

The Divers

Will (Garth) Ramsden was a very experienced deep air diver and totally fearless, a solo diver day or night. Born in North Queensland, he was a farmer boy who wasn't nicknamed 'Garth' for nothing. If you've ever read the 60s comic strip of the same name, you'll understand why. He had the body and looks that most men wish for and women crave – tall and handsome with curly dark hair and built like a brick shithouse. In the year 2000, he'd be a match for Arnold Schwarzenegger, only much better looking.

We often called upon his exceptional strength. He was, however, somewhat lacking in the empathy department. He didn't suffer fools lightly and tended to get into arguments. I could never understand how it was that he got along with John.

Lindsay Hill was also a deep air diver solo diver who was capable of 90 metres (300ft) plus air dives without any apparent effects of narcosis or oxygen poisoning. He was a tall, skinny guy, but wiry with seemingly unlimited stamina...but having said that, most commercial divers would fit that description.

His usually ruffled and uncombed dark blond hair hung down to his shoulders. A good-looking guy in a rugged sort of way, and with his charm and easy-going manner, he had no trouble attracting the ladies. His diving skills were second to none, a fearless diver capable of extreme depths. He was also very knowledgeable in the use of explosives.

Boat Crew

John Clark was ex-navy (SMN), and his main functions onboard were the operation and care of the dive tender, diving equipment, and general shipboard duties. He was also our enforcer. At just 5'6' (168cm) tall, he had a round, moon face, which was always badly shaven, and was built like a beer barrel with match sticks for legs. He was a thrashing machine when it came to fighting, and his solid body could take a lot of punishment. He was absolutely fearless when it came to meeting any opponent regardless of size and when necessary, could be utterly ruthless. He would break a bone or take out an eye without a second thought.

His heavily tattooed body, long mullet haircut, and his very apparent mean disposition meant getting a legitimate job was virtually impossible. So, to him, the boat and its crew were his family and home. He was not the brightest cherry on the tree, but interestingly, he got on well with everyone on board – except when drunk.

Papua New Guinea Crew

Joe was chief helmsman and performed general ship duties. He was also an occasional shallow water diver. He had been with me for many years, and I trusted him implicitly. Joe was a Wari Islander, a man of great stature. He was tall, well built, and handsome. Joe also had a good command of English, and his knowledge of local reefs and anchorages was excellent. He was a friendly and extremely likeable guy.

Jack was also a helmsman and attended to general ship's duties. Jack was also a Wari Islander, and like Joe, I also taught him to dive with both hookah and scuba. Like most of his clan, he was at home in the water. He was a short, stocky man, well built, and strong, but Jack had a very different demeanour than Joe. Jack was more the archetypical man with a chip on his shoulder. He was often quite surly and quick to scowl when things didn't please him. But in the days when there were no reliable autopilots, having a good helmsman was very important, so we learned to live with his idiosyncrasies.

Cookie, as the name suggests, was the ship's cook, and also cabin boy and occasional helmsmen. He found it difficult to get work because of a clubfoot. It just so happened that one day we were desperate for a cook, so I put the word out while in Samarai. He was the only one who applied. It was a short expedition to Jomard, so with some reservation, I put him on. It turned out to be the right decision. Apart from us getting used to his limping around, his bad foot didn't seem to hamper him much at all. He was grateful for the job and turned out to be a hard and loyal worker. He was from Samarai Island, and also the oldest person on board.

Milne Bay boys, overall, were popular as boat crew in New Guinea as most had a missionary education and spoke reasonable English. They also had excellent seamanship skills and local reef knowledge. More importantly, they were, on the whole, a good-natured and friendly people.

Fritz Herscheid

The Emperor's 'Golden Lily' Syndicate And The Japanese Navy

The stunningly successful way the Japanese army and navy had looted its way across China was ultimately not lost on the Japanese Imperial family. So it was, that in 1940, in conjunction with other privileged families, the Imperial family created a top-secret organisation codenamed 'Golden Lily'.

The single aim of the organisation was to rape conquered countries of their precious metals and gems and funnel the wealth to the Imperial family and other favoured families in Japan. The organisation was headed by Emperor Hirohito's brothers, Prince Chichibu and Prince Takeda.

According to history, the plunder of countries occupied by the Japanese was absolute and total. The Japanese army and the private army of Emperor Hirohito went on a pillaging and looting spree that was unparalleled in modern history. This included China, Manchuria, Thailand, Burma, Malaya, Borneo, New Guinea, Singapore, the Dutch Indies, in fact, everywhere they went.

They systematically emptied treasuries, banks, factories, monasteries, temples, museums, pawnshops, art galleries, private homes – nothing was sacred. Even the bodies of the dead were violated. Gold teeth were ripped out; fingers with rings were cut off. This amassing of treasure continued right until the day Japan surrendered.

The International Court of Justice in the Hague declared that the Japanese had looted approximately 250,000 metric tons of natural resources, including copper, lead, tin, zinc, rubber, oil, and rice from South-east Asia and the broader Pacific region.

According to various post-war estimates, a conservative figure of gold bullion looted by the Japanese was between 4,000 and 6,000 tons. Speculation over the years on the total worth of this war loot ranged up to $3 billion in 1940s dollars, the equivalent of well over $100 billion today. However, the 6,000 tons estimate does not take into account the 'Black Gold' that was and still is, rampant in Asia.

Throughout history, Asians have had contempt for paper money. Add to this 6,000 tons the more significant sum of 'Black Money' that existed in Asia such as unreported assets, criminal profits, black market proceeds, and secret hordes of gold and gems. These are estimated to have been three or four times as much as the official figure. As an example of Asians dislike of paper money, during the war, even Japanese officers required payment in either precious metals or gems.

The Japanese looting was in direct contravention of the Hague Conventions of 1899 and 1907 to which, incidentally, Japan was a signatory. The convention obliges military forces not only to avoid the destruction of enemy property but to provide protection for it.

Theoretically, to prevent such looting, unclaimed property is moved to the safekeeping of the 'Custodian of Enemy Property' to be taken care of until it can be returned to its rightful owner.

Since the looting was illegitimate, the Japanese needed to disguise the stolen treasure as quickly as possible. All semi-precious metals and coinage were quite openly melted into ingots at Japanese-run, land-based smelters.

However, for more precious and valuable metals such as gold, platinum, and silver, more secrecy was called for. So, the Japanese came up with a plan to convert suitable freighters into refinery ships. They chose the most modern and fastest freighters for that purpose. These ships were usually cleverly disguised; this way they could operate mostly undetected in occupied territories.

Most of the converted Japanese freighters worked in southern Asia including Borneo and the Dutch Indies. One such ship was the *Hakkai Maru*.

The *Hakkai* was a modern, diesel-powered merchant vessel launched in 1938. She was virtually new and capable of a top speed of 16.5 knots. In 1941, she was requisitioned by the Japanese navy and 'officially' converted to an auxiliary Navy repair ship. However, she was also fitted with three large modern furnaces and kilns in the forward hold.

The *Hakkai* was also the only refinery vessel known to have operated in New Guinea waters, and we only know this because she was sunk there! Most of the refinery ships worked exclusively in southern Asia and the Philippines.

In the early days of the war, the *Hakkai* also spent much of her time cruising Asian waters, including Indonesia. In late 1942, she returned to Japan for further modifications to enhance her submarine-repair and service capability. She also carried additional stores such as torpedos, etc. Her submarine-repair role was fast becoming more and more important.

After her refit in early 1943, she went to the gold-rich Russian Kuril Islands. On the 12th November 1943, she was sent to New Guinea waters. Her career came to an unexpected and abrupt end on the 17th of January 1944. She was hit in the engine room by a massive skip bomb that almost tore her in half. She sank quickly by the stern and now sits upright on the bottom of Rabaul Harbour.

Salvage Pirates

Rabaul and the *Hakkai Maru* Treasure

Fritz Herscheid

Chapter 1

Rabaul and the *Hakkai Maru* Treasure

M y name is Simon Jaeger, I am the owner and captain of the salvage vessel the *MV Scorpion*, and this is the story about the recovery of the treasure from the *Hakkai Maru* in Rabaul harbour, New Guinea.

* * *

I had no idea of the extent to which the Japanese Navy and Army had plundered the riches of the countries they conquered, nor had I ever heard of the Emperor's 'Golden Lily Syndicate', or the Japanese refinery ships.

Until one day, while researching the Manila Galleons at the University of Sydney library, I accidentally stumbled across a reference to the Japanese looting of Asia and the gold refinery ships, this was interesting.

As I read on, the name of one ship struck me like a ton of bricks – the *Hakkai Maru*. In all the wartime records, she was only listed as a submarine repair ship, but now I might just have discovered her real, but clandestine role.

I had dived the *Hakkai* a few times. She was a beautiful ship but of no interest to me from a salvage or scrap perspective. Her propeller was missing, having been blown off by a local operator. Being a modern-diesel vessel meant that there was very little copper piping on the ship. Most importantly, her heat-exchanger would only amount to a few tonnes of scrap copper, simply too much effort for the reward.

Discovering that the *Hakkai* may have had the capacity to refine gold was exciting, and it put a whole new perspective on the wreck. I began thinking, according to the records, she had sunk very quickly, and her loss was completely unexpected. It follows that if there was gold on board the ship, the crew might not have had enough time to remove it before she slipped below the surface. Now, that was enough to gladden the heart of any salvage pirate.

Escaping the miserable weather, we were experiencing at Samarai, the lure of the chase, and the possibility of striking it rich was all the excuses I needed to make a trip to Rabaul. It was time for me to convince the crew that we should consider spending some quality time in Rabaul and do a spot of treasure hunting while there.

In the salvage business, moving from one project to another can sometimes be challenging. Salvage crews sign on for one specific project at a time, from beginning to end. They are not paid a wage, only a percentage of the salvage proceeds. Any changes to the itinerary and the possible loss of income had to be agreed to by all. However, on this occasion, I didn't expect too much trouble convincing them. There were already grumbles about the weather and lack of scrap coming on board. The South-East trade winds had been blowing hard for months, and our time for working the wreck per week was measured in hours, not days.

As it was, the *MV Scorpion* had already left the windy and uncomfortable reef anchorage near the wreck and was now safely in the calm, all-weather anchorage at Kwato mission. Here we were only a couple of miles from Samarai Island and at least some form of civilisation, especially the Samarai Club and friendly local ladies.

The rotten local weather, together with the lack of scrap coming on board, and the thrill of returning to Rabaul, not to mention the possibility of millions of dollars in gold and silver, easily clinched the deal with the crew. It was agreed as soon as there was a lull in the weather, we would make a run for Rabaul.

Chapter 2

Samarai to Rabaul

Anyone, who has experienced it will tell you that bad weather when at sea, is always more frightening and feels worse at night. No matter how rough it gets during the day, it just always seems worse at night. Not being able to see and then compensate for the rogue waves is always a worry. Now, as the Trobriand Islands slowly slipped past our stern, and we entered the Solomon Sea, the southeast swells gradually become larger and closer together.

Soon the wind picked up, and it began to whip the tops of the waves. I now almost regretted leaving the calm anchorage at Boli Point at Kiriwina Island. And if that wasn't bad enough, the seas were now coming at us directly on beam, and the *Scorpion* was rolling mercilessly.

From my bunk, I watched in silent amusement as Joe, the helmsman, stood spreadeagled wrestling to keep the ship's course while trying to take the larger waves on our forequarter. It took a lot of skill in these conditions. I could not help wondering how Tony, our landlubber engineer, and John, my enforcer, were faring. Both were prone to seasickness.

My bunk was in the wheelhouse. I'd strategically positioned myself against the scupper to stop myself from falling out. Blondie was in the bunk with me, and thankfully, she was fast asleep and oblivious to it all. She was securely tucked in behind me. As long as I didn't fall out, she was going to be okay.

I had scored a nice bit of flesh there. She was a real stunner, some 55 kg, long blond hair, magnificent little body, shapely legs, and perky tits. She was a trophy I wanted to keep – well, for a while, at least.

I first spotted her in the Port Moresby Yacht Club. I immediately tried to strike up a conversation, only to be told in no uncertain terms to 'bugger-off'. She said she was engaged to a patrol officer. My ego was bruised, and it only made me more determined not to be fobbed off so easily. The *Scorpion* was going to be on the slip for at least a week for a refit. I was confident that it would give me enough time to penetrate her defences.

I was smitten and wasn't going to let this stunning little horn-bag get away that easily. So, every day I returned to the club, and every time I saw her, I persisted with planned, but seemingly accidental, encounters. Sometimes, there was a short, dark-haired guy with her. He would often be holding her hand, so I suspected he was her fiancé. As the days went by and familiarity crept in, the scowls were replaced by a simple 'Hi' and sometimes a smile. Then one fateful day, the 'Hi' turned into a full-blown conversation. She told me that her fiancé had left for a three-month patrol to the remote highlands. He told her it was an opportunity he couldn't refuse, and then simply left her to her own devices in Port Moresby. She was seriously pissed-off. I could feel the venom in her voice. I made the most of it by going in for the kill.

'How on earth could he leave a defenceless woman in a dangerous shithole like Moresby?' I asked, and that was no bullshit.

She looked at the floor as tears welled in her eyes.

'Seriously,' I said, 'How on earth could anyone do this to someone so beautiful and vulnerable. I would never leave any women, let alone someone like you, in such a dangerous place.' ...but that wasn't entirely true!

I thought she was going to cry. All she could say was, 'Really, what am I going to do?' as she put her head on my shoulder.

She did look beautiful, but at the moment, she also looked small and vulnerable. I had to pull myself together. I was starting to feel sorry for her. Shit, I must be getting soft! Better concentrate on the skimpy pink shift dress and her bare nipples that were now poking into my chest.

'Just look at you,' I said, slowly moving her away at arm's length and looking deep into her eyes. 'You are magnificent; there's no one in this club that looks anywhere near as spectacular as you.' I changed tact and said. 'Let's have a drink and celebrate your freedom,' as I lead her to a quiet table.

The drinks and conversation flowed freely, and I could sense victory was in my grasp. Many of her drinks were double strength, and it was not long before she was getting very animated and playful. I took the plunge and suggested she might like to come and have a look at the *Scorpion,* which was now alongside Steamships Jetty.

She was drunk, but still in charge. 'Why not? I'd like that,' she said.

A short taxi ride later and a few more stiff drinks on the back deck, and it was time to show her the bridge and my bunk. A few passionate kisses and fondling, and as quick as that, she was naked in my bunk. After that encounter, I knew that I wanted to keep her.

In the morning, I suggested that there was nothing to keep her in Moresby now, and she might enjoy cruising the tropical islands of New Guinea. Believe me, *Adventures in Paradise* is dull in comparison to the picture I painted.

Her world had collapsed. She was alone in an unfriendly city, and she felt deeply rejected by her now ex-fiancé. The truth is, there was nothing to keep her in Port Moresby now. My offer of a tropical island adventure was a means of escape. She could see that the *Scorpion* was a good-sized and comfortable vessel. So, without too much ado, she agreed. So, that's how it came to be, with the rocking and rolling motion of the boat, that her perky little tits were now rubbing into my back.

We could expect another six hours in this infernal washing machine before the sun came up. Experience had taught me that, at sunrise, it would just feel like just another bad dream. Joe's voice woke me. I glanced at my watch, and it was 4:00 am. I could hear him whispering to Jack, who was taking his turn at the wheel. I took note that the boat's movements were not quite as violent as before, and it felt like the wind had died down. I quickly nodded back off to sleep.

It was 5.30 a.m. when I awoke. The monotonous rhythm of the main engine reverberated reassuringly throughout the boat, but that was not all that was throbbing. So, I made sure the curtains to our bunk were closed and gently turned Blondie around. I couldn't help thinking what a great arse, just before I thrust deep inside her.

9

I had never met a woman so willing to have sex, anywhere, anytime. Soon, she was keeping rhythm with me and quietly groaning. She reached back, digging her fingernails into my arse. That ensured it would not be long before I did my number. What a great way to start the day!

The golden glow in the eastern sky signalled the beginning of a new day. Soon the sun would creep over the horizon, and everything would be better. I took the wheel and asked Jack to wake Cookie and get him to bring me a coffee and start getting breakfast ready. A few minutes later, Jack returned and resumed his stint at the wheel, and I moved to the chart table to study the charts. Cookie limped up the ladder and into the wheelhouse with my coffee.

With the sun now just over the horizon, the New Britain coastline was visible in the distance. Well actually, what we were seeing was the mountain ranges. It would be some time before we saw the coast. However, it was reassuring to see land in the distance.

We were still some 35 nautical miles offshore. I could, at this point, have chosen to change course to starboard, making for a slightly shorter trip. But by maintaining our current course and getting closer to shore, we would enjoy a more comfortable cruise to Rabaul.

Tony came onto the bridge deck with his cup of tea and seemed to be surprised to see land. He surveyed the horizon, 'How long do you reckon before we reach the coast and get out this bloody sea on the forequarter?' he asked.

'About four hours,' I replied.

He glanced towards my bunk with a smirk on his face. 'How's Blondie handling it?'

'She'll be okay. I stuffed my pillow under her back to help stop her from rolling out,' I replied.

Tony chuckled as he bent over the chart table to check our latest position marks. 'I'll go down to the galley and check on Cookie and see how he's going with breakfast. What you want?' he asked as he got up to leave.

'Bacon and a couple of eggs on toast will do me,' I replied. And with that, Tony left the wheelhouse.

A short time later, a shout from below told me that breakfast was ready. The galley was at the rear of the boat and opened up to the back deck. The table and benches took up the whole width of the stern section. It was a convenient and comfortable set-up.

My breakfast was waiting for me, and only then did I realise just how hungry I was. Cookie handed me a fresh cup of coffee, and I was enjoying my breakfast when John stuck his head around the corner.

'Morning everyone, I'll have some Weet-Bix and a white coffee with three sugars, Cookie,' He bellowed in his typical, loud, cheerful way as he sat down.

John Clark had been with me for over a year now. He was a short, barrel-chested, thickset man of great strength. He was the black sheep of his family and viewed much the same by the crew. Most of them were very guarded when around him.

John was an ex-Navy seaman, dishonourably discharged for striking an officer. His other exploits included being an ex-motorcycle gang member, and he had served time for attempted murder, grievous bodily harm, theft, ... the list goes on. Except for Blondie, he was the only non-diving member of the White crew. He was petrified of sharks, and, in fact, he was terrified of just about anything in the ocean!

His duties onboard were simple, but they took a massive load off the divers. First and foremost was to ensure that the dive tender was ready at all times. His other duties included filling the scuba tanks and ensuring the dive regulators were clean and prepared for the next day. Like the Wari boys, he also had deckhand and helm duties.

The job he relished the most was being my hitman. It seemed to give him pleasure to inflict pain. I've never met anyone like him. He could be laughing and joking one minute and totally and utterly ruthless the next. When asked to do so, he would break a person's arm or poke their eyes out. No questions asked.

It's interesting how we became acquainted and the reasons for his misguided loyalty to me. One afternoon after many hours at the Sydney University library studying shipwrecks, I was on my way to King's Cross in Sydney for some amusement. I'd been unable to find the car park close to the Cross and had to park a short distance away. As I was walking towards the Cross through some dingy alleyways, I came across a group of thugs beating the shit out of a little fat guy.

It didn't look right, so as I got closer, I sang out 'Hey! What the fuck's going on here?'

And with that said, two of the men immediately peeled off from kicking the little guy and made advances to me, telling me to 'fuck off', or I'd be in for the same. But it was to be their unlucky day. Little did they know that I was a black belt in the art of karate.

I easily blocked the first guy's clumsy round-house punch and dispatched him very smartly with a blow to the throat that left him gasping for breath. The second guy went down almost immediately afterwards with a beautifully timed sidekick that smashed into his knee. The crack was like a rifle shot.

These guys must have been really dumb. A third thought he could do better than his friends, but he was dispatched almost as quickly with a knuckle punch that smashed his nose. Blood exploded all over his face and into his eyes, blinding him, and before he could react, a knee straight to his balls left him groaning and rolling on the ground.

By this time, the little guy, who I could now see was more stocky then fat, had recovered somewhat and was getting stuck into the other two. It was comical to watch, head back, chest puffed forward, his arms were punching like pistons – crude but effective.

It was his thickset body that had enabled him to withstand the punishment that the thugs had been levelling at him. Moments later, they were limping away into the dark, making threats as they went. And, as quickly as that, the fight was over.

I invited him to join me for a drink, which he accepted. Holding out his hand, he said, 'Thanks, I'm John. Who are you?'

'My name's, Simon, 'I said with a smile, shaking his hand. 'Pleased to meet you, John.' I noticed he had a very firm grip.

Later, at a popular girlie bar, I got his long story. He had joined the navy after school but found the discipline difficult. He was dishonourably discharged for bashing a young, snot-nosed officer. Back on shore, he drifted into a bikie gang, which was making a fortune selling drugs, and life was good for him. A turf war ended all that, and he got caught stabbing a rival bikie member in the neck and subsequently landed in jail.

He had just been released from Long Bay jail a few hours earlier after serving a two-year sentence, which he described was for 'assault occasioning actual bodily harm'. He was on his way to the Cross to party, but mainly to find a prostitute, when some rival gang members recognised him and jumped him. After a couple of beers, I discovered that he had nowhere to go and no home. Although he was not the brightest cherry on the tree, I thought his boating skills and laid-back attitude to breaking bones might be an asset to us on the boat. So, I asked him if he would like to join us in New Guinea. His answer was a simple, 'Sounds good to me. Got nowhere else to go.'

Now some twelve months later, John had proven himself an invaluable member of the crew. He takes care of the 100 other menial tasks that the divers or I would otherwise have to do.

Seated on the back deck, John turned towards me and mumbled with a mouthful of Weet-Bix made with disgusting powdered milk, 'How long before we change course and get this damn sea off our beam and stop this bloody rocking?'

'Won't be long now,' I replied, 'Probably a couple of hours. I want to get as close to the coast as possible before changing course for Cape Orford. That way we'll have a much calmer ride to Rabaul.'

'How long before we get there?'

'It'll take about 20 hours for us to make Rabaul. We should be at anchor around two in the morning,' I said.

The monotony of life on board continued as the nautical miles slowly slipped under the keel. The two-hour watches for the crew and my checking our position every hour by running fixes or the sextant was all that there was.

It was around midday when Blondie surfaced, hair unkempt, but in a very sexy way. She was dressed to kill in a skimpy bikini. Fuck! I was going to have to watch the crew!

After a late breakfast, she went made her way to the top deck where she lay stretched out on her deckchair trying to get a tan – topless, of course. Her perky nipples were reaching for the sky. I was watching her through the rear window of the wheelhouse while checking the charts. *Shit, she looked good!* My thoughts were interrupted by Garth, who had also just surfaced from his cabin.

It was almost time for his two-hour stint at the wheel. Garth was my big worry when it came to Blondie. He was a tall, handsome guy, 24 years old, and with miles of testosterone and muscles to spare. It was the muscle between his legs that worried me.

Garth had been with me on several salvage expeditions. He was an absolute whiz kid at repairing or making all sorts of things. He'd become fond of inventing booby-traps ever since an episode we had with a competitor while working the American submarine *S39* at Rossel Island.

Now, I wasn't so sure that having him on board was a good idea. He was a real lady's man, smooth as silk. I would have to watch him very carefully, especially if Blondie has had a bit too much to drink. I get the feeling she tends to be anybody's then.

Right on cue, we changed course. With the sea now on our starboard forequarter, it was much more comfortable. We were now hugging the New Britain coast and once again settled into the routine of steering watches and course corrections. When not on watch or the helm, there was always a game of backgammon or chess to help pass the time. Tony, however, was usually busy when we were underway. He was always covered in sweat and grime, checking things in the engine room and regularly pumping the bilges.

At 9:30 p.m., right on cue, the regular and reassuring flash of the Cape Gazelle lighthouse came into view. We were now only a few hours from our destination. Knowing these waters well, I set a course to run close to the lighthouse while rounding the Cape. After that, I will be able to change course directly for Rabaul Harbour. And in just four hours, we will be anchoring in dead calm water a hundred yards from the Rabaul Yacht Club.

17

Chapter 3

Rabaul

It was an uncanny feeling waking up in the morning; my brain needed time to adjust to the change of circumstances. From day after day, listening to the continuous and monotonous roar of the 300hp Caterpillar diesel and the incessant rocking and rolling. To the boat being absolutely motionless and deadly dead-quiet.

Glancing at Blondie peacefully sleeping beside me as I rolled out of the bunk. I stopped a while to admire her naked body so beautiful and flawless – hair askew and utterly dead to the world. As I gently slipped the sheet over her, I couldn't help thinking, *How could anyone sleep so much?* I tapped her on the arse and went to survey my surroundings.

Standing on the bridge deck and soaking up the scenery, I could not help but be in awe of this magnificent harbour. No matter how many times I experienced it, it never failed to mesmerise me.

In the early morning hours, the waters glistened like a shining mirror. There was hardly a ripple to disturb the reflection of the surrounding mountains and smouldering volcano. It felt like a powerful magic had cast a spell and stopped time. There was a large freighter tied up alongside the main wharf, some smaller inter-island coasters, and smaller pleasure craft riding at anchor, several local native families fishing from their canoes – a beautiful and tranquil scene.

I lazily made my way down to the galley and put the kettle on the stove. While waiting for it to boil, I made a quick survey of the ship. I checked the anchor and made sure everything else was shipshape before heading back to the galley to make myself a steaming, aromatic, cup of coffee. I sat down and enjoyed my coffee and the quietness of the surroundings while soaking in the ambience. It was good to be back in Rabaul.

A little later, Cookie arrived in the galley to begin preparing breakfast. The clanging of pots and pans broke the spell and spoilt the moment. It was 9:00 a.m. before the crew surfaced from their slumber and ambled out to the afterdeck. Blondie being last was no surprise. With everyone gathered and a big fresh pot of coffee brewing, we discussed the day's coming events.

Everyone, it seemed, was keen to go shoreside and have a look around the town, so I asked John to get the tender in the water and suggested a counter lunch at the Yacht Club might be in order. There, we could discuss our plans in more detail and explore Rabaul township afterwards.

We were anchored just a few hundred metres from the Yacht Club jetty, the manicured lawns and the large, covered veranda were clearly visible from our deck. It looked very inviting, especially after Samarai and months at sea. We were all looking forward to a huge steak and ice-cold beer. Our kerosene fridge on board didn't exactly keep things very cold.

There were quite a few clubs and pubs in Rabaul, but the Yacht Club was handy, being so close and easily accessible for us. The counter lunches were huge, and the beer cheap. We staggered in single file like drunken sailors down the jetty, our sea-legs not used to the level ground. It's a funny sensation as the brain tries to compensate for a movement that doesn't happen. Being the ladies man he was, Garth put his arm around Blondie to steady her, his hand creeping very close to her tit. She did the girlie thing and giggled as she pulled herself close to him. I couldn't help but look at Lindsay and raise my eyebrows. He just grinned.

We found a large table on the veranda set a little away from the main crowd and made ourselves comfortable. Blondie took our orders and went to the counter to order lunch for everybody. She used to be a waitress at some point in her life, so she had a good memory for this sort of thing. John had made a beeline directly to the bar and was already on his way back with a tray of ice-cold beer.

With everybody comfortably relaxed at the table, I glanced around to see that no one was in earshot and then described what we were up against and emphasised that it was nothing insurmountable. Still, we would have to be careful on several scores. I went on to explain.

The *Hakkai* is deep, so we have three diving options: limited decompression dives, extended deep diving, or repetitive dives. Both of the latter were dangerous and increased decompression times, and I was not a fan of repetitive dives.

I proposed that we should restrict our dives to 'limited decompression'. This would severely limit each diver's bottom time for the dive, but it was the safest option. And by diving solo and in a relay, we could increase the bottom time by the number of divers in the relay. Usually, this is necessary when placing explosives, which can be a long and tedious job.

The *Hakkai* is sitting upright on an incline with her head down. The bow is at 56 metres, and the stern at 47 metres. We will be diving on air, Mixed gas was not available to us, neither were dive computers. To ensure the best possible safety margin, we must strictly follow the *US Navy Dive Tables* when calculating our bottom time.

In our search for the kilns, those visiting the forward hold, which is at 56 metres, would restrict their bottom time to 10 minutes with a five-minute decompression at 3 metres. Those in the shallower aft hold, which is at 47 metres, can stay for 15 minutes and also do five-minute decompression at 3 metres as an added safety precaution.

When working in and around the shallower, continuous deck and cabin area, we can use the table for 42 metres. This would give each diver a good 20-minute bottom time. To err on the side of safety, we would factor in a ten-minute decompression stop at 3 metres.

Each diver would work two dives per day, one early in the morning and another in the late afternoon, effectively giving each diver 40 minutes in the water. The surface interval between the dives will enable most of the residual nitrogen to clear from our system.

'How am I doing so far? Any questions?' I asked, looking at everyone in turn. There was a nodding of heads, so I went on. 'I don't think we should tie up to the *Hakkai* buoy. A better option is to move the *Scorpion* to an anchorage close to the wreck. You know, out of sight out of mind and dive the wreck from the tender.'

Everyone agreed that being tied up directly to *Hakkai's* buoy for an extended period would only arouse curiosity and suspicion, especially if little or no scrap was coming to the surface. People would start to wonder what the hell we were doing.

I went on to say, 'I know of a good anchorage just a few hundred yards from the *Hakkai.* It's a small, sheltered cove. We can drop the anchor in 3 metres of water and very close to shore. The boys can swim ashore anytime they want and get a half-car into town.'

Utilities in New Guinea are called 'half-cars' and were the local equivalent of taxies. They were cheap transport and plentiful. Not the safest or most comfortable form of transport, but plentiful.

I turned to Garth and Lindsay, 'It's obvious that the local divers will want to talk to you guys from time to time about your diving experiences etc., and sure as eggs, the conversation will get around to what we are doing in Rabaul. Just tell them that we are going to pull a few condensers for Pat Roberts, especially the *Hakkai.*' I went on, 'It might give us some breathing space and legitimise our being on the wreck for a while, at least until we started blasting.'

'Yes, what about Pat Roberts?' Garth asked. 'Don't you think we should talk to him?'

'Absolutely, I intend to,' I replied. 'Tony and I'll go over and see him tomorrow after the morning's dive. I don't think there will be any issues about us pulling condensers for him. It's just how much he's prepared to pay.'

'Look,' I said. 'we're getting ahead of ourselves. First and foremost, we have to confirm that the *Hakkai* is indeed a refinery ship. That should be relatively easy, in fact, we should be able to do that on the first or second dive. We only need to find the kilns and smelters.'

'Finding the bloody strongroom might prove to be a bit more difficult,' Lindsay said as he downed the last of his beer.

There was a raising of eyebrows and murmur of agreement from everyone on that score.

I asked for quiet and went on. 'If we establish the *Hakkai* has smelters onboard, we are going to have to do something to keep the local divers away from the wreck for a while.'

Souveniring portholes and collecting scrap, non-ferrous items from the *Hakkai* was a popular pastime for some local divers for many years, mainly on the weekend.

'How are you going to stop them?' Tony asked.

'Very simple – booby traps, of course. Everyone knows there is a lot of unstable ammunition on board, and it has a habit of going "boom" every now and then. Everyone knows this,' I said with a wry smile. 'As soon as we get back to the *Scorpion* this afternoon, we'll move anchor close to the *Hakkai,* and

tomorrow we do our first dive. Let's hope we find what
we're looking for.'

Chapter 4

The Problems with an Illegal Treasure Hunt

No one must suspect that this is a treasure hunt, that always conjures up images of easy money. And that's especially true when it comes to my salvage competitors. If they were to find out the *Hakkai* was a gold refinery ship, they would think nothing of muscling in (as would I, if the shoe was on the other foot). And with no legal recourse to keep them away, the guns would be out, and it would be on for young and old.

A huge dilemma for any salvage pirate is that if your potentially valuable and 'illegal' project becomes common knowledge, your competitors are naturally going to try and get a bit of the action. And, if they don't steal it from you and the government finds out about it, then they will. Worse still, the government will almost certainly give you a hefty fine, and probably confiscate your boat, and throw you in jail, just for good measure!

No salvage pirate ever wants the government to become involved. The unwritten law among salvagers is that if you can't scare a competitor away with some dynamite or a few rounds of gunfire, then you're better off making a deal with them and share the work and proceeds. But deal-making is the last resort. Firstly, you use whatever means necessary to protect your turf. Usually, the winner is the one who is the most ruthless, or the one who lands the deciding blow.

My two main roving-salvage competitors in New Guinea waters were Barry and his crew on the *Mv Swan*. They are currently working a destroyer in Bougainville. The other is Dave on the barge *Santo*. The last I heard, he was working wrecks somewhere near Aitape. Both were dangerous rivals and would stop at nothing where money was concerned.

To a lesser degree, there are a few divers in Rabaul who regularly salvage scrap on the weekends for Pat Roberts. He owns the salvage rights to most shipwrecks in the harbour. Pat doesn't work the wrecks himself but uses local sports divers to scrounge non-ferrous from the shipwrecks.

Last but not least, there was the harbourmaster. He is God as far as ship movement, and to a lesser degree, the use of explosives in the harbour. He and the local divers would be keeping a very close watch on us.

And who could blame them? As far as the local diving community was concerned, my piss-ant little salvage vessel coming to town was, to them, the equivalent of the *Queen Mary* visiting Rabaul for the rest of the population.

The *MV Scorpion* was a beamy, 20m, coastal cargo vessel, converted to salvage work. She had a ten-ton side lift and a twenty-ton stern lift, dedicated dive equipment/compressor room, some 20 scuba tanks, oxygen decompression equipment, a secure and hidden explosive room capable of holding two-tonnes of high explosives, comfortable crew quarters, a galley and salon, a bridge deck with wheelhouse, and a large skipper's bunk. We also had a differential magnetometer, dive tender, hookah gear on board, the list goes on... To the local scrap-scrounging divers, we were a big deal and a potential threat to their weekend scavenging.

The main concern for us was, should anyone else discover that the *Hakkai* was more than just a Japanese Navy repair ship, but also associated with the Japanese illegal refining of precious metals, the game would be up.

The *Hakkai* sank very quickly during a famous raid on Rabaul called 'Operation Cartwheel'. She sank stern first and disappeared below the surface in less than an hour. It is highly probable that if she had any gold or silver bullion on board at the time, she sank so quickly that nothing could be transferred from her. In which case, there were potentially millions of dollars in precious metal stored somewhere in the dark recesses of her hull.

After returning to the *Scorpion* from an afternoon exploring Rabaul's main street, we left the Yacht Club mooring and motored a mile or so to a little cove on the western side of the harbour, only a few hundred metres from the wreck. I dropped the anchor in just 2 metres of dead calm water and a few metres from the black sandy beach.

It's worthy to note that the *Hakkai* was recognised as one of the finest shipwreck dives in New Guinea, possibly in the world. The visibility was usually excellent, and the depth to the cabin structure was within acceptable sport-diving limits. There was, however, very little penetration into the ships holds as her steel hatch combings were still firmly in place, and it was dark and dangerous in the holds.

The wreck, like several others in the harbour, has been permanently buoyed for years. A group of local sports divers first used conventional ropes and buoys, but the local fishermen would free dive down and cut the ropes and steal the floats. The ropes made great anchor lines for their canoes.

An enterprising old navy diver who was pulling copper lath-stock from the wreck at the time came up with a unique solution. He scrounged some discarded 50 mm nylon mooring line used by big ships at the main wharf. Because of its size, the rope was useless to the local fishermen. It was nylon, which floated, so no need for a buoy. The mooring would typically last a couple of years until the marine growth became so heavy that it sank. Then a new one was procured, and all was good again. The wreck being buoyed was very convenient and saved us having to put one on it. But it did mean that the local sport divers also had easy access.

Tomorrow morning, some of us will get reacquainted with the wreck, and for others it will be the first time. This will essentially be an orientation dive, a chance to get an overview of the ship. For a lot of reasons, everyone must have a good knowledge of the ship's general layout, as this will help establish points of reference that we can all relate to.

Chapter 5

Diving the *Hakkai Maru*

I t was 5:30 a.m., and John and the Wari boys were busy getting the dive tender ready for the morning's dive. That included taking care of all the tools, scuba tanks, dive weights, regulators, etc. There is nothing more frustrating than being suited up in the hot tropics ready for a dive only to find that some vital component, like the dive weights or masks, is missing.

So, when everything was ready to go, Blondie and the local crew lined the deck to bid us farewell. It was with some excitement that we cast off. A quick sharp pull on the starter cord and the outboard sprang to life. In just a few short minutes, we were at the *Hakkai's* buoy.

As we approached the mooring line, John scrambled past the divers to the front of the tender and securely tied us up. With everyone keen to get into the water, there was a jostle to get tanked up. We checked and set our dive watches for our entry time, and, in typical diver's fashion with divers on either side of the tender, we hit the water in unison.

Descending the mooring line, I couldn't help marvelling at how clear the water was, especially considering this was a harbour. In seemingly no time, the top of a mast came into view. I checked my depth gauge and noted it was about 25 metres. I levelled off and glided past the first mast in the direction of the bow. Soon another mast appeared out of the gloom and came into view. It was the forward topmast. Moments later, I could see the whole topmast and its goalpost. Swimming down to the goalpost level, I could see the ship's holds with their thick steel roller hatches firmly shut. I marvelled at the huge winches and derricks that still looked like new, and the spiderweb of steel lifting cables that were still in place. Suddenly, my attention was drawn to the cannon at the bow its barrel pointing slightly upward was now also clearly visible.

I wanted to get an overview of the whole ship, so to conserve air and increase my bottom time; I levelled off at around 20 metres. As I continued to glide and slowly fin towards the deeper bow, I spotted an anti-aircraft gun on the deck still pointing menacingly towards the sky. As I got closer to the bow, I was surprised that there was no damage to the forecastle area. I could see one anchor was still firmly stuck in the hawsepipe, and in the other, the anchor chain disappeared into the gloom and, I suspect, the anchor was buried in the mud at the bottom. I turned around and headed back towards amidships. I then found a huge cylinder bolted to the foredeck. It looked like it might have been a decompression chamber. I'm amazed at how intact the shipwreck appeared – the main masts were complete with derricks and davit-falls, and there were winches, and the hatch covers all firmly in place. One could easily imagine that you could simply raise her from her watery grave and steam away.

But, the illusion was shattered when swimming past the funnel. The damage done by the skip bomb on the starboard side was visible, and the breech that subsequently sent her to the bottom was huge. The bomb had smashed smack-bang amidships and torn a massive hole in the engine room. It was no wonder she went down so fast.

As I glided through the rear goalpost, soon I could clearly see the stern gun. I couldn't help thinking of what a magnificent ship this had been. It was no wonder she was so popular with the sports divers. I looked at my watch and 40 minutes had disappeared as if it had only been five. It was time to start finning back in the direction of the mooring line. I still had a five-minute decompression stop at 3 metres.

Back in the tender, Garth was first to let fly. 'What a fuckin' great dive! Shit! That's a fantastic wreck. This has to be one of the best I've ever dived.'

'Told you it was a good dive. She's a beauty, all right, and where did you end up?' I replied.

'Spent most of my time in the aft section. Lindsay was with me. What do you reckon, Lindsay?'

Lindsay shook his head, 'Simply fantastic, but I think it's going to take some time to find that bloody strongroom. This is a modern ship. I noticed that the Japs used steel instead of timber flooring on the bridge decking. That's going to make it a bit more difficult and dangerous to check out the dark cabins below.'

I shot back, 'I know, but maybe that's a blessing in disguise, given the amount of sport diving that the locals do on the wreck. Fortunately, they restrict most of the diving to the shallower bridge and accommodation area. Most are looking for souvenirs, and none are looking for a hidden treasure room. Fortunately for us, the *Hakkai* has steel hatch covers, and most of the locals are too afraid to do deep penetration dives into the dark holds.'

Tony chimed in, 'I had a quick look around the bridge and cabin area trying to find the watch bell. There's a fair bit of damage there, and Lindsay's right. Checking those cabins is going to be difficult.'

Back on the *Scorpion* and in the comfort of the aft deck, we discussed the morning's dive, and one thing everyone agreed on was it would probably take a couple of dives to orientate ourselves to the wreck – especially the amidships accommodations. Tony suggested maybe we should make 'mud maps' of the areas that we visit, but this was not well received.

Getting up to have a shower, I said, 'This afternoon, let's see if we can get into the holds, Tony and I will take the forward hold, and you two,' I pointed to Garth and Lindsay 'take the aft hold.'

'Sounds like fun,' Garth said as he laughed in anticipation of another exciting dive.

We now had some nine or 10 hours to kill before the afternoon dive. I was keen to talk to Pat Roberts. The local crew, including Lindsay and John, were eager to explore Rabaul. We left Cookie to baby-sit the boat while the rest of us piled into the tender. The plan was that we would drop the boys off at the Yacht Club jetty, and from there, they could spend the day exploring the town, taking a half-car back to the *Scorpion* later in the day and swim out to the boat. Tony, Blondie, and I would carry on to Pat's wharf.

Pat's wharf was easy to find being the last small-ships wharf on the north-west side of the harbour before the larger CPL wharf, which was some distance away. After finding a safe spot to tie the tender, we made our way to his office. Vicky, Pat's wife, was sitting at a desk diligently working at something. She was pleased to see Tony and being a big girl, she almost made him disappear when she hugged him. Vicky was an educated, girl from Bougainville – a Buka. Like so many of her clan, she was as black as the ace of spades.

After some small talk, she pointed to the workshop where she said we would find Pat. Pat Roberts had built up a thriving business on the Rabaul waterfront. He was a very enterprising businessman. Once, he even salvaged a Japanese cargo submarine, which he converted into a water carrier to service the international ships at anchor. Pat was also an exalted person, a member of the famous Australian commandos, Z Special Unit, better known as 'Z Force'.

As we entered the workshop, Pat spotted Tony and waved, he hobbled over to greet us. Pat was a physically large man. He had difficulty walking, partly due to size, but it was exacerbated by his damaged Achilles tendons. However, he appeared to be cheerful enough.

Tony explained that we had heard he was looking for divers to pull condensers from his wrecks in the harbour, and that was all the excuse we needed to leave the rotten weather in Milne Bay for some well-deserved R&R in Rabaul. We may as well earn some extra money ripping the condenser out of the *Hakkai Maru* for him and still have plenty of free time shoreside. His eyes lit up as he shook my hand, saying he would have no issue with us pulling the condenser out of the *Hakkai* or any other ship for that matter. He agreed to pay us 30 cents per kg landed at his wharf.

I was happy enough with this. The price per kilo could have been better, but having Pats' approval to work the wreck was more important and would go a long way to legitimising us being there. After we took our leave from Pat. Tony dropped Blondie and me back on the *Scorpion,* and he returned to the Yacht Club jetty.

We spent the rest of the day just relaxing onboard doing odd domestic jobs. There is always something that needs attention on a boat. It was mid-afternoon before the boys came back, and like good little Vegemite's, they had also been to the market and returned with a whole lot of fresh fruit, including a heap of fresh, young, drinking coconuts. These were a welcome sight, as the drinking coconuts go very well with white rum or tequila!

John went about his task of pumping bottles and getting the tender ready for the afternoon's dive.

* * *

Shallow shipwrecks in tropical waters attract the same beautiful corals that you find on any coral reef in the world. However, wrecks at depth like the that of the *Hakkai* present a different danger. A seemingly innocuous thin layer of coral with small, prickly, glass-like coral branches only a few millimetres tall cover virtually everything.

If you are not careful and brush up against them, they have the habit of puncturing your skin and breaking off. If you do not dig these coral splinters out and treat them immediately, you will most likely end up with some severe tropical ulcers, particularly on the arms and lower legs.

Wreck divers quickly learn to wear some sort of protection when penetrating shipwrecks. A thin, 3 mm neoprene suit will usually do the job. Gloves are mandatory. Some wreck divers, like Tony, on the other hand, preferred to dress as many salvage divers of the day – in jeans and a long-sleeved, Aussie football jersey.

So, appropriately dressed, we were ready for our first real penetration dive on the wreck. Within minutes of leaving the *Scorpion*, we were once again tied up to the wreck buoy. Everyone was keen to get into the water, and moments later, we were gliding down the mooring line.

A school of good-sized barracuda swam past, and I thought to myself, *Hell, I wish I had my speargun with me.* But moments later, the fish are quickly forgotten as the topmast came into view. Tony and I effortlessly glided to hatch number one.

The steel hatch coamings on the ship were still firmly in place, but fortunately, for us, they were now small rust holes in many places. We head in the direction of the largest hole in the forward hatch. It's just big enough for a diver to squeeze through, but only after taking off his scuba tank and passing it through the hole first with the diver following. We did that, and once inside, with practised ease, we replaced our scuba tanks and continued our dive. Slowly, our eyes adjusted to the gloom. Streams of light were filtering through hundreds of small, fist-sized holes in the hatch, giving us just enough light to orientate ourselves in the upper decks.

The *Hakkai's* holds consisted of three decks: an upper deck, a 'tween-deck', and lower deck. At one time, each deck consisted of heavy timber flooring that accommodated various bits of machinery, but the timber had long since rotted away.

Each deck was used for a different purpose. Now electric cables dangled dangerously from rusty beams throughout the ship's holds, the fixtures having long since rusted away. These were like a giant spider web waiting to snare the unwary or careless diver.

More worrying, was the heavy machinery, some of which now balanced precariously on the steel bulkhead beams, just waiting to fall and crush divers in the lower decks.

Being mindful of the machinery above, we drifted into the darker, lower deck only to find more confusion as equipment from the upper decks lay scattered amongst the original lower-deck equipment. Fanning the narrow beam of my torch into the forward section, it was evident that this must've been a woodworking shop, so was no interest to us.

Cruising back up to the tween-deck, we make for a small hole in the transverse bulkhead and swim through into the number two hold. There was more machinery on the top and tween-deck. I shined the torch around and down into the lower deck. The searchlight beam unexpectedly highlighted part of the evidence we were looking for – the foundry. There were three large furnaces, all still mostly intact, with funnels heading to the tween-deck level, and metal moulds were scattered across the lower deck.

Now where the hell are the kilns? My torchlight no sooner stabbed into the dark recesses towards the transverse bulkhead, when three tall kilns almost jumped out at me. This is the last bit of evidence we needed.

I wanted to get a quick, closer look. I exhaled, allowing myself to sink deeper into the hold. As I descended, my torch flashed across sheets of iron balanced precariously on the tween-deck. They must have fallen from their racking against the hull above and now posed a potentially dangerous threat to any diver in the lower hold. Should they shift and fall, especially during an earthquake, which were a regular occurrences in Rabaul... Well, you'd be dead meat – mincemeat in fact.

I saw that several sheets of iron had fallen from the transverse bulkhead giving easy access to number three hold. I shined my torch at Tony to get his attention away from the kilns and then swam to the opening. Shining my light into number three hold, I saw it had nothing of interest for us. I noticed Tony's torchlight fanning the starboard side. He pointed to what looked like a charcoal bunker in the corner.

I would have liked to continue exploring this marvellous shipwreck, but our 20 minutes was almost up, and it was time to find a convenient exit. We found it via a raised hatch and doorway that led to the continuous deck. We then made our way to the surface.

As we approached the 'deco-stop', I saw that Garth and Lindsay were already decompressing. We made gestures in crazy sign language akin to charades, trying to tell them what we have found. But in the end, I think the 'Okay' signal said it all. Back in the tender, Tony couldn't contain himself and blurted out, 'We have found three bloody smelters and furnaces in number two hold!'

'You fucking beauty!' John shouted, doing a bad imitation of Indian dance.

There was relief and excitement all-round. We were now one step closer to realising our goal and the possibility of some very serious money. At this point, it looked like our trip may not have been wasted after all.

* * *

Back on the *Scorpion* and in the comfort of the after deck and with the Bacardi rum and fresh coconut water flowing freely, Garth and Lindsay recounted their exploration of the rear holds.

Garth began. 'The forward rear hold, hold four, was easy to enter as the area was badly damaged by the bombing that sent her to the bottom. There appeared to be several large freezers or cool rooms fixed to the hull on the top deck. On the lower deck, there were three big diesel generators. That deck must have been very noisy and uncomfortable for the crew.'

Then, Lindsay added to the account by saying, 'Both the top and tween-deck of hold number five looked like they were used for crew accommodations. That was evident by the many broken and rotten bed bunks. The lower deck had a lot of machinery, much of which had probably fallen from above. There appeared to be a lot of dive gear equipment including several large air compressors.'

Garth finished off the account by recalling, 'One, in particular, was a huge, 2-metre horizontal monster and almost certainly was used for pumping torpedoes. The half-dozen, massive Long Lance torpedoes in the lower hold made that assumption easy. These things were not easy to miss being some 9 metres long and

610 mm in diameter with half a ton of high explosives stacked in the nose. Shit, they could do some damage if they went off. But more worrying was the depth charges still neatly stacked in front of the torpedoes.'

In the after-holds, Garth found what he thought might have been a bottling machine. A whole heap of what may have been beer or sake bottles were laying around. He brought a bottle of what he thought might be sake to the surface, always the optimist. But even though the cork was still firmly in place, a quick taste test proved the contents were spoiled. Garth was adamant he would bring up some more, given the time and depth constraints, not something I was keen on him doing.

We had found what we were looking for, so I saw no reason to venture back into the deeper holds, except possibly to search for evidence of the strong-room. There was now no question of the *Hakkai's* metal-smelting and refining capability. The only questions were, did they get the opportunity to refine any precious metals, and if so, was there still any gold or silver onboard? And the million-dollar question was, if so, where the hell is it?

The celebrations were getting a little out of hand. The second bottle of Bacardi was almost empty. Blondie was getting very animated and beginning to slur her words. Every time she leaned over the table to refill her drink, her tits would fall out of her loose top, causing her to blush and giggle as she put them away, much to the crew's delight.

Bloody hell! She was a flirt! It was time to drag her away and give her time to sober up. Tonight, we will celebrate with dinner at the Travelodge.

Chapter 6

The Search for the Bullion Room

I was convinced that unlike gold bullion stored on general cargo ships where it was necessary to keep safe from thieves, passengers, and crew, that was not going to be the case in a Japanese warship.

In cargo ship of years gone by, anything of value, especially gold or money, was usually always stashed in the vessel's darkest crevice. Often, a cofferdam or a secure space in the lowest part of the hold where it could subsequently be covered with cargo making it impossible for anyone, including crew, to get at it. Sometimes, gold and silver bullion was even hidden in the coal bunker.

However, on a Japanese warship, it would be unthinkable for a sailor of the Japanese Imperial Navy to steal from the Emperor. This was, however, not always the case for ranking officers. It follows that some effort would have been made to keep any rendered down gold safe and secure. And concealed away from prying eyes, especially so when it wasn't strictly legal. At the same time, it had to be relatively easy to get at and accessible to the main deck. This was crucial to transfer large amounts of heavy material quickly.

We all agreed that the bullion room would most likely be somewhere in or around the deckhouse, possibly in a cabin or room under the continuous deck. So, from now on, we decided to concentrate our efforts in and around the accommodations area.

The trouble is, it doesn't take a lot of space to hold a million dollars' worth of gold bullion. One standard 400 oz gold bar is about the size of half-carton of cigarettes! With a ship the size of the *Hakkai,* the saying, 'Like looking for a needle in a haystack' seemed to be an understatement.

I don't think anyone got much sleep that night, dreaming how they would spend their share. I also made Blondie a few promises, and she was especially grateful. I briefly wondered where the hell did she learn the tricks she was now practising on me. But Lord Tennyson's quote sprang to mind, 'Ours not to reason why, ours but to do or die.' So... I let her have her way with me. Afterwards, she seemed to be a lot clingier, but I guess that's how women are where money is concerned!

*   *   *

It was 6:00 a.m. and another beautiful day in paradise. The water is glassed out, and there is barely a ripple on the surface. When breakfast was done, we were all quickly suited up and ready to go, and within minutes, we were speeding across the dark blue surface to the wreck. Everyone was in top spirits and, as always, keen to get into the water.

This morning the water was cool and refreshing. The exhaust bubbles rushing past my ears felt reassuring, and life, in general, felt good. If possible, the water looked even clearer than yesterday, and in seemingly seconds, the mainmast came into view and moments later the funnel. As I continued deeper, the whole of the wheelhouse and accommodation area was visible. I watched Garth and Lindsay peeling off to the starboard side of the ship. Tony and I headed for the upper port passageway.

Looking down the passageway towards the front of the ship, the deeper end, one thing was immediately apparent – this was going to be a little more dangerous than I first imagined, and, in more ways than one. Everything was covered in a layer of volcanic mud. Its consistency was like the most delicate talcum powder. It covered everything. Stir this up, and visibility in the cabin will turn to zero.

Copper wires and light fittings dangle from the ceiling, waiting to snare a diver's equipment. A rusted steel plate balanced precariously on slender beams, seemingly waiting to fall and cut a diver in half. And if that wasn't bad enough, the entire area was covered in small marine growth and in particular a thin cement-like coral with short, sharp, needle-like spikes that are ready to stab you and break off in your skin, ensuring that a tropical ulcer would follow. Last, but not least, hidden in the crevices, lionfish, sometimes called scorpionfish, *Pterois antennata*, were lurking. These little buggers refuse to move away from a diver, and their 13 venomous dorsal spines can easily penetrate wetsuits. If you don't see them and accidentally venture too close, they will, in a blinding flash, 'jump' out and butt you with their needle-sharp spines, piercing you deep into your flesh and injecting venom. This is an excruciatingly painful experience, as some of my divers can attest.

And, if that was not bad enough, there were two sections of steel sheeting above what appeared to be the radio room. They look like they may have fallen from the bridge deck above and now balance precariously on a couple of slender beams. Diver's bubbles might be enough to dislodge them, so we needed to be extremely careful when visiting this area.

Finishing on the upper passageway, we glided down the ship's outer hull to inspect the lower passageway on the continuous deck. It was much darker there than the deck above, and the front entrance to the cabins contained a mass of debris consisting of rotting timbers and steel beams. All of which prevented access to the forward cabins.

I signalled Tony to give me a hand and see if we could move some of this junk. We pushed and shoved, even used our legs to kick and push, but no luck. A sledgehammer might have been enough to loosen the cement-like coral that was binding everything together. Still, I had a sneaking suspicion that we might resort to a bigger hammer – dynamite. I glanced at my watch and noticed that our 20 minutes bottom time was up, so we headed for the surface. Right on cue, I saw Garth and Lindsay doing the same.

*   *   *

Back on the *Scorpion,* it was time to discuss our findings and take notes. Garth and Lindsay had split up. Garth swam down the top starboard passageway to a large door on his left. He had entered a companionway, and looking upward towards the stern, he could see the flickering light from Lindsay's torch. Lindsay had entered the companionway on the opposite side via a cabin where the roof/floor had rusted away.

Being careful not to stir up too much silt, they checked out several cabins on this level but found nothing to suggest a strongroom or large safe. Limited bottom time prevented them from investigating further.

Putting his beer down, Garth repeated his earlier words, 'This is not going to be as easy as we thought. There's a jumble of rotten timber, steel plate, and mud. The earthquakes have shifted a shit load of stuff.'

'Yes,' Tony responded in his Pommy accent, 'With only 20 minutes bottom time, it's going to be a bugger moving that steel blocking the forward cabin on the port side as well.'

'Worst case, we will just have to use explosives,' I said, 'But before we get ahead of ourselves, you guys,' I was talking to Garth and Lindsay, 'need to get into the accommodations on the deck level and check the internal passageway and cabins. That'll be a little more difficult and darker, so make sure your torches are fully charged, and take a spare one, each.'

'That will be fun. I think we should do it without fins. We'll stir up less mud that way,' Garth said.

'I agree. Let's see what you come up with after that dive. It should give us a better picture. Tony and I will see if we can move some of that rubbish blocking the port entrance.' I said.

'I wouldn't mind a look at the bloody engine room,' Garth chimed in.

'All in good time,' I replied, 'Twenty minutes doesn't give us much time to play tourist and muck about. Hopefully, after this afternoon's dive, we'll have a better idea of the wreck and be able to map out a plan.'

I directed my attention to John. 'Don't forget to put a couple of small sledgehammers in the tender. Tony and I are going to try and move some of that junk blocking the front two cabins.'

'Long handle or short?' he shot back.

'Short handle, John. We'll be working in a confined area.'

'Still want to look at the engine room,' Garth quipped with a grin on his face.

I chose to ignore him. 'Not much more we can do this morning, so let's rest up. I am going to take Blondie and show her around the town. Anyone want to come for a ride?'

Everyone, including Jack and Joe, was keen to go shoreside. Someone had to stay onboard, so again, Cookie volunteered to look after the *Scorpion*.

Tony was married and had two young daughters. He never showed any interest in womanising, so, I guess he would socialise at one or more of the many local clubs or pubs. There was no doubt that Garth and Lindsay were going whoring. Rabaul had a virtual smorgasbord of available women, both single and married, and in all colours and persuasions. There were beautiful local girls, absolutely gorgeous Asian and mixed-race girls, to countless single and married European women. Nurses had a reputation for being especially horny.

The local crew would also have no trouble finding women. The worst-case scenario for them was to sample the local 50-cent hookers' dubious delights, called '50-cent Mari's'. The girls usually hung out on the Palm Theatre steps; many White guys also took advantage of these girls, especially for a quick blow job.

'Okay, John, get the rest of the dive gear out of the tender and have it ready in 30 minutes,' I ordered, and followed that, with 'That should give everybody time to get ready.'

*   *   *

I was keen to show Blondie around the town and what it had to offer. Rabaul was a friendly town and an idyllic place to live. It had a welcoming, local, Asian and European population.

Rabaul's World War II history was evident everywhere, from the Wreck Wharf (*Komaki Maru*) to hundreds of Japanese caves and tunnels just begging to be explored. Yamamoto's command bunker was always of interest. The Japanese submarine base with its caves on the surface and a 300-metre drop-off was another must-see. There were small Jap tanks that still littered the side of many roads. It was an exciting place to be a boy.

It was late 1969 and Rabaul had, apart from the local Tolai people, a large expatriate and Chinese mixed-race population of over 2,000. It was universally considered one of the most progressive and beautiful towns in the Pacific. Its superb natural harbour was ringed by extinct, and also a couple of not-so-extinct, volcanos! It was a garden town, filled with tall, beautiful, tropical, flowering trees and shrubs. But there was more to Rabaul then just stunning tree-lined avenues.

It was also the commercial centre of New Britain and the surrounding islands. It was rivalled only by Port Moresby. Mango Avenue, the main street, was flanked by large modern shops, supermarkets, hardware stores, banks, restaurants, souvenir shops, and cafes. Everything you would expect from a vibrant, modern town could be found there – bakeries, newsagents, theatres, the list goes on.

In Chinatown, you had the best local produce markets outside of Fiji. Every possible tropical fruit or vegetable imaginable was available there, especially on the weekends. All were displayed under shaded roofs or giant mango trees. I swear that the best mangos and paw-paws I've ever had in my life came from this market.

The Chinese shops across the road would sell just about anything, from a machete to one cigarette with two matches and a striker!

There was no broadcast television, so, by necessity, Rabaul was a very social town. So social, I might add, it was a proverbial 'Peyton Place,' if you can remember back that far to know what that is. On the southern end of Mango Avenue, you had the Yacht Club. Next door to that was the upmarket Travelodge motel, which had the best air-conditioned coffee shop in the town. A large pool in the centre courtyard was available if you were a guest or bought a beer or two.

There was also the ever-popular Chang's Chinese restaurant, the Ambonese Club, the Aviat Club, the Returned Serviceman's Club, and Rabaul Golf Club with its awesome fairways next to the airstrip. Then there was the upmarket New Guinea Club with its mirror-finished teak floors with its billiard hall, popular with white-collar workers like the 'Bank Johnnies' and business types. There was also the Palm Theatre, the popular Ascot Hotel, and coffee shops and world-class restaurants like Joe's Steakhouse.

Rabaul's supermarkets included Burns Philp, Steamships, and Carpenters. Then there was Andersons on Malaguna Road for the best quality European products including yoghurt, proper milk, although it was frozen, real cheese, and the best beef steaks in the town. It was also the first and only air-conditioned supermarket in town at the time.

There were beaches such as the ever-popular black sand beach at Pila-pila, just over the Tunnel Hill road, or the Kulau Lodge resort on the way to Ratung on the north coast. The old Jap sub-base was good for swimming and scuba diving, and the stunning panorama of the harbour, the excellent roads made it just about the most fantastic place on earth.

* * *

Today, I thought it might be interesting to take Blondie to the golf club. It was only a few kilometres away, opposite the Lakunai Airport. They had an excellent reputation for lunch, and it was a pleasant setting overlooking the fairway. It was a little too far to walk in this heat, so it would have to be a taxi or the local form of transport, commonly called 'half cars' – in other words, utilities.

The road past the airport and on to Matiput village was always busy, so it did not take long to get a lift. Blondie wasn't too pleased and rolled her eyes back in her head as she was prone to do. But she took it like a trooper, and soon we were bouncing along in the back of a utility truck with a dozen locals.

When we were getting close to the club driveway, everyone in the back started yahooing and shouting at the driver. Those that weren't shouting were banging on the roof of the cab. It was the usual practice, but possibly a little more animated for the benefit of the 'dim dims', as White people were called, but it was all in good fun.

Lunch was a pleasure, the ambience relaxing, and even more so after a few beers. I was feeling decidedly sleepy. Blondie noticed this and whispered, 'I think you have had enough.'

'Give me a break. I've only had a couple.'

'Don't forget you've got to dive this afternoon,' she said, giving me that 'you're stupid' look.

I changed the subject. 'I wonder if Garth and Lindsay have found a couple of stray females. That shouldn't be too hard. there's enough of them here.'

Blondie's face showed a hint of anger as she went into attack mode. 'Jealous, are you?' Highlighting her displeasure by rolling her eyes and shaking her head.

Boy, women can be fickle, so I feigned innocence. Desperately thinking up an appropriate reply, I finally blurted out, 'For God's sake, give me a break! I've got the horniest piece of flesh in the country. What the hell do I want with a bit of stray?'

But little did she know that there were some very tempting bits of female flesh in Rabaul, and most of it ready to fuck at the drop of a hat. I must have come up with the right answer, for she leant forward and gently rubbed my leg under the table. 'Wait till I get you back on board,' she said with a mischievous grin.

It was 3:00 p.m. by the time we got back. With the two cooling fans directed right on my double bunk, I again let Blondie work her magic. After half an hour of full-on humping, I fell asleep exhausted, naked, and dead to the world. The next thing I knew, I woke with a start, John was shouting my name and banging on the cabin wall. He must have suspected that Blondie and I had been up to no good, so that's why he didn't come up to the bridge deck to wake me.

I felt quite good after the catnap and was raring to go. I looked at my watch, and, bugger! It was already 4:30 p.m. No time to muck about. Time to get suited up and ready for this afternoon's dive.

* * *

We needed to do something about that jumble of steel beams and girders blocking the entrance to the forward cabins. So, instead of fooling around with sledgehammers, I decided to use a bigger sledgehammer – some AN60 dynamite.

Today I would take it upon myself to make up the charges. This was something I usually left for the others to do. It's not a pleasant job, especially in the hot tropics. Our explosives were all nitro-glycerine based and very effective. However, working with nitro-glycerine explosives in the tropical heat is 'fucken horrible'. It's also potentially very dangerous, especially if it starts to sweat. The poor bugger, who in the explosives industry is called the 'powder monkey', making up the explosives is usually in for a super headache induced by the nitro-glycerine fumes. This is known as a 'bang head'. It feels like your temple is going to explode.

Thankfully, today there was a bit of breeze on the front deck, which helped dispel the fumes. Sitting cross-legged on the hatch, I quickly made up six separate explosive packages of 1 kg each of AN60. When finished, I cut a length of Cordtex detonating fuse, Cordtex a strong, flexible cord with PETN exploding at 6400 m/ss and used to 'daisy-chain' a sequence of explosives. After I'd made a couple of detonators and a new role of bell wire, we were ready to go.

* * *

The afternoon's dive would be a little different from the usual. Garth and Lindsay would enter the water together and continue their inspection of the superstructure concentrating on the port side, while Tony and I would place the explosives.

Placing explosives and connecting them is a time-consuming task. So, to maximise our total bottom time today, Tony and I would work in a relay. I would go down first and set as many explosive charges in place as time allowed and join them with Cordtex.

Tony would follow some 15 minutes later, bringing down the detonating wire and detonators. His job would be to check to ensure all the explosives were securely in place. Once that was done, he would attach the detonators to the explosives, connect it all up, and return to the surface trailing the wire behind him. It was just as simple as that.

It was almost 5:15 p.m. when I finally entered the water and started my rapid descent to the wreck. It's quite amazing spiralling down into the darkening deep waters by yourself. It clears the mind, there is only one focus, 'Get to the bottom'.

In the darkening, deep blue, there is no sense of depth, up or down, just nothingness – everything is the same. Only the air bubbles give you an indication of the vertical and a sense of orientation. Then, like magic, when the wreck slowly comes into view, dim, dark and foreboding, everything falls back into perspective, and again, like magic, the brain kicks back into gear.

The extra weight of the explosives I was carrying helped to 'torpedo' me towards the gangway. I inhaled quite deeply, thereby increasing my buoyancy to slow my descent and save myself from crashing into the deck rail. Once there, I took a moment to compose myself and then take stock of my surroundings. In the dim light, I checked for the best places to tie the explosives and immediately start attaching them for maximum effect with bits of wire that I had brought down for the job.

I was into my fifth placement when Tony arrived. He could see where I'd been working and immediately started threading the Cordtex, leaving me free to place the last charge. A few minutes later, I was finished. I signalled Tony that I was heading back to the surface. After a 10-minute decompression stop, I surfaced. All we had to do now is wait for the boys to come back up.

Garth and Lindsay are close behind me, and 15 minutes later, with Tony safely onboard, John scratches the detonating wires onto the battery terminals, and bingo, it's done. It's a bit of an anti-climax, the only indication that the explosives have detonated is a small crack on the hull of the aluminium tender as the shockwave hits.

There is barely a ripple on the surface. But 40 metres below, it would be a very different story, and tomorrow morning's dive will quickly tell us how successful the blast had been.

*　　*　　*

Back onboard the *Scorpion* and even before I've had a chance to get out of my wetsuit, Blondie attacked me. Boy, was she pissed off. Then, as if it was my fault, said, 'There's a "fucking Peeping Tom" onshore with binoculars. He's been watching me for ages.'

The boys all looked at each other with mock amusement.

'What the hell makes you think he's looking at you?' I asked bewildered.

'Of course, he's looking at me. Who else would he be looking at?' she spat back. 'I was sunbathing naked on the deck chair, trying to get rid of my bikini line for you. Who else would he be looking at?'

Lindsay could not contain himself and burst out laughing. It was contagious, and soon there were giggles all around. Trying to defuse the situation, I looked at her in all seriousness and said. 'Us, of course, you silly woman. Someone might be looking to see if we're pulling scrap from the wreck. And please don't go running around naked on the boat. I told you before, tits are okay with the local culture, but exposed thighs are a big no-no, let alone, a shaved pussy.'

Like a viper, she spat back, 'Fuck em!' and stormed off towards the galley wriggling her arse as she went. Everybody except me was amused.

'Shaved pussy? Now, that's nice,' Garth mimicked, nodding to the boys.

'Yea, yea. Stop ogling. You've seen it all before,' I found myself mimicking Blondie by raising my eyebrows in mock disgust and mumbling under my breath, 'I hope she doesn't punish me tonight.' There were a few smirks as we headed off single file down the narrow passageway to the galley for dinner.

*   *   *

Waiting for us was a huge pot of spaghetti Bolognese, and it looked like Cookie had made enough for 10 men. I guess he intends to give the same to the local crew. They usually ate fresh fish or tin fish with rice, or sometimes or bully beef with rice. I wondered how they would like it.

Talk at the dinner table soon centred on this afternoon's dive. There was not much that Tony or I could add. We would need to wait until tomorrow to know the results of the blast. However, Garth and Lindsay had been able to have a quick look at most of the cabins on the starboard side. There was nothing obvious that they could see which may have been used to store precious metals. There were two hatches at the rear. The smallest was locked and the other open, but time didn't allow further scrutiny. That would have to wait until tomorrow.

Blondie again brought up the subject of the guy spying on us, and I had to admit that we needed to be careful. I think it was also time to seriously consider setting a couple of booby traps. We also would have to bring up a bit of scrap for Pat Roberts, not a lot, just enough to keep him happy and make our dives appear legitimate.

*   *   *

It was another magic morning in Paradise. The rising sun sent a golden glow across the smooth waters of the harbour. There were a few native canoes off in the distance fishing on the shallower wrecks, a very tranquil scene. Soon, we were once again tied up to the wreck and getting ready to dive.

This morning we hit the water in unison, powering down to the *Hakkai*. The quicker we got down, the longer our bottom time. Saturation starts the moment you enter the water. The wreck was familiar to us now, so there was no getting lost, and in a few minutes, we were levelling off at the outer port passageway.

The results of the blast had been quite dramatic. Virtually all the coral growth from the immediate area had disappeared. The steel girders, beams, and other rubbish blocking the doorways had blasted through the forward opening and now lay strewn along the front deck like so many matchsticks.

The blast had worked better than expected, and the doorway to the internal passageway was now clear. I noticed another large steel sheet balancing on the upper level. I swam up and tried to dislodge it, but it would not move. I took a mental note to keep a close eye on it.

Entering the passageway, I noted that it ran from port to starboard. I could see the light greyish water on the other side, filtering through the debris. To my right, another much longer passage ran fore and aft with rooms to the outer bulkhead. I noticed that the internal walls had at one time been lined with timber, but this had mostly now rotted away.

Because the *Hakkai* was down by the head, the superstructure's front bulkhead had become a dam for the volcanic mud and other rotten debris. It was difficult to guess what may lay hidden under it. Hatches that might lead to hidden rooms below sprang to mind.

To explore this area properly, we would have to dredge it. We have a large, 15 cm dredge powered by a 2,000 kPa compressor on board that could easily do the job, but that would mean anchoring over the wreck. An alternative was to use smaller air dredges and power them from scuba bottle. The only trouble with these is that they are prone to blockage, mainly from oyster shells and other bits and pieces of rubbish hidden in the mud.

Shining the torch along the bulkhead, I could see nothing of interest protruding from the mud that might be used to hold gold bullion – not that I expected it to be that obvious.

Chapter 7

The *Lyon Maru* Condenser

We were now on our third day of searching the deckhouse area and still no sign of anything that looked like a safe or treasure room. There were some grumbles among the crew, but this was mainly frustration rather than discontentment.

We did have one stroke of luck. Garth, I guess trying to win 'brownie points', promised Blondie lobster for dinner. So, after the morning's dive, he and Lindsay had gone off to the other side of the harbour to dive a previously cut-up shipwreck in shallow water. Broken-up wrecks are always an excellent place to find lobsters or coral trout.

The *Lyon Maru* was a large freighter for its day being some 10,000 tons. She was sunk at the entrance to Rabaul harbour by US land-based aircraft in 1944. And because she was obstructing the main shipping lane, she was also the first ship in the harbour to be cut up by Japanese salvors in 1957.

In 1956, the Australian administration permitted Japanese salvage companies Okadigumi Salvage Co. and Nayo Boeki Kaisha to salvage and cut up shipwrecks in Rabaul Harbour. Clearing the shipping lane was a significant consideration for issuing the salvage rights. As it turns out, whichever company had worked the *Lyon Maru* must have been in one hell of a hurry to get to better pickings, because they left some very valuable stuff behind.

The boys quickly discovered that the ship's whole stern section, aft of the engine room including the keel and propeller shaft, had disappeared entirely. This part of the ship had protruded into the shipping lane. However, everything forward of the rear hold, including the engine room, had only been cut to the ship's waterline. In the engine room, the enormous, cast-iron cylinder heads from the three-stage reciprocating steam engine were missing, but the crankcase and complete condenser remained attached to the base of the motor. They could not believe their eyes. This condenser would easily top 10 tons.

The lobsters and possible favours from Blondie were quickly forgotten as they raced back to the *Scorpion* for explosives and manpower. Two hours later, the cast iron casing that encapsulated the condenser was shattered, and like a freshly peeled egg, the bright, copper condenser gleamed in the sunlight ready for lifting.

By 5:00 p.m. that afternoon, towing it with lifting bags, they had it alongside Pat's wharf. The next morning, we were $4,000 richer, which was nothing to be sneezed at. This was the equivalent to a tradesman's annual wage in 1969.

There would be another 4 tons to follow, including the massive weir pump and valve assembly plus a couple of smaller heat exchangers and copper piping. Finding the condenser and loose copper on the *Lyon Maru* was a serious lesson and prompted us to agree to check out other cut-up wrecks in the harbour to see what else the Japs may have left behind.

Chapter 8

Pesky Visitors

Another morning dive on the Hakkai, we were halfway through our inspection of the cabins when I heard a loud bang. My first thought was that it was John on the surface giving us the warning signal, as he had been trained to do, firing a sawn-off .303 pistol under the water. One-shot meant 'Danger, be careful'; two shots meant 'Return to the surface immediately'. We kept the gun in the tender specifically for that purpose. Or, of course, it might not have been John at all. It might have been someone who had just shot a shark close by with a powerhead.

A few minutes later, we had our answer as a couple of local divers came into view. They kept their distance but continued to watch us. I guessed that they were waiting for us to run out of bottom time so they could zoom in and have a closer look at what we were up to.

This was not good. They would be asking themselves, why the hell are they blasting the accommodation area? We would have to do something about this. I decided it was time to break a leg or two.

Back on the *Scorpion,* I gathered the boys for some serious discussion, but first of all, I had to get Blondie out of earshot.

'Let's have lunch at the club,' I suggested, and the boys nodded in agreement.

'Make yourself beautiful for me and make those cretins shoreside jealous,' I said, squeezing her arse.

'Okay,' she said with a smile, and with that, she was off to the wheelhouse. I didn't want to involve her if things went wrong.

The crew were well aware that too much was at stake for us to allow the constant snooping to continue. It appeared that it was mainly from the same two guys who have been watching us from shore. The spying would only get more brazen if we did not nip it in the bud. I called the boys together and in a low voice, turned to John, 'You recognise the guys?'

'Yes, the fat one and his mate are regulars at the Yacht Club. He and his mate often pull stuff up for Roberts.'

'Okay... John, tonight you break one of those guy's fucking legs. That will keep the prick out of the water.' Looking menacingly at the crew, I added, 'Any objections?'

There was a chorus of 'No' and shaking of heads.

'Okay, then... As soon as Blondie's ready, we'll head off to the club for lunch. John and I will check out how best to get to these 'wankers', and then we'll come back tonight for dinner. Let's hope one or both are at the club.'

'A counter lunch and beer sound good to me!' Lindsay said, poking me in the ribs as he saw Blondie coming down the passageway.

* * *

The club was busy. It must have been today's special – T-bone steak with chips. That sounded just like what the doctor ordered. With the meal finished and a couple of beers down the hatch, it was time to go and check out the 'hit area'. I gave John the nudge,

'Have to go for a piss,' he said in a voice loud enough for Blondie to hear.

'John, can you please be a bit more civil?' Blondie objected in a frustrated tone.

'I'll come with you,' I said, quickly defusing any arguments.

The toilet block was close to the Travelodge fence. The first thing we noticed was the Travelodge employees apparently use the club showers and toilets. They had long ago cut a hole in the chain wire fence and parted the thick Poinciana hedge directly behind the toilet. John walked over to the opening and stepped through. He walked down the track a bit and then came back.

'I'll get a good view from back there of anyone visiting the piss house. Not a problem,' John said with a grin.

Back in the clubhouse, I needed to apologise for coming back tonight and said to those at the table, 'Shit. I've lost track of the days,' I said, 'It's bloody Friday, so let's come back tonight for the $10 special. And it's my shout.'

There was, of course, total agreement. The boys knew exactly why we were coming back tonight, and it wasn't just for the meal.

* * *

Back on board, there were still several hours before we would return to the *Hakkai* and resume our search. I turned to John. 'Go down the hold and find a short length of water pipe, one with enough length and weight to break a leg. I don't care if you break one or two. Just make sure whatever you do will keep the prick out of the bloody water.'

It was a simple plan. I told John to wait on the Travelodge side of the fence and keep a watch for our targets. As soon as the opportunity arose, he would crack him over the skull, drag his unconscious body into the shadows, and break his legs. I stressed we needed to make it look like a robbery, so I told him to take his wallet, pull out the cash, and throw the wallet away.

'Not a problem,' was all he said. I'm sure his eyes get closer together when he gets the opportunity to do harm.

'But be careful, and make sure that no ones around to see you,' I warned. I turned to Lindsay, 'We also need to set some booby-traps – not enough to kill anyone but to seriously scare the shit out of them or at least take out their eardrums. That will keep them out of the water.'

It was not unusual for munitions on wartime shipwrecks to explode. Most World War II explosives had a tendency to leach and become unstable with age; the slightest knock can set it off.

I put my coffee down and looked at Lindsay. 'Rig up a couple of sticks of AN60. Set them somewhere close to where we are working. I suggest you put the main switch at the top of the mast, or maybe better still, the funnel. That way we can easily disarm it on our way down and rearm it on the way up. Put the mercury trip switch near the port entrance and the explosive some distance away. We don't want to kill anyone!'

'It'll be a pleasure. I'll put something together now and take it down. Two sticks of AN60 should do it,' Lindsay said with a devilish grin.

'Okay, boys and girls, time to rest up for this afternoon's dive,' I said as I stood up 'sculling' the last of my beer.

* * *

It was 4:30 p.m., and we are cruising over the still waters to the wreck. We had decided not to set the 'booby trap' this afternoon but wait until early tomorrow morning. Most pleasure divers don't get to the wrecks until midday on Saturday, giving us plenty of time to do it in the morning. A blast or two will make them less likely to visit this wreck for a while.

Even this late in the afternoon, the visibility was still quite good near the surface, but it got progressively darker as we went deeper. Upon reaching the wreck, torches were necessary. It would be pitch black in the lower cabins.

Tony and I first headed for the bridge deck and searched for a suitable place to leave our flippers. A fallen beam provided the perfect spot, so we jammed our fins under it. Then we quickly pulled ourselves along, hand over hand, down the outside of the ship to the continuous deck. Doing this always reminded me of spiders crawling down a wall. Once there, we swung over the gunwale onto the passageway, right at the cabin entrance.

Entering the doorway looking to the left, we saw a lot of volcanic ash collected in the deeper end. What we thought were water pipes sticking out of the mud turned out to be a stack of Japanese rifles, two of which we pulled out of the mud and left near the entrance for collection later. Turning to the right and making our way up to the shallow end, we came across remnants of three or four cabins, timber stumps, and some wall material still sticking out of the mud.

This was most likely the officer's accommodation, and it would be interesting to dredge it and see what personal effects we might find – but for now, we had to stay focused. To the left of all this were the engine room entrance and funnel enclosure. There was nothing there.

At the end of the passageway, there were two cabins to our right. A toilet and a bathroom, all of which were no interest. We needed to be extra careful because copper wire and electric heaters were dangling everywhere. I noticed that there was some bomb damage to the rear bulkhead. This would make a good emergency exit. It's even large enough to swim through. We then turned left towards the starboard side and continued slowly so as not to stir up the sediment. Upon glancing to the right, we saw Garth's torch flicker and acknowledged by Morse code that we saw him.

Against the starboard bulkhead, there were several huge cooking pots. As Tony swung his torch around, he highlighted an open hatch. We turned to investigate, and when we did and were just a few feet away, Lindsay popped his head through the hatch like a 'Jack-in-the-box'. It was so sudden and unexpected, I nearly had a heart attack. Tony did a double-take and stumbled back, his scuba regulator catching on some copper wire that was dangling overhead, which caused a massive cloud of dust.

It's bad enough being in the dark bowels of a shipwreck at 40 metres, let alone to have some 'fuckwit' scare the crap out of you. It is very common to find giant groper and, even scarier, giant moray eels in shipwrecks. And my history with moray eels over the years has not been enjoyable.

After untangling Tony, we took a closer look into the hatch and saw what appeared to be containers. I reminded myself to speak to Lindsay about that when we returned to the surface. Lindsay was still looking up out of the hatch and had a big grin plastered all over his face. To take the smirk off his mug, I slowly leaned forward and in an instant, ripped off his mask. In a microsecond, he snatched it back out of my hand and disappeared down the hole like a gopher.

It was time to return to the surface. As we looked around for the fastest exit, I spotted another hatch. It was under a lot of debris and securely locked – and then I remembered Garth had mentioned this yesterday. While shining the torchlight around the area, I also spotted a large electric winch system directly above the hatch, and this set me thinking.

But it was time to leave, I tapped Tony on the shoulder and pointed to the large hole in the rear bulkhead, a quick exit point. With no fins, we pulled ourselves quickly along the deck to the hole and continued like that to where we stashed our fins. We quickly put them on and then swam back up to the decompression stop.

Back in the dinghy, Lindsay still had a huge smirk on his face and made that stupid, snorting noise he called a laugh. To me, it sounded more like a hyena with hiccups.

'Didn't you see me?' He said in between his snorting laughs while removing his scuba tank. 'I was watching you guys for ages.'

'I didn't even see your bubbles,' Tony said. 'You scared the crap out of me, and then I got tangled in some bloody copper wire. Not funny!'

'It was so sudden and unexpected, I thought another moray was having a go at me,' I laughed.

'But seriously,' I went on, directing my comments to Lindsay, 'how much further does the upper tween deck extend under the superstructure?'

'From that hatch, it's only about 30 cm to the engine room bulkhead and stacked along the hull there appears to be what looks to me like refrigeration units,' he replied.

'So, that means the other hatch is not accessible from the rear hold,' I said out loud, not speaking to anyone in particular, and then continued. 'And that winch mechanism above that hatch... Now that's interesting.'

'Yes, that's a bloody big winch and directly over that small hatch. Strange!' Tony remarked, his face showing that he was deep in thought.

'Okay, boys, we know where we are going to concentrate tomorrow,' I said, and then I turned to John. 'Get us back to the boat. Let's get ready for tonight's episode at the club.

Chapter 9

Let's Break a Leg or Two

It was just getting dark as we walked across the road to the club. John peeled off and made his way towards the back entrance of the Travelodge Hotel.

'I'll catch up with you later. Just want to have a word with a mate at the Travelodge.' he said as he walked towards the thick Poinsettia hedge that separated the Yacht Club from the Travelodge.

The area behind the hedge was quite dark, but the toilet block had an outside light facing the club. This would allow John to easily watch people as they came and went to the toilet without being seen. Once he spotted his mark, he would use the hole already cut in the fence to enter the toilet area.

It was just over an hour before John joined us at the table. He had a big smile from ear to ear, so we guessed that a diver was going to be out of action for a while.

'What something to eat?' I asked.

'Yes, I'm famished, but a drink first would be great,' he replied, rubbing his hands.

'I'll get the shout. Come and give me a hand,' I said, standing up. I was keen to know how it went down. 'What happened?' I asked when we were out of earshot. I had to keep Blondie out of this.

'It was even easier than I thought,' John replied. 'Like most blokes, he didn't go into the stinky toilet, but instead came to the back of the toilet block to piss against the wall and on the grass. He was only a couple of feet from the opening in the fence. As soon as he had his cock out, I crept up behind him and slammed the bar into his head. I knocked the fat prick out cold. Then, I had a quick look around, but no one was coming. I grabbed his wallet, pulled out the bills, threw the wallet over the fence, and then smashed both his lower legs with the bar. I could tell by the angle they ended up in that they were broken. He was still out like a light when I left. The fucken prick didn't feel a thing.'

'Hope you haven't killed him!'

'Nah, they'll find him soon and patch him up. Eventually, he'll be as good as new.'

Sure enough, while we were on our way back to the table, there was a commotion outside. All the club's staff was running around. I went over to the garden entrance and spoke to a guy standing by the door. 'What happened?' I asked.

'Bob Brown has been beaten and robbed,' he replied.

'Will he be okay?'

'Think so, but it looks like they might have broken his leg. Probably someone from Oscar Tammur's Mataungan Association. They've been playing up a bit lately.'

'Bloody-hell!' I replied as I left to return to our table.

I sat down and said to everyone there, and making sure that Blondie was listening, 'Looks like the Mataungan's beat the shit out of a guy behind the toilet block and robbed him.'

'He must have been a target,' Garth said. 'From what I know, the Mataungan's don't just randomly hurt people.'

'Oh well, nothing to do with us. Let's enjoy our meal. How about another round, Lindsay?'

'Good idea. Same, everyone?' With everyone nodding yes, he went to get the drinks.

Chapter 10

The Treasure Room

The morning air was fresh and clean. It was 6:00 a.m., and there is a welcome gentle south-east breeze this morning causing just the smallest ripple on the harbour. It was time to talk a bit more strategy.

I looked at Lindsay. 'You concentrate on getting the 'booby traps' set up and running this morning. The rest of us will work on the hatch.'

Looking at everyone, in turn, I said. 'This hatch is almost exactly how I envisaged the scenario would be. The strong room would be difficult to get into. And as I anticipated, it would be impossible to do so unnoticed while at the same time having easy access to the continuous deck for discharge. This hatch ticks all the boxes.'

'I agree,' Garth replied. 'I checked that out yesterday, and it's quite suspicious. Why on earth would they need such a heavy winch for such a small hatch opening?' he went on. 'But there's a fair bit of rubbish covering the damn thing, so it might be a good idea to use a couple of small charges to loosen everything up.'

'I think that's a good idea, Garth. You go and make up a couple of 1 kg charges and take down a couple of extra couple of sticks just in case.' I went on, 'The three of us will dive this in a relay. Tony will go down first with a sledgehammer and shove or kick anything he can to the shallow end. I will follow when he comes out and tie off the explosives. Garth, you follow last to finish up with the detonators. How does that sound?' There was a general agreement, and 10 minutes later, everyone was ready to board the dive tender.

'Just thinking,' I said. 'No sense in Garth and I coming along and twiddling our thumbs in the tender for 30 minutes, waiting for you guys to come out of the water. You go, do as much as you can and come back here. Then, we can talk about what you've managed to get done over a cup of coffee, and then Garth and I'll go down.' And with that, they were off.

*   *   *

Thirty minutes later, they were back and in high spirits. John immediately went about getting things ready for the next dive, while Tony and Lindsay joined us at the back deck.

'I was able to move a lot of stuff away from the hatch, but we do need to loosen the coral and cut the locks,' Tony explained.

I interrupted Tony. 'Yes, lucky she's down by the head. I guess all you had to do was give it a good shove, and it skidded down the passageway towards the forward bulkhead.'

Tony laughed. 'Yes, that's about it. And, I had a good look at that winch arrangement. That's a bloody big electric motor on that winch. It looks like it would easily lift a ton.' John poked his head around the corner to let us know everything was ready, and with that, Garth and I left to do our bit.

I jumped in first and swam down to the funnel to check the booby trap was still disabled. Then, I headed for the back of the cabin superstructure and down to the deck. I entered via the bomb hole in the rear bulkhead – a much quicker entrance to the work area than the deeper door at the front.

The visibility was good, and I quickly began to place the charges. Tony had certainly cleared a lot of the shit away. I had only just finished when Garth arrived with the shot wire and detonators. I gave him a wave and was on my way back to the surface.

Soon Garth was also back in the tender. John fired the shot, reeled in the detonator wire, and we were on our way back to the *Scorpion*.

Chapter 11

The Hiptimco

Each day we had almost nine hours free time between dives and having just one tender was proving to be a bit inconvenient. It was simply not enough to satisfy everyone's needs – Garth and Lindsay with their many girlfriends, Tony and his Japanese cave exploring and souvenir collecting, Blondie and me for our shore-side excursions. The dive tender was also an uncomfortable and wet ride, especially if the wind got up in the afternoons.

What we needed was something bigger, faster, and more comfortable. Tony spotted an advert on the Yacht Club notice board that he thought might be of interest. It featured a 7.5m fibreglass, inboard-outboard cruiser for $3,000. It looked good in the photos.

I made a quick phone call to the number on the advert and found out that the boat belonged to a Chinese accountant in the town named David Wu. He confirmed it was a Hong Kong built Hiptimco and was fitted with a Volvo Penta inboard/outboard. We could come and discuss it with him at his house tomorrow.

He was not much of a salesman. During the course of the conversation, he mentioned that he was having some trouble selling it. Apparently, the locals didn't trust it because it was manufactured in Hong Kong, and also the hull appeared very thin.

The name 'Hiptimco' struck a bell, and I remembered seeing one of these for sale at Tutt Bryant's in Rabaul a few years ago. In all probability, this was the same boat. I remember the price at the time was around $8,000. I was interested,

Before viewing the boat, I decided to talk with the Tutt's salesman and see what he could tell me about the Hiptimco. To my surprise, I was taken aback by his enthusiasm for the boat. According to him, the Hiptimco had a revolutionary hull. It was made of hand-laid epoxy over woven fibreglass matting, instead of the usual cheaper and inferior Polyester. The epoxy ensured a thin, light, but a very strong hull.

It had a huge flared bow, making it a very dry boat. It was powered by an economical 145-hp, four-stroke Volvo Penta motor and a Volvo outboard leg. The interior has two forward bunks, a toilet, and a salon area. It could power along at 30 kts in calm weather.

All right, I was interested, but $3,000 was more than I was prepared to pay. However, I had a hunch that Mr Wu might be willing to negotiate. By his own admission, he was having difficulty selling it. I thought it was worth checking out, so I phoned him back and made arrangements to view the boat the following day.

*   *   *

It was a particularly gorgeous day, not a cloud in the sky, and I might add, a bit of a hot walk to Mr Wu's house. We arrived at the address around mid-morning.

John commented, 'Bloody nice house, but can't see the boat.'

'He's a fucking accountant. Do you expect him to live in a shack? The boat may be around the back,' I replied as I knocked on the door.

This was not your typical high-set, New Guinea house like so many others, but rather a large, single-level dwelling set amongst beautiful tropical gardens and surrounded by large, shady trees. This was nice. I could hear footsteps on the timber floor, and a moment later, Mr Wu opened the door.

'Aar, you must be Simon, here to look at the speedboat. I'm David. Come on in and let me show you some photographs and details first and tell you a bit about it.'

I didn't let on that I'd already spoken to the guys at Tutt Bryant.

Leading us to the back patio, he asked. 'Would you like a beer?'

'Yes, thank you,' we both chimed in unison as he showed us out to the patio which fronted onto a good-sized swimming pool and manicured gardens.

'This is my wife, Suzie, and please call me David,' he said as he pointed to a brunette relaxing in the pool with a glass of wine.

Again, like parrots, we both chimed, 'Hi, Suzie.'

David returned with two ice-cold beers and pointed to some cane chairs, asking us to sit down. He'd brought with him a photo album and some brochures. He spread the photos on the coffee table and explained the pros and cons of the boat.

Meanwhile, Suzie came out of the water and went to the bar fridge to get herself a wine refill. I could not help admiring her slender body and large breasts, which were having a little trouble remaining in her rather skimpy bikini top.

She came over to where we were sitting and stood with legs apart, water dripping down her slender legs, her left hand on her hip, just watching us. She projected power and confidence. I got the impression she was older than David, but then Asians tend to age well, so that may not have been the case.

I was trying to guess her age when she winked at me. I suddenly realised I had been staring. Bloody hell! I have to get my mind back on the job and concentrate on what David was saying.

Fortunately, David was enthusiastically engrossed in describing his toy boat's attributes to notice that I was ogling his wife.

I snapped back to attention and said, 'Can we have a look at the boat? Didn't see it when we came in.'

'It's in the water, down by Toboi Slipway. You can take it out for a test run if you like.'

'I haven't felt well today. In any case, John has more experience with inboards. He'll take the boat for a spin and report back.'

'I'll take him down and show him around. There's a trick to getting her started sometimes. I'll just put on some clothes.' And with that, he left to get changed.

I pulled John aside and whispered, 'Be gone an hour, no less, or you're dead meat,' John smiled and nodded in agreement.

David came back neatly dressed in a white t-shirt and shorts. 'Help yourself to the beer. We won't be long.' And with that, they left.

* * *

Suzie had slipped back into the pool with her wine, and I ambled over to the edge.

'The water is great. Why don't you join me?'

'I haven't got any swimmers.'

'Don't let that stop you,' she said with a smile, as she whipped off her top to reveal her full, round breasts.

Getting undressed when you're only wearing shorts, an open shirt, and thongs is quick and easy. I'm glad it was because I was already at half-mast and didn't want to embarrass myself. I dove into the water in two seconds flat.

I surfaced close beside her and immediately wrapped my arms around her waist and pulled her in close. Before she had a chance to react, I cupped her breast with my left hand, and I kissed her deeply and passionately. My tongue found hers, and she responded in kind.

I was like someone possessed, crazy, craving – it was simply nothing less than sheer, animal lust. I moved from her mouth to suck her now-erect nipple. Not a word was spoken. This was raw, blind sex.

One of her hands found my fully erect member and was rubbing him furiously. Her breathing became erratic, and she giggled as I ducked underwater and removed her swimmers. Back on the surface, I immediately started kissing her again as my eager fingers quickly found her moist pussy. She willingly spread her legs to make it easy for me. I could not believe it. I was like a teenager at his first fuck and unable to control himself.

Without further ado, I sank my shaft deeply into her. She moaned in desperate passion and then something I had never experienced before; she started to contract her muscles and pulsate her vagina. I was horrified I could feel myself on the verge of coming. Fuck-off! It had not been two seconds! I was in a panic and pulled out, forcing 1,000 random thoughts through my mind – anything to stop myself from uselessly filling the pool with cream.

She sensed what I was doing and relaxed. Thank Christ, it worked. How embarrassing. I needed a little more time to cool off.

In a hoarse voice, I said, 'Hop-up and sit at the edge of the pool.' I grabbed her by the waist and helped her up.

'Now, lay back and get comfortable.' I pulled her closer to the edge and swung both of her legs over my shoulders. I immediately buried my head deep between her thighs. Soon, she was virtually crying. Her body was heaving in rhythms, and in just a few minutes, she came in waves. Her sweet nectar almost drowned me. Exhausted, she just lay there, but once is never enough. I tried to continue, but she begged me to stop. She was too sensitive.

I couldn't restrain myself any longer, I pulled her back into the water and turned her around. She was leaning with the palms of her hands on the edge of the pool. Her back arched as I thrust deep inside her cupping both her breasts at the same time. My rhythm became faster and faster – wilder, deeper, and harder until I virtually exploded. It was a climax one remembers for a lifetime. After a few moments, we dragged ourselves out of the water and lay exhausted at the edge of the pool.

*   *   *

After what seemed an eternity, she got up. 'Would you like a cold beer?'

'Thought you'd never ask.'

'Make yourself comfortable on the cane lounge,' she purred as she handed me the beer.

I gladly accepted the beer and moved over to the cane lounge and sat down to enjoy the drink, but she was not finished with me yet. Suzie started to fondle me gently, and when that was not enough to get me to full mast, she began using her tongue 'Do you like that?'

'Stupid question. Keep going.'

Then she straddled me and guided my now fully erect member into her as she went to work. I have never experienced a woman with such pussy control. The rhythmic pulsations together with the deliberate slow up-and-down motions was sheer ecstasy.

I buried my face deep into her breasts. I was in heaven. My mind was not my own. It seemed like an eternity before I exploded deep inside her a second time. Slowly, as my dick shrivelled, I also drifted back to reality.

The heat of the day ensured that it was not long before the pool's cooling water beckoned again. Still naked, we dove into the cool waters. Standing there in chest-high water, I hugged and kissed her passionately.

I couldn't help but tell her what a fantastic encounter it had been, it was only then that I learnt that her husband hadn't serviced her in over a year, or at least that's what she claimed, and she believed that he only kept her around as a White trophy to show off to his friends. It seems his passion was what Suzie called 'jungle bunnies,' not an entirely pleasant phrase for local Black girls.

It looks like he had quite a few. In a way, I could not help feeling a little sorry for him. Outwardly, they looked like an ideal couple. Suzie was one hell of a good looker and sure had some great sex tricks. I suspected that she had a very secret and colourful past. I was hoping that we might have another casual encounter sometime before I left Rabaul.

*   *   *

When David and John returned, Suzie was back in the pool, and I was casually sitting on the lounge reading a magazine, hopefully not appearing too casual or guilty.

It was apparent from the grin on John's face that he liked the boat. 'She's a beauty. A bit fancy for us, and we'll need to strip much of the interior, but a good-handling boat. With a hooker mounted on the bow, she would be a great dive tender when working further away from the mothership.'

97

'Okay,' I said, turning to David, 'I'm a cash buyer. How does $1,500 sound?'

He coughed and spluttered a bit. 'No, no, cannot do.'

'Well, what's your best price? Your asking price of $3000 is too much for something second hand and out of Hong Kong.'

Looking very unhappy, he thought for a while and replied, 'Lowest price,' he said, 'is $2,500 cash.'

'No, sorry, David. I'll meet you halfway. $2,000 cash today, right now. But that's it.'

David looked troubled like he was a lost child and then relented. 'Okay, $2,000 cash.'

'John, pay him please.'

John had three bundles of $1,000 cash stashed in his pockets. He pulled out two wads of cash and handed them to David.

'Can you please count the money and give me a receipt? A handwritten one will be okay, and I'd like the brochures on the table. Also, could you please call a taxi to take us to Toboi?' I asked.

With the receipt, paperwork, and keys in my pocket, we said our goodbyes and were on our way to the Toboi Slipway to pick up the Hiptimco. I let John drive her back to the *Scorpion* while I asked the Taxi driver to take me to the Yacht Club jetty to pick up the tender.

* * *

Everyone was keen to have a look at the new acquisition, even Blondie. John had been right. There was too much useless shit in the boat. It just made it too heavy. It was going to be a lot more responsive once we lightened the load.

I said to John, 'Get rid of the toilet and bunks in the forecastle, piss off the table and bunk arrangement, and rip out that built-in fridge. Leave the helmsman's chair and the two rear seats either side of the engine cowling.'

Blondie was beside herself. 'I don't believe it! You're going to destroy this beautiful boat.'

'We don't need all that fancy shit. This is a workboat, and taking all this useless crap out will lighten her substantially and make the boat much faster and responsive,' I replied.

Tony also thought I was crazy, but I had no use for a fancy boat. It had to be a practical workboat.

'Do you want me to keep any of the stuff?' John asked.

'Just the stainless-steel water tank from the forecastle. Dump the rest over the side.'

Chapter 12

Opening the Treasure Room

Later that afternoon, while relaxing with a cold beer, we mapped out the evening's dive. Tony and I would dive together, taking down a couple of short-handled sledgehammers, a big chisel, and a crowbar. If the hatch was not already open after the blast, our job was simply to pry it open.

Meanwhile, Lindsay would come down with us and enter the engine room via the massive hole in the side of the hull that sunk her. He will have a look to see if there is an entrance to whatever this hatch leads to from down there. Meanwhile, Garth will stay out of the water just in case we needed to send someone down to blast the hatch.

The extra weight of the sledgehammers meant we were in for a superfast express ride to the wreck. Slowing down was always a challenge, but we have had a lot of practice.

It is interesting to note that quite often when taking tools down, we would load them into a bucket for an express ride down. When finished, we would upend the bucket, fill it with air, and get a lift back to the surface. All of our scuba bottles were steel, and they would become slightly neutral-buoyant when full, so getting to the bottom was easy. Coming back up, especially from a deep dive, could be a challenge when carrying tools. We learnt many years ago that buckets were great elevators, like mini lifting bags. Yes, you got that right, buckets. There was no such thing as BCD's in the '60s and early '70s. They simply hadn't been invented, and the horse collar Fenzy didn't really qualify as a BCD.

*   *   *

We entered via the hole in the aft bulkhead and headed directly for the hatch. The first thing we noticed was the area surrounding the hatch was as clean as a whistle. The blast had done a great job of clearing all the shit away. The bright shining steel was just starting to get small rust blooms. However, the bloody hatch was still firmly in place.

When looking at it before the blast, and while it was smothered in rust, coral growth and rubbish, everything appeared severely corroded. I was confident that the hinges and locks would have come off with even a small blast, and if not, then they would be so weak as to be easily broken with hammer and chisel – but I was wrong. Everything was still in good condition. It looks like the Japs used some quality steel on this job.

We gave it a few futile bangs, mainly to see if the blast had cleared the coral and rust from under the lip of the hatch. We could achieve nothing with just a couple of hammers, so I let Tony know that I was going to have a look down the passageway. He acknowledged, 'Okay,' and by hand signals let me know that he was going down to the engine room.

I took both hammers and swam past the engine room entrance, which was to my left and headed towards the ship's front. I stopped to inspect what looked like medical equipment in a collapsed metal cupboard.

I carefully fanned the silt with my hand to see if anything of interest lay under the mud. Soon, several small glass vials with long necks popped up and, like dolls, danced in tune with my fanning. They most likely contained heroin but could have been something even more dangerous, so I left them. Then, something glass but more substantial became visible. I carefully dug my hand into the mud and pried it out. It was a very nice, long-necked research glass with 'cc' markings along the side and Japanese inscriptions. It looked interesting, so I decided to keep it, and tucked it into my shirt.

With my souvenir glass tucked away, I picked up the sledgehammers and continued downhill. I then saw where all the bits of steel and rubbish had fallen. Most of it was jammed up against the fore bulkhead. It is actually a blessing that the ship was down by the head. That saved a lot of hard work lugging the rubbish away from the work area. As we might need the hammers again, I left them just outside the doorway against the scupper board before heading to the surface.

Lindsay and Tony reached the decompression stop just as I was about to make my way into the tender. John took my tank and glass souvenir, and with a strong flip of my fins, I slipped up and sat on the gunnel for a moment before dropping into the tender. I removed my shirt top to catch the last rays of the sun while waiting for the boys to come out of the water.

We were on our way back to the *Scorpion* when I asked Lindsay, 'What did you find in the engine room?'

'Nothing much, I only went down to the first level below the continuous deck. There's a lot of small machinery there. I also noticed many large tools bolted to the hull. I followed the mezzanine floor to a dead end, by the look of it, about where the hatch is, but definitely not quite as far.' He went on, 'There was something strange, though. There used to be a large doorway into whatever was behind there, but it was welded shut.'

'That's a bloody good sign. They obviously wanted to keep people out of there,' I said.

It was now 5:00 p.m., and there was no time to muck about. We needed to get Garth into the water as quickly as possible. So, it was a combined effort to get the explosive charges made up. That's a bloody strong hatch and combing, so I was not going to muck about. 'Let's use four bundles of AN90, each with 2 kg of high explosives,' I ordered. 'That should shift the fucken thing.'

Because we only had one diver in the water and limited bottom time, we made up the charges all ready to go on the surface, complete with a detonator and 'detonating wire'. All that Garth had to do is take them down, jam them in place, and slowly make his way to the surface trailing the detonating wire behind him.

'I want you to place one bundle under each hinge, one at the lock, and the last one under the lip of the lid on the same side. That should move it,' I told him.

'No problem,' Garth replied as he stuffed the explosives and roll of wire under his wet suit.

'Don't blow yourself up,' Tony joked as he handed him the torch.

'You wish,' Garth shot back with a grin.

'Okay, Garth, let's go,' John said.

And with that, they were on their way to the wreck. Joe and Jack immediately began to clean up and put the leftover explosives back in the locker. For the rest of us, it was time to have a shower and relax. Dinner would be ready when they came back.

Showers for the guys in speedos or underpants were usually taken on the front deck under a hose strapped to the ships derrick. It was popular with the divers and crew. However, Blondie preferred the claustrophobic privacy of the bathroom, which I always found quite strange as she had no issues showing off her body any other time.

Chapter 13

The Tiger Shark Incident

It was 6:30 p.m. I was relaxing with Blondie in my bunk waiting for Garth and John to return when all of a sudden, there was one hell of a commotion as the tender crashed into the *Scorpion*.

John shouted at the top of his lungs, 'Garth's been attacked by a shark! Hey, Simon! Garth's been attacked by a shark!'

I jumped out of bed like a jackrabbit, with visions of severed arms and legs, 'What the fuck are you talking about?' I yelled.

My heartbeat returned to something like normal when I saw Garth climbing on board with no visible parts missing or blood spurting on deck. Tony and Lindsay appeared on the front deck, both with bewildered looks on their faces.

John was still beside himself, stomping around in circles. 'For Christ's sake! Calm down, John!' I yelled as I pushed past him. John is petrified of just about everything in the ocean, and sharks, snakes, and eels were top of the list.

'Garth, what the hell happened? You haven't been bitten, have you?' I said, looking him up and down.

'No, but fuck! It was close. Let's get comfortable on the back deck, and I'll tell you all about it. Have Cookie bring a bottle of rum or vodka,' he said as he looked down at his outstretched hand that was still shaking.

We sat down, and Cookie plonked a bottle of Bacardi and five glasses on the table. Garth immediately snatched the bottle from the table and poured himself a drink that disappeared in one mighty gulp. He filled his glass again, but I grabbed hold of his arm, forcing him to slow down.

'You're no good drunk. What happened?' I said in an earnest tone.

Garth took a deep breath and began to settle down and began. 'It was already quite dark when I got down to the wreck, and black as hell in the superstructure. Not a problem though, but getting the explosives locked against the hinges took a bit longer than expected. I had to find a couple of pieces of scrap steel to hold them in place, then one of the fucken detonators dropped out.' He took another sip of rum.

'Go on,' I prompted.

'By the time I had everything in place, I looked at my watch and noticed I'd been down for 20 minutes. I wasn't worried. I'd just spend an extra five or so minutes decompressing.'

'What about the shark?' Lindsay interrupted in a frustrated tone, keener to learn the meaty bits.

I shot daggers in Lindsay's direction and prompted Garth to continue,

'I was quite happy hanging onto the 'deco line' in the twilight playing with the bioluminescence, when all of a sudden, I noticed a shark swim by in the gloomy distance. It was quite stunning with a phosphor-like trail coming from its tail. At first, I wasn't worried, but when it got closer, I saw that it wasn't a pesky reef or nurse shark, but a bloody tiger!'

Garth looked around and continued, 'Now, I was getting a little worried. I couldn't pop directly up to the surface because I didn't want to risk the bends. As it made its second pass, things began to look serious. This thing was huge – at least 4 metres, almost as big as the tender. It was circling close to the surface, and I was desperately hoping that John would spot it and scare it away with the .303, but no, he was up there pulling his fucken dick!'

'Fuck off! It was dark,' John retaliated, and by the look of it felt a bit guilty that he had been goofing off instead of paying attention. Garth took another sip of his rum.

'For fuck's sake, go on!' I prompted.

'He circled me for a while, very calmly, very deliberately, like he was testing me. I knew I would have to be prepared just in case he had a go at me. I wrapped my legs around the buoy line and took my weight belt off and clipped it to the D- shackle. I then tied off the detonating wire to the mooring and let some 15 metres play out from the reel and stuck it back into my wetsuit. I then took my scuba tank off and stuck it under my arm.'

'Unfortunately, there was no rock for me to hide under. Instead, I was dangling like a juicy bit of bait under the tender. Your episode at Rossel flashed in mind,' Garth said, looking at me.

'You remember. We were working the sub, and you shoved your movie camera down that shark's throat. Well, I had something better, my scuba tank. I was confident that it would do the job if the shark tried anything.'

Garth continued. 'He made another pass and then disappeared into the gloom. I sighed in relief, thinking that he had left, but that was short-lived. I saw him reappear out of the gloom. This time he was coming straight towards me. When he was about 2 metres away, he slowly and deliberately opened his mouth. As he did so, I lunged forward and shoved the scuba bottle, backpack, and regulator into his open jaws.'

'Like lightning, he snapped his jaws shut. It must have frightened the hell out of him when his jaw clamped down on that bloody steel bottle. There was an awesome explosion of power, as he made a 180-degree turn that almost knocked the wind out of me. One second he was there, and the next, he just simply disappeared.'

'At that moment, I didn't care about bottom time. All I could think of was air and the safety of the tender. I covered the distance to the surface in seconds and exploded out of the water like a penguin. I belly-flopped onto the deck. I don't even remember touching the gunwale.'

Garth looked at the now empty glass of rum and turned to Cookie. 'A cup of coffee, Cookie.'

The tension drained from Garth, and the mood around the table was much better. Some jokes were made at his expense, and things slowly got back to normal.

Although it was for Garth's benefit, I spoke to everyone at the table but looked at Garth. 'You know, what you experienced just now with the tiger shark is typical of the species. It's quite different from reef sharks that show their displeasure by darting around like blue-arse flies before coming in to take a chunk out of you when your back's turned. Tigers and great whites are very different in their approach. I guess it has a lot to do with their size. They take their time, calmly sizing up their prey with several passes. When ready, they simply come closer until a short distance away and calmly open their jaws then surge forward to take a huge chunk out of you. You were lucky to have pre-empted it, Garth. Good job!'

'Just changing the subject,' I said. 'did someone remember to pop the charges?'

'I did,' John replied.

'Good, let's see what tomorrow brings.' I turned to Cookie in the galley. 'Come on, Cookie. Let's get some food on the table. We're all hungry.'

Chapter 14

The Silver

The next morning, all thoughts of the shark incident were long forgotten. We were like naughty children heading to the candy store. I was first in the water and powered down to the wreck, squeezing my nose to compensate for the rapid pressure change. The rest were not far behind me, following in line. Everyone wanted to get to the hatch first.

I dived through the break in the rear bulkhead, the bright beam of my torch zeroed towards the hatch. I was greeted with a perfect result.

The hatch cover was nowhere to be seen. It had simply disappeared. I briefly looked for it in the immediate area but saw nothing. It had been blown clean off. I made a beeline for the open hatch and without hesitation, dove headlong into the darkness.

My scuba tank squealed as it scraped against the now-shiny metal opening. Still upside down with my legs dangling out of the hatch, I shined my torch around the room to get my bearings and to make sure there are no 'nasties' ready to chew my head off. Giant gropers come to mind.

I could immediately see that I'm in a small room some 3 metres by 5 metres and some 3.5 metres tall. Apart from my bright torchlight beam, there was not a skerrick of light filtering in from anywhere. As I shined the torch around the room, I could not help thinking, *Where the hell did the mud come from?*

The first thing I noticed against the hull were two large safes. Then, as I moved the torch down to illuminate the deeper end of the room, I saw what looked like a jumble of small bricks poking out of the mud. My heart skipped a beat. My first thought was...gold!

I immediately dropped to the bottom of the room and gently rested on my knees, being careful not to stir things up too much. I bent down and carefully pulled a brick out of the mud. The first thing that came to mind was how heavy it was. On closer inspection, I saw it was the wrong colour for gold, but looked more like lead.

I took my heavy divers' knife and bashed into the brick a couple of times, then shined the torch directly at the cut. I instantly recognised it as silver. I glanced around the room. There must be hundreds of these silver bricks buried in the mud.

A flood of searchlights flickered around the room, and I knew the boys were behind me and wanted to come in. I turned around and looked up, showing them the bullion, making the 'Okay' sign with my free hand and punching the air – well, water. I must have had a grin from ear to ear as their blinding torchlights flashed across my face. I signalled the boys not to come in until I was out of the room. We couldn't afford to stir up too much mud, or visibility would turn to zero, and then we might have trouble finding the exit.

On my way out, I stopped momentarily to make a quick mental note about the safes I guessed to be about 2 metres high by 1.5 metres wide and 1 metre deep. I could also see that the tops the safes were securely welded to the hull.

I'd seen enough for this dive, and with the silver bullion tucked inside my shirt and sitting securely on my weight belt, I squeezed past the boys and made my way to the surface.

Even before allowing me to get into the tender, John was firing off questions. 'Did the blast work? Did you get into the room?' he asked, as he took my scuba tank and, like a mini-crane, swung it onto the deck.

'Yes, it was perfect. The hatch just disappeared, leaving a nice clean hole in the deck. And, before you ask,' I continued, 'yes, we did find the ship's safe. There are two, in fact, and also hundreds of these,' I said, smiling, as I pulled the silver brick out of my shirt and dumped it on the deck.

John's eyes nearly bugged out of his head. 'You fucking beauty!' he yelled. It was John's stock reply whenever he was seriously pleased with something. He had a peculiar way of speaking the phrase which was unique to him. He said it with a drawn-out 'y-o-u' and put emphasis is on the 'beauty', which sounded like 'be-u-teeee', with long gaps between each word.

A few minutes later, Garth, Lindsay, and Tony joined us, each with a silver bar. They could not have stayed down any longer even if they had wanted to. With the scramble to get a block of silver each, the visibility quickly turned to zero. They were smart enough to form a human chain and allow the leader to follow his air bubbles to the ceiling. Then, like blind men, fumbled for the hatch and made their escape.

In the tender, we were in high spirits discussing the find, the four of us each polishing the silver to make it shine. I noticed John looking on in a forlorn way, and I thought it was time to take the mickey out of him.

'Looks like these are about 5 kg,' I said, juggling the bullion in my hand and looking at John. 'At the current price of $1.70 per oz and 32 oz to the kg, that makes each ingot worth around $270. Now, we have one each. It looks like it's time for you to go down and get yours.'

'Fuck you! Sometimes you guys piss me off. I have to burn up here in the stinking hot sun while you guys go for your cool dip. Give me yours,' He said, making his way past the jumble of scuba tanks lying on the deck to reach for my ingot.

Even I had to be a little careful when it came to dealing with John sometimes. He was, after all, a bit crazy. 'Okay, okay. Don't get your knickers in a knot. Here, take a look. I'll bring one up for you tomorrow. This one's for Blondie,' I said with a grin as I handed him the silver brick.

John snatched it from me. Suddenly it seemed it quite small in his big hands. He carefully placed it on the seat next to him, giving it a little pat. Watching him pat the silver and actually talk to it just confirmed my suspicions about him. I knew all along he was crazy. All the way back to the *Scorpion,* he appeared to be mesmerised by the metal.

Back on deck, I reclaimed the ingot and handed it to Blondie. The weight took her by surprise, and she nearly dropped it. It would not have been pleasant if it had fallen on her foot or worse still mine.

'Your new silver doorstop,' I said with a grin.

She rolled her eyes and gave me that 'You're stupid!' look again, holding out the silver ingot for me to take it back.

'This dirty little chunk of metal, my dear is worth over $250. Not something to be sneezed at,' I said, taking it back from her.

She looked surprised and then smiled. At that moment, Cookie sang out to say that breakfast was ready. I only then realised just how hungry I was.

At the salon table, a huge pile of toast, a pot of hot baked beans, and scrambled turtle eggs were waiting for us. I don't like turtle eggs, so I snapped at Cookie, 'Where the hell did you get the turtle eggs?' As I scrapped them to one side of the plate and started on the baked beans.

'The market boss.'

'I'll have them,' Lindsay said as he reached for my plate to get the eggs.

'Piss off. Blondie might want them.'

It was time to talk a little strategy, but first, I turned to Lindsay. 'I think it's important we should make sure that we don't leave the booby trap switched off like we have done the past few days. Lindsay, it's your job to make sure it's switched on after each dive.

'Okay, not a problem "boss",' he chuckled, mimicking Cookie.

It was not going to be easy getting the silver out of the room. The hatch opening was small, and it opened into an enclosed space. Also, only two people could work comfortably in the room, and the micro-volcanic mud was a real problem. Pulling the silver bars out of the mud would turn the visibility to zero, just as the boys found out this morning.

We had no option at this point but to dredge. After throwing the idea around the table for a while, we agree to make a small 50 mm air dredge with a 15-metre tail. This should be long enough to get it roaring because the longer the tail in an upward direction, the greater the expansion of the rising air, and the more powerful the suction. We would power it using scuba bottles to power the dredge.

While digging around in the mud, none of us had come across any oyster or clamshells, which was great, as they are the bane of underwater dredges, constantly clogging them up. They are especially bad if they are stuck halfway up the tail.

By working in relays, two divers at a time, we should have the room clear of mud in a day or so. Also, Tony suggested that it might be a good idea for each diver to take down a small lifting bag while dredging and return to the surface with two or three ingots per dive.

After breakfast, Garth and John got to work on building the dredge while Blondie and I went shoreside to buy the 50 mm ribbed hose for the tail. We had to visit a couple of different stores, but eventually, we found what we were looking for at Steamships. They had some 50 mm water suction hose that was perfect for our needs.

Blondie and I took the opportunity to while away a couple of hours at the Travelodge coffee lounge. From there we moved next door to the hotel's pool. At this time of day, it was easy to find a couple of deck chairs and relax. And before I knew it, two bottles of wine had disappeared.

While I was getting sleepy, Blondie was getting quite loud and racy. Her playfulness when drunk was good fun under normal circumstances, but it was proving to be embarrassing in public, and some guests were starting to take notice.

Bloody hell! She was drunk and wanted to play, keeping her hands off my crotch was bad enough, but her habit of not wearing a bra was becoming a problem. Every time she leant over to kiss me, her tits kept falling out, and worse still, her dress was riding up almost to her waist. She was in 'lolly-land', oblivious to anyone else. All she was interested in was playing, and the only playing with her was sex.

It was time to make a quick exit. I dropped the money on the table, which I hoped was enough and scooped her up in my arms and carried her out via the back entrance and down to the jetty.

She was wriggling like a worm and still trying to kiss me and chew my ear. Somehow, I managed to get her to the *Hiptimco* without falling over. As soon as I cast off and stepped back into the boat, she pulled my shorts down and went to her knees. I knew only too well that all that mattered to her now was sex, so I had no option but to oblige. We were drifting in front of the Yacht Club, the blowjob was amazing, but it was time for some real sex. Fortunately, the helmsman's chair was just the right height, so I picked her up, bent her over it and went to work doggie style.

*   *   *

It was almost 2:00 p.m. before, somehow, we made it back to the *Scorpion*. Garth was there to catch the ropes. He hauled Blondie out of the *Hiptimco* and onto the deck like a rag doll and held her steady.

'Throw her over your shoulder and get her into my bunk,' I ordered.

I was almost jealous at the ease of which he was able to carry her, fireman's style, up the ladder.

Before following her to the comfort of my bunk, I left instructions with John to ensure that everything should be ready for a 5:00 p.m. dive and to have someone wake me.

I needed a couple of hours of sleep to recharge. I was a little concerned that alcohol may induce a bit of narcosis. I would have to be both cautious and careful. Amazingly, Blondie was already off with the fairies and sprawled all over the bunk. I shoved her to the one side and lay down next to her.

It had indeed been an exciting afternoon, but it demonstrated that I would need to keep a close eye on her at parties, especially if there was alcohol around. I must've been in a very deep sleep, for I woke up with a start to find Joe shaking me by my shoulder and calling my name. For a microsecond, I didn't even know where I was or why he was waking me.

'Wake up Simon. We have to get ready for the dive,' Joe whispered in my ear while trying to avert his eyes from Blondie's half-naked form. I mused at how embarrassed the locals get when looking at women's thighs.

'Okay, okay,' I replied. 'Give me a few minutes to wake up. Go down to the galley and have Cookie make me a strong, black cup of coffee.'

With that, Joe left the wheelhouse. It did not take long for me to pull my wits together and get down on deck. I stopped to look at the tender and noticed that it was already fully loaded, including extra scuba bottles and the air dredge. Everything seemed to be ready and only waiting for me.

I found the dive crew relaxing and chatting on the back deck, all suited up and ready to go. I asked Cookie to get me my Lycra suit and dive boots while I drank my coffee and quickly got dressed. Ten minutes later, we were in the tender on our way to the *Hakkai*.

Our dive plan was simple. Lindsay and I would take down the dredge and two scuba bottles and get everything ready to work. My job was to take the suction end of the dredge into the treasure room and ensure a sufficient length of hose in there to work the whole area. Lindsay, meanwhile, had to find a convenient porthole and poke the tail of the dredge through it. Then he had to go out of the wreck and take the tail up as high as the length allowed, fastening it somewhere near the bridge deck. He had to make sure it was securely fastened, or it would whip around like a loose garden hose.

On Lindsay's signal that everything was ready, I would fire up the dredge and work as long as my remaining bottom time allowed. Tony and Garth would follow, as soon as we surfaced, each taking a full scuba bottle to feed the dredge.

The dredge worked like a beauty, and I could easily have accidentally overstayed my bottom time. But very fortunately, Lindsay's tap on the shoulder reminded me it was time for us to make for the surface, taking the empty scuba bottle with us.

As soon as I was in the tender, the first question Tony threw up at me was, 'Where's the ingots you guys were supposed to bring up?'

'Bloody forgot. With getting the dredge ready and then starting work dredging, I simply lost track of time. As it was, I would probably have over-stepped my bottom time if Lindsay hadn't prompted me. Fucken lucky!' I replied.

A few minutes later, Lindsay popped his head above the surface. John quickly leaned over the side and grabbed his scuba tank and lifting bag with two ingots, allowing Lindsay to swing his lean body on the gunwale facing the ocean, while he cleared his nose and washed his hands. Tony and Garth almost immediately disappeared below the surface on their way to the bottom.

*   *   *

And so, the monotony of dredging continued one diver after another. But on the bright side, our haul of silver onboard grew. It was not until after the morning of the third day that the silt was gone, and twenty-five ingots were safely on board. It was now time to retrieve the bulk of the silver. But first, we had to dismantle the dredge and as quickly as possible. It stuck out of the starboard porthole like a beacon and roadmap to the treasure room.

Recovering the silver was a physically hard and challenging job. It was all compounded by the darkness, the confined space in the treasure room, and the small hatch opening. Each bucket load of silver has to be manually hauled up out of the treasure room, then dragged uphill to the bomb hole at the rear bulkhead, all the while being careful not to drop it into the dumbwaiter hatch near the cooking pots. It then had to be lifted up and over the bomb hole and dropped onto the back deck. From there, it was easy airlift to the surface.

And all the time we were doing this, we had to be vigilant of the sport divers who might be visiting the wreck. Everything we hauled out of the treasure room each day had to go all the way to the surface. We could not leave anything on the back deck for prying eyes to discover.

This treasure hunting business was turning into bloody hard work, but the relay system was working well. The diver in the treasure room would put six ingots into a fire bucket, the diver at the hatch opening would haul it up. The next diver would drag the bucket to the opening at the rear bulkhead. The last diver would load the ingots to a bigger basket ready for airlift to the surface.

This way, we managed to pull up around 200 kg per dive. By day two, I was exhausted, so much so, I was even refusing Blondie's advances – and that is saying something!

But by the end of the third day, I dropped the last silver ingot into the bucket. I moved to the hatch and gave Lindsay the thumbs-up and then the cut-throat signal pointing below. Lindsay understood, and the bucket was on its way. My torchlight flashed across a huge smile on his face as the last bucket disappeared through the hatch.

One hundred and seventy-five silver ingots now nicely carpeted the floor of our explosive magazine – out of sight, out of mind.

Now it was time to discuss how on earth we are going to open the safes.

Chapter 15

Working the Two Safes

Relaxing on the back deck with the crew, I made a quick estimate of our haul so far. We had a total of 175 silver ingots safely locked away in the explosive magazine. This represented about $30,000, although we were aware that we would be lucky to get somewhere around $25,000 on the black market.

Whether this project was worth the effort, now depended on what we find in the safes. More thinking out aloud than talking to anyone. I said. 'Would have been great if the "arseholes" had just stacked the gold on the deck. But no, they have to put the damn stuff into two, huge, fucking safes and then weld the damn things to the bloody hull. Bugger me!'

'It's better than not having them at all.' Blondie chimed in.

'What the fuck are you talking about?' I retorted in an annoyed tone.

'Well, at least you found two safes. That's better than not finding them,' She replied, looking at me in defiance.

'Fuck me... Why state the obvious?' was all I could say, as I shook my head and turned to the boys.

'Yes, it's great to find the safes, but we still got to work out how to get the fucken things open and out of there. Let's go down in the morning and assess the situation. We will then be in a better position to make a decision.'

'It's going to be bloody difficult to blast those safes open down there,' Tony said, shaking his head.

I spoke to Garth and Lindsay, 'What do you guys think?'

Lindsay looked up from the table. 'I don't know, but it sure looks like the safes are securely welded to the hull.'

'Yes, and that's unusual. Every safe I've ever come across has simply been bolted to the deck.' I went on, 'Makes me suspect they did that because of the weight. I guess they didn't want them falling over in rough weather.'

'That's probably right, Simon. How thick you reckon the safes' casings are?' Garth asked.

'I've no idea, but these are solid, old-fashioned, key safes," I said. 'I'll take my camera with me tomorrow and take some photos, and I'll see what I can find out.'

We agreed that I should enter the water first. That way, I should be able to get some decent photos before the room silted up. Tony would come down a few minutes after me, followed by Garth.

After dinner, a relaxing game of cards, and a few stiff drinks, Blondie was ready for a nap, and I was physically tired, so I followed her to our bunk.

* * *

First thing in the morning, I got my new Nikonos II underwater camera ready, complete with flash holder and a sock full of spare flashbulbs. I would use black-and-white film, as this can be developed in Rabaul. Colour film and slides must go to Australia for processing.

With the camera slung around my neck, Lindsay and I went down first. Lindsay headed off in the direction of the funnel to disarm the booby trap, while I glided towards the rear of the accommodations area and made my way directly to the treasure room. I shined the torch into the hatch, and thankfully the mud had settled, and the water was crystal clear.

I slipped through the manhole as far as my ankles and hooked my feet to the hatch rim. I was, in effect, hanging upside down. I didn't want to disturb even the little bit of mud that's left inside. My torch highlighted each safe in turn. They were old and huge. The weld across the top was clearly visible. I took my first photo.

I then dropped into the room and concentrated on each safe, taking four photos as quickly as I could reload the flash. Each flash, in the confined space, momentarily blinded me. When my eyes returned to normal, I used my torch to get a closer look at each safe in turn. They appeared identical and stood on short, thick legs. Both safes were fully welded on top and down each side, but not underneath.

Each safe had only one, big door. There were no combination locks, but instead, these safes required a key. The keyhole was smack-bang in the middle of the door. To the left of each keyhole was a very sturdy looking handle for opening the safe. As I ran my hands against the steel door, I inspected the strong, bulky hinges that protruded to the front. I know I would be wasting my time blasting the hinges. They were not what's holding the door shut, inside are some very solid steel bars!

I brushed the dust off the copper nameplate just above the keyhole hoping I might be able to get a name, but unfortunately, it was printed in Japanese. Next, I banged on the door and the side of the safe with the backend of my diver's knife, and that rewarded me with a solid 'clunk', very solid, – no tinny clang here. This was a very solid and robust piece of work.

I was now ten minutes into my dive and had seen enough. It was time to exit. I wanted to take some other, more general snaps of the wreck for prosperity.

Just as I was about to exit the hatch, my orch flashed across Tony's smiling eyes waiting to enter.

As Tony disappeared down the hatch, I took a photo of the three large cooking pots. Moving across to the head, I took a picture there, and then I swam down the passageway to the port doorway, where, surprise, surprise, I find the hatch that we blew off.

I exited the port doorway, took a photo of the companionway, and then swam over the gunwale and upward on the ship's outside towards the funnel. I took a couple of snaps as I went and then slowly finned my way back to the surface.

Lindsay was already in the tender. We relaxed while waiting for Garth and Tony to arrive. Some twenty minutes later, back on the *Scorpion,* we again huddled on the back deck discussing our findings.

Then, something strange happened. Blondie put her two-cents worth in and suggested it may not be such a smart idea to get the photos developed in Rabaul.

'What the hell are you talking about?' I snapped in a sarcastic tone.

'Because, "stupid" ... the operators check each photo for quality, and underwater pictures of a shipwreck will naturally create quite a bit of interest. I know what I'm talking about because some "arsehole" in a photoshop allowed naked pictures of me to end up on the street.' There was venom in her voice as she spoke with her head held high and looking defiant, and there's that 'stupid' bit again, I'll have to talk to her about that.

The boys burst out laughing, Garth quipped. 'Do you have any to show us?'

Blondie, as cool as a cucumber shot daggers his way and said, 'You've already seen more than most people.'

Fuck, what did she mean by that? But we had to agree she was right. Rabaul is a small town, and a series of photos taken on a shipwreck in the harbour with many highlighting a huge safe would surely get tongues wagging. So, taking photos was a wasted exercise. Thinking about it logically, we didn't need the images anyway. I had seen enough to make a judgment of what was probably the best course of action. Trying to open the safes in the room just was not an option. It was not that it was impossible, there were just too many constraints. The obvious answer was to get the safes out of the room and away from the ship.

It was not rocket science, and I suggested the only logical conclusion was to surgically remove that section of the hull to which the safes are welded and send the whole kit and caboodle to the ocean floor. From there, it would merely be a matter of lifting it away from the wreck and dropping it in shallow water a short distance from the *Scorpion,* where we would be free to work all day without interruptions.

With everyone in agreement, we then had the awful task of making up the explosive charges. For this blast, we would use the best underwater explosive we have in our arsenal, Sakura 90 dynamite. It was a very fast and water-resistant plastic explosive especially useful for cutting steel.

For a job like this, the trick would be to stuff the explosives into lengths in sections of a fireman's hose. In this case, we would need four short lengths, each about 3 metres long. Each length of firehose would then first be threaded with two strands of Cordtex, the ends of which would protrude about 500 mm from each end of the hose. The whole thing would then be stuffed intermittently with explosives and sand. Interestingly, the sand is included to add weight. This makes it easier to set the charge in place and saves us having to use weights. Once packed and the ends tied, you have a massive 'explosive sausage', as we like to call them.

*   *   *

It's 9:00 am, and, at long last, the four lengths of firehoses, each filled with explosives and sand, together with their little Cordtex tails, were all neatly stretched out on the front deck. Everything was ready for us to take them down. There was no sense in rushing to place them as most of us have a cracking, nitro-glycerine headache, so we will just have to wait for a couple of hours.

All too soon, it was time to hit the water and set some serious charges. Because of the weight of the sausages, each diver would take down one explosive sausage. Tony volunteered to 'bounce dive' and return to the surface for the detonating wire.

When considering how best to place the charges, we decided to take advantage of the hydrostatic pressure and ensure the optimum placement. We will be setting the charges from the inside. The resulting backpressure should cause the safes to be thrown clear of the wreck. It will be interesting to see the result.

Once in the treasure room, the sausages were quickly secured in place. One across the top, and one down each side of the safe. The most difficult was the one underneath the safes, by the time I got that right, Lindsay and Garth had already daisy-chained the sausages together with the Cordtex tails. I pulled four detonators out of my shirt and tied one to each Cordtex knot. This would ensure an almost instantaneous blast.

Tony was back with the det-wire, and as soon as he handed me the end, he was on his way back to the surface, slowly trailing the det-wire behind him. I made the connection, and everything was ready. It was time for us to head back to the surface.

*   *   *

Detonating 100 kg of explosives in one blast can create a little problem in Rabaul, especially if you want to keep it secret. The Rabaul Vulcanological Observatory monitors all seismic activity. An explosion of this size would register on their instruments, and by simple triangulation, they would be able to determine that the epicentre was the *Hakkai Maru*.

We had a bit of a chuckle in the tender, Tony saying that if Pat hears about the blast on the *Hakkai*, he'll think it's his condenser and be happy. As soon as all the bums were off the seat, John did the honours and detonated the blast. This time, there was a loud hard crack on the tender hull and a big upwelling of dirty water. One thing for sure this blast went off with a real bang, but we would have to wait until tomorrow to see the result.

Chapter 16

The *Santo* Comes to Town

After the blast, all the boys went shoreside, and Blondie and I decided to relax and chill out on our deck chairs at the top deck, catching a few rays of sunshine with a glass of wine before the afternoon's dive. Even better still, Cookie had outdone himself by putting a platter of nibbles together before he left.

The sun wasn't far from dipping over the mountain ridge. I looked across at Blondie and couldn't help thinking just what a magnificent creature she was. She was lying there on her stomach, propped up by her elbows, her silky blond hair slightly rippling in the afternoon breeze, deeply engrossed in one of her girlie magazines. Her back arched, revealing her perky tits, which did not quite reach the deck chair, the sight was enough for me to start getting the urge.

Still lying on my left side, I positioned myself a little closer and reached over to her, I ran my hand through her silky hair and gently down her smooth back. I slowly continued to her firm arse, where I slipped my hand in under her bikini and continued down towards her pussy. She gave a little wriggle without looking up, slightly repositioning herself and making it easier for me. At that moment, I knew I was going to be 'in like Flynn'.

I was already hard but restrained myself and decided to give her a massage first. She always liked that. I needed some lubricant, and what better than the coconut oil she's using to help her get a golden tan? I got up and sat side-saddle on my deck chair and poured a generous quantity of oil down her back. I then proceeded to give her a shoulder and back massage.

I didn't hurry, but all the while slowly working my way down her spine to her arse. Soon, I dispensed with the bikini and began gently massaging the cheeks of her arse and down to her pussy. It was producing the desired result. She stopped reading her magazine and was now flat on her stomach, enjoying the sensations that were rippling through her body.

My dick was now so hard I thought it was going to explode. There's nothing sexier than a good doggie, and it was time to stick it in. I got up and straddled her, poured more coconut oil down her crack, and concentrated on getting my rod into her pussy, being very careful not to make a mistake here. Then, with both hands planted firmly on her arse, I began to start pumping harder and harder, all the while looking down and admiring her beautiful body.

I looked upward to thank God for sending me this amazing woman, and at that moment, in the distance, I spotted a small barge cruising past Matiput Point. I thought to myself, *Shit, that looks like the* Santo. *But, no, it couldn't be.* I briefly stop pumping Blondie and blinked my eyes and looked again. The barge has disappeared, but only momentarily, as she quickly re-emerged from behind the Beehives and continued into the harbour. Now I'm sure it's Dave's salvage barge, the *Santo.*

Well, that was enough to totally and utterly destroy my desire, and my once-proud rod very quickly shrivelled and was now no more useful than a piece of slack rope. Even Blondie's desperate pleading and encouragement had no effect. The magic of the moment gone. I could not believe it, not at this point in the salvage. This was the last thing we needed. We could deal with the locals, but a professional salvage operator was an entirely different matter.

It was close to 4:30 p.m. In the distance, I recognised the signature, white spray from *Hiptimco's* flared bow, the boys were on the way back to get ready for work. I watched as they made a detour towards the *Santo* and then cruised alongside it for a few minutes before changing course back to our anchorage. Well, at least Dave would know we were in town, although he would have found out soon enough, anyway.

A few minutes later, the boys pulled alongside, and as expected, there was a fair bit of excitement. There was no way out of it, we would have to go to the club tonight. It was the only way we were going to find out what the hell he was doing here. So, at 6:00 p.m., *Hiptimco* was skipping over the smooth waters of the harbour to the Yacht Club jetty.

*   *   *

The *Santo* was now anchored close to the club. We slowed down on the way past to see if anyone was still on board. A local crewman stuck his head over the gunwale as we approached. 'Where's Dave?' I shouted.

'Him he go long club,' he answered.

'Okay,' I replied.

A few minutes later, we were doubled-up alongside Dave's tender at the jetty. We had only just crossed the road and entered the manicured club grounds when there was a wave and shout from the deck.

'Hey "arsehole"! What the fuck are you doing here? Come and join us!' Dave yelled.

A few more chairs and another table were jammed up, and soon there were ten of us at the table. Tony ordered a round of drinks from the waiter, and after introductions, I asked Dave, 'And what brings you to Rabaul? I thought you were working the wrecks at Wewak.'

'We were, but we heard stories of two Jap destroyers sunk at Cape Gloucester. The *Ariake* and *Mikazuki*, and sure enough, after a bit of research, we found a photo of the *Mikazuki* sitting high and dry on the reef. I couldn't resist that. We immediately stopped working the Sugar Charlies, which, as you know, are just a group of small, 500-ton Jap cargo ships, at Mushu Island. We refuelled and victualled at Wewak and made a bee-line for Cape Gloucester.'

'When are you heading back?' I asked.

'In a month or so. We heard that Pat Roberts wants someone to pop a few condensers, so by coming to Rabaul, I can kill two birds with one stone – get rid of the scrap onboard, and get paid while having some well-deserved R&R.' He went on, 'And what about you guys?'

'Actually, much the same. The south-easter had been blowing its ring out for months, all the way along the Sunken Barrier, and Samarai was getting a bit boring. Then, out of the blue, we got word that Pat was looking for someone to pull a few condensers for him before his salvage rights ran out. According to him, the local divers aren't capable of pulling any of the big stuff. So, since it would take a while for the south-east "trades" to die-off, we agreed to take a paid holiday to Rabaul.'

'There are enough nurses and office girls here, not to mention unsatisfied housewives, to please a whole platoon, let alone a few horny divers,' Garth said with a smirk.

Ignoring him, I went on, 'We had a bit of luck with the *Lyon Maru*. We pulled a 10-ton condenser out of her and have just started on the *Hakkai*. It's probably only going to get us a small four- or five-ton heat exchanger, but that alone will pay the bills. We're not in a hurry, and we're in a nice secluded cove close to the wreck.'

'Yes, I'm keen to dive the *Hakkai*, too,' Dave said.

That was not a good sign; I know everyone would like to dive the *Hakkai*. I had to think of something and fast. Firstly, and most importantly, I had to pretend we had no objection to them visiting us or diving the wreck, so I said. 'You should come for a dive after you get rid of your cargo and get settled in. In fact, when you do, I'll join you.'

'That'd be great,' was Dave's reply.

The evening progressed with everyone swapping the usual salvage stories of accidents and near-accidents – telling lies of good salvage results and bad ones. All too soon, it was time to leave and head back to the *Scorpion*.

Chapter 17

Depth Charge

As soon as Blondie was out of earshot, I said to the crew, 'We're going to have to keep Dave out of the water, at least for a week or two.'

'What do you suggest?' Tony asked with a worried expression.

'Do you remember what happened to Dick Graham and the *Pacific Pearl* out of Giso?'

'Yea, Bluey Childers sank his boat at Buin with a 100-lb American bomb.'

'Exactly, I'm going to do a quick jump on the *Hakkai* tonight and pull one of those depth charges out of the rear hold and stuff it right up Dave's arse.'

'Bullshit!' Garth exclaimed in disbelief.

Everyone looked at each other with scepticism written all over their faces. Tony was the first to say something. 'You're not serious, are you?'

'You fucken watch me. As soon as he is nicely tucked up in that cove at Matupit, he's going to have a bloody serious accident.'

'Fucken hell! This I've got to see. I'll come with you and give you a hand,' Lindsay immediately offered with a mischievous grin.

'Hang on Simon, not so quick,' Tony said in earnest, 'Forget about the *Hakkai* depth charges. They're too deep and dangerous. What about that Jap sub chaser in Karavia Bay, the *CHA 7*? Last time I looked, there were six still strapped on the back of her deck, and she's only in 20 ft of water.'

'Fuck me. I forgot about that. Thanks, Tony.'

I turned to John, 'Get the 500-kg lifting bag, slings, torches, and some rope, and get the tender ready,'

'Tony, get six sticks of Sakura AN90 and remove the wrappers. I don't want any tell-tale pieces of wrapper floating around after the blast. Bundle them together with some string. Put an instant detonator in the centre of the charge and tie off the 'det-wire' so it can't pull out of the bomb. Oh yes, and a new 300-metre role of bell wire.'

I went up to the bridge, kissed Blondie and let her know that Lindsay and I would do a quick night dive on a wreck in Karavia Bay but would be back soon. I pulled my thin, one-eighth wet suit from the draw and put it on.

I was back on deck in seemingly no time. I asked John, 'Ready?'

He smiled and nodded in the affirmative.

'Okay, then let's go and pick up a depth charge.' And with that, we were off.

* * *

It was almost 10:00 p.m. A clear blue sky and the full moon shimmered on the surface of the water. I was very fond of night dives, especially when there was a lot of bioluminescence in the water. It's quite spectacular when streaming from your fins like sparklers.

It did not take long to locate the wreck, and minutes later, I was swimming and half pulling myself along the deck towards the stern, and the depth charges. Lindsay remained behind waiting for me to find a suitable depth charge before bringing down the bag.

On inspection, there didn't appear to be much difference between any of them, but I eventually chose the deepest one because it would be easier to rig the lifting bag. Lindsay must have got tired of waiting for me and snorkelled down to see what was happening. He tapped me on the shoulder, I turned and gave him the thumbs-up, and he disappeared to bring down the lifting bag.

The cradles which held the depth charges were of an old design. When released, the depth charge simply rolled down the rail and into the water. The contraption was cast from a high-quality, non-ferrous, copper metal alloy called 'gunmetal'. It doesn't corrode, so it was very easy for me to remove the safety pin and open the gate that securely held the depth charge in place.

Fortunately, the small coral growth on the cradle rail stopped it from rolling away once the gate was open. It was easy getting the sling around it and then attaching the lifting bag. We immediately began to fill the bag with air, but the depth charge refused to budge. There was seemingly nothing holding it, but a thin layer of cement-like coral was enough to stop it coming off the cradle. This meant giving the cradle a couple of sharp whacks with a sledgehammer. That action was not very good for the heart, but then the brain was already numb to the danger.

The trick now was to stop it bouncing into the other depth charges before it started to rise. It was nerve-wracking enough having an unstable, thirty-year-old depth charge bounce on the cradle, let alone into other depth charges. That definitely would increase the chances of a big bang! But soon, it gently floated the short distance to the surface. Lindsay moved it across to the tender and John temporarily secured to the gunwale.

For moving scrap secretly, the tender had special lifting holes in the keel, they would come in good use now. It did not take long to shackle the depth charge to the keel. I had to have a silent chuckle. I'm sure John had no idea just how dangerous this depth charge was. I think most people would have shit themselves. No, the reality was, most would be smart enough not to do something so stupid!

The Japanese depth charge is a very crude weapon. It is essentially a 22-gallon drum filled with high explosives. The detonating fuse is pre-set to a given depth and fired based on a predetermined hydrostatic pressure. Naturally, the fuses, which are called 'depth charge pistols', were not installed. They wouldn't be until it was time to deploy them. But these depth charges on the *CHA 7* were over 30 years old, and explosives have a habit of becoming very unstable with age.

It was not until midnight before we were back alongside the *Scorpion.* It was an uneasy feeling to have a live, unstable depth charge loaded with 350 lb of Shimose powder dangling below the tender and not 1 metre from the *Scorpion's* hull.

Blondie was ignorant about any of this, and anyway, I didn't want to scare her. Also, I didn't trust her enough for any serious shit. If our relationship soured, she could have a field-day – blackmail, and jail comes to mind.

* * *

It was another beautiful morning. We were a little late getting started after last night's little escapade but weren't concerned about it. We were confident that Dave would be occupied most of the day discharging cargo and moving to Matupit. Everyone was keen to hit the water and check out the blast's results on the treasure room. Other than working out how to sling the lift, we had nothing planned for this dive. It was more of a pleasure dive than work, and it was also the excuse we needed to take *Hiptimco*, leaving the tender and its cargo, safely alongside the *Scorpion*.

Like torpedoes, we glide past the mainmast to the starboard side and head directly to the treasure room from outside the ship's hull. We were greeted by a perfectly cut opening in the ship's side that opened up into an empty room. Nothing of interest there now, so we immediately shot to the bottom where we found a sight to behold. Two safes, still intact and firmly attached to a small section of the ship's hull, laying on the bottom of the ocean floor some 15 metres from the side of the ship – perfect!

We took a few minutes to check how to best sling this slightly awkward lift and think about what we might need to bring down on the next dive. Back in the tender, we agree that it might be prudent to leave lifting the safe until tomorrow. The lift may go wrong, and if so, we would leave ourselves exposed. Better, we take care of the *Santo* first.

Chapter 18

Bomb the *Santo*

So, while Blondie was away having her shower and getting ready for our trip into town, I briefly went over the plan with the boys. This time, Joe, my most trusted local, would play a significant role. At 6:00 p.m., John would slowly make his way in *Hiptimco* just south of the bay where the *Santo* is anchored. There, out of sight, he would wait for me.

Joe and I would take the tender as close as possible to the *Santo's* stern and drop the depth charge in shallow water. After which, we would move the tender behind the little sand spit where the *Hiptimco* was waiting. I would then transfer to the *Hiptimco* and return to the *Scorpion* as quickly as possible, and Joe would detonate the charge.

All the divers, including John and Blondie, would then immediately leave for the club, where we would once again join Dave and his crew. It would be very difficult for him to blame any of us for his misadventure when we are having dinner with him!

Joe's instructions were to wait until 8:00 p.m. before detonating the blast. After which, he was to quickly reel in the 'det wire' and hightail it back to the *Scorpion*. All very simple.

* * *

It was just after 6:15 p.m. when Joe and I left the *Scorpion*. It was only a mile from our anchorage to the shallow cove at Matupit where Dave was now anchored. Even with the 160-kg depth charge dangling under our keel, it did not take us long to get there. As we slipped past the Beehives, the stern of the *Santo* was visible in the fading light.

But something wasn't right. At first, I couldn't figure out what it was, then I realised Dave wasn't anchored. Instead, he had driven the bow onto the beach, and his ramp was down. I guessed he must have done this, so his crew had easy access to the shore. I assumed he must also have put his stern anchor out so he could pull himself off when it came time to move.

I couldn't believe my luck! If by any chance an explosion were to occur, it would be obvious to anyone that his stern anchor must have dragged over some old, WW2 bomb or other ordinance.

As we got closer, I quietly manoeuvred the tender to about 30 metres aft of the *Santo*. On my signal, Joe slipped into the water and quickly cut the rope holding the depth charge. It dropped to the bottom like a stone.

With Joe back in the tender, we quietly motored our way in the direction of the sand spit at the southern point. All the while, Joe carefully playing out the detonating wire. We rounded the point, which was about 140 metres from the *Santo*. I ran the nose of the tender onto the black sand beach.

From here, Joe would be somewhat protected from any shock waves by the sandbank, while still watching the blast. Hopefully, he would also be out of the direct line of any shrapnel or large waves resulting from the explosion.

I handed Joe the 'det wire' and said, 'it's now 7:00 p.m., At 8:00 p.m., you pop the blast and don't forget to reel in the det-wire. And watch out for any flying shrapnel.' With that said, I jumped into the *Hiptimco,* and John and I headed back to the *Scorpion* at full speed.

It was just on 7:15 p.m. as we were walking up to the clubhouse. I could see Dave and his crew in the same spot on the veranda. Walking into the club, I said. 'Fish and chips for everyone. What about a beer?'

There was a collective agreement, so I sent Blondie off to order the meals and John to get the drinks. The rest of us ambled over to Dave's table.

'I noticed on the way across that you are anchored in that small cove at Matupit. Good spot. It puts you close to the *Italia Maru*,' I said, breaking the ice.

'Not anchored,' he replied. 'I put the nose on the beach so the boys can come and go as they please.' Dave looked over towards Blondie who was, as usual, dressed to kill. 'Boy, that's a fine-looking piece of arse you have there.'

'Yes, she's a good sort, and I want to keep her for a while, so hands off!' I replied in good humour.

Some knowing smiles and snickers came from the table, and even bigger smiles of approval when Blondie leaned over to put the drinks on the table. Nothing was left to the imagination as her tits were clearly visible. Bloody hell, she's a flirt!

Just making idle chatter, I asked Dave if he had surveyed the *Italia Maru*. I'd dived the wreck several times a couple of years ago. She was an easy wreck to find as there was always an avgas slick that rose to the surface. You could smell it from some distance. One had to be careful diving the wreck because the avgas would burn your skin if you came into contact with it. The wreck was lying on her side, and if that monster three-stage steam engine was on top of the condenser, it would be a bloody difficult and potentially dangerous job to recover it.

'If the condenser is easy to get at, shouldn't take more than a couple of days to pop it and get it to the surface,' I said, 'but if it's under the engine...' I continued letting the sentence trail off into nothingness.

'If it's under that 60-ton monster, Roberts will simply have to get me five or six boxes of Hydrogel, and I'll pulverise the fucking thing,' was Dave's off-the-cuff reply.

'Want another?' I asked Dave, pointing to his drink.

'Why not?' was his quick reply.

'Can you go and order another round of drinks please, beautiful?' I said to Blondie, with particular emphasis on the 'beautiful'.

'Ok, honey. Give me some money,' she said with a sexy drawl as she stood behind me, each breast cupping my ears and rubbing her hands down my chest. Then, with a clean new, twenty-dollar bill in her hands, away she went.

Just as Blondie was about to pass out the drinks, all hell broke loose. There was an almighty explosion that rocked the building. Glasses and bottles smashed to the floor. Blondie stumbled in fright and dropped her tray of drinks. Rabaul residents instinctively fearing that Mount Tavurvur, the local volcano, had erupted again, all ran outside.

At our table, everyone looked at each other. John looked alarmed and burst out, 'What the fuck?!' I was unsure if he was genuinely frightened or merely making a show, but I suspect the former.

It was apparent that the explosion was not from our side of the harbour, so I said to Dave the first thing that popped into my head. 'Shit! Sounds like your explosive magazine just went up in smoke.'

The colour instantly drained from Dave's face. It was as if time itself had stopped. Then, a few microseconds later, he sprung to his feet, knocking bottles and glasses off the table and raced out of the club and down towards the jetty with his crew behind him in single file trying to keep up with him.

In that instant, I was also curious to see the result of the blast, so I shouted to the crew, 'Come on, quick! Let's have a look.'

Virtually everyone in the club and Travelodge made their way to the foreshore in the hope of catching a glimpse of whatever just happened. I had Blondie by the hand and was dragging her along at a pace she has never run before. Garth, being the athlete he was, reached the jetty first and jumped headlong into the *Hiptimco*. He immediately started the engine, and the rest of us followed while John and Lindsay cast-off the mooring lines. Moments later, we were right behind Dave and his crew. The *Hiptimco* was much faster than Dave's dive tender, and soon we were powering ahead.

The sight that greeted us as we entered the cove was beyond belief. A tsunami-like wave had flattened the smaller vegetation on the foreshore. The *Santo* was now almost three-quarters of her length high and dry. Worse still, she had crushed a few smaller coconut palms on her way up, and her bow was in the air.

I was awestruck, all I could say was, 'Fuck me! He's got a job ahead of him now.'

Once we got over the initial shock, there was a bit of sniggering on board, much to Blondie's bewilderment. I was now just quietly hoping that Joe was okay because this had been one hell of an explosion. We had used ordinance before, but only at depth, so the immediate effect was never as spectacular as this.

We were standing at the barge's stern in ankle-deep water when Dave and his crew pulled up. At first glance and apart from the fact that she was almost high and dry, it didn't appear that she had suffered any serious structural damage.

We walked up the starboard side inspecting the hull as far as the bow ramp and caught up with Dave and Johnno, his officer, there.

'Fuck me! This is going to be one hell of a salvage job, Dave. Wonder what caused the explosion?' I said with as much sincerity I could muster.

'Fucked if I know,' He said.

'Did you drop out a stern anchor?'

'Yes, both of them.' he replied.

'Shit mate, maybe you dropped one on some kind of explosive ordinance, a bomb maybe.'

Dave wasn't in talking mood, and I couldn't blame him, as he continued his inspection. I shone my torch at the loading ramp and looked at the small palm trees under the hull. They were flattened as the barge was driven ashore. Two big palm trees ultimately stopped her in her tracks.

There did not appear to be any damage to the bow or loading ramp, and I could not see any cracks or holes in the hull. However, even though the *Santo* was only a small, 20-metre barge, this was still going to be a big job. But I knew Dave was up to it, and in any case, he had no choice.

I had seen enough and took my leave, promising Dave we'd help where we could. I left to round up the crew, and we headed back to the Yacht Club to finish dinner, the conversation naturally revolved around Dave's dilemma.

Lindsay, the idiot, said. 'I hope Joe's okay.'

Blondie, not being totally dumb, looked puzzled and asked, 'Why, shouldn't Joe be okay?'

'Some problem with a local girl, a Mari,' I jumped in, shooting a scowl in Lindsay's direction and not giving him time to think of a stupid answer.

The crew were busting to gloat about the explosion, but we had to bite our tongues, at least until Blondie was out of earshot. One topic we could talk about was how the hell he was going to get the *Santo* back in the water.

* * *

Later, back on the *Scorpion*, Jack and Joe were at the gunwale, ready to catch the mooring lines. Joe had a grin from ear to ear. It was obvious he was quite pleased with himself. Blondie headed directly for the shower, which meant I was going to be in for some great sex.

We pulled Joe up to the bow, and out of earshot in case Blondie finished quicker than usual.

'That was a hell of a big blast, Joe. I hope you didn't get hurt by any shrapnel,' I said while pretending to check him for any signs of injury.

'No, boss, no injury, but it did hurt when the tender fell on top of me.'

Puzzled, I asked, 'How on earth did the tender fall on you?'

'Well, I moved the tender just a little further back from the sand spit, and pulled the nose up on the beach, but the det-wire was a bit short. So, I walked across the spit and straightened the wire over the top of it instead of around it.

'I was standing in knee-deep water on the right side, holding the tender steady, waiting for the time to fire the shot. I had the battery already in front of me and one terminal already attached. When it was 8:00 p.m., I touched the other wire on the battery. There was a loud crack. At first, I thought something was wrong, and before I could look up, it was followed by a massive explosion. Boss, I don't know where the water came from, but it just went up and up and up. I couldn't see the *Santo,* and the next minute, a huge wave swept right over the top of the sand spit, and almost capsized the tender.'

Joe stopped for a moment, Lindsay. being impatient, prompted him, 'Go on, go on.'

'The wave pushed the dinghy right over the top of me and ripped the det-wire out of my hand. When I surfaced, I looked for it under the water but couldn't find it. I knew you would be really mad if I didn't reel it in, so I quickly pulled the tender to shore and ran to the spit and luckily saw a bit of it sticking out of the sand. I pulled it in as fast as I could. It was all tangled, so I threw it overboard near the Bee-Hives.'

I held John by the shoulders with both hands and with as much sincerity I could muster said, 'You did a bloody good job, Joe, but you must never speak of this to anyone. Do you understand?'

'Yes, boss. I understand,' he replied with a grin. 'I don't want to go to jail either.'

We all cracked up laughing. Joe was one hell of a smart cookie.

'Okay, it's time for bed. We have an early start tomorrow.'

And with that, we all disappeared to our little cubby holes.

Chapter 19

Lifting the Ship's Safes

It was an unusual sort of a morning for Rabaul, overcast and drizzling, a bit miserable really. But we were all in good spirits.

With the 'Dave issue' taken care of, we were now able to concentrate on lifting the safes to a shallow working depth. I estimated that the lift would weigh somewhere around four or five tons, which unfortunately meant using our ten-ton lifting bag.

Normally, I would have moved the *Scorpion* over top of the wreck and used our heavy stern lift, but that might set tongues wagging and draw attention to where we drop the safes. It was better to play it safe and use the tender and lifting bags.

The safes were on the bottom at about 50 metres. This presented a problem because when using a lifting bag that was almost twice the capacity of the lift, it would take just a little over half the volume of the bag to get to rise off the bottom. As the lift continued its upward journey, the decreasing surrounding pressure would cause the volume of air inside the bag to expand, and in doing so, the bag would increase speed exponentially. The danger was that the bag would pick up so much speed that it was unsafe for Lindsay to ride on top of the bag to operate the vent – a severe case of embolism comes to mind. Worse still, well, maybe not worse than an embolism, but still bad, with the inertia, the bag will fly right out of the water like a rocket, and because of the design, deflate and sink back to the bottom like a big bag of shit.

The only answer was to do two lifts, thereby reducing the amount of air expansion and subsequently, the speed. We would suspend the bag at around 30 metres for the first lift and lift it to the surface. Once the bag is floating on the surface, we would tow it towards the cove until the safes scraped along the bottom. That should be approximately 20 metres. The whole kit and caboodle would then be sent back to the bottom, and we would then lift from that point to the surface.

My instructions to John were, 'Get two of the long, 5-metre slings, the big crowbar, and also a 3-metre length of 10 mm reo-bar and put them in the tender.' I continued, 'Then get out the 40 mm nylon tow rope and make up a 30-metre lift line, splice eyes at either end.

Tony interjected, 'Simon, we've got a length of silver rope about 30 metres long. It's not as strong as nylon, I know, but will easily take five tons. It's just a shame to cut up the expensive tow rope.'

I agreed. It was indeed wasteful to cut the tow line. John was left to organise the gear and make up the silver-rope lift line. It was now time to ensure that each diver knew his role.

'Okay… Lindsay and I will go down first and get the slings in position. Tony, you and Garth better stay topside until we get back. We'll explain what we've done, and that way you'll know exactly what to do when you guys go down.'

Turning to Lindsay, I said, 'Lindsay, you take the slings and reo bar, and I'll take the crowbar.'

Tony laughed. 'Someone's in for an express ride down.'

'Shit, you're right about that. I better get John to tie a lanyard at the bevelled end. I don't want to drop it.'

Twenty minutes later, John stuck his head around the corner. 'All's ready, and I have the 6 mm, yellow and blue rope for the crowbar.'

Just then, Blondie appeared on deck dressed in a skimpy bikini. 'Can I come along?'

'Not a problem,' I said. 'But you better slip on one of my long-sleeve shirts. It gets very hot out there, and you'll burn like a crisp. Look at John, long-sleeve shirt and Mexican hat. You should bring a hat as well.'

She went off to fetch her stuff while we got dressed for work. Soon, the four of us were on our way to the wreck. Tony and Garth stayed back onboard the *Scorpion* to get the lifting bag and ropes ready.

Lindsay had the easy job, bringing down the slings and reo bar, but I was in for an express ride. I had to make sure that I torpedoed in the right direction, or it was going to be a long walk underwater. At 50 metres, I didn't have the luxury of time.

Both Lindsay and I were in the water hanging onto the gunwale, waiting for John to load us up. Here came the trick. I hung onto the gunwale with both hands. John placed the crowbar in the crook of my elbow and then tied the lanyard to my wrist with a slipknot. I'd already rinsed my goggles to prevent them from fogging up. He checked my mask, making sure there is no hair under the seal.

I looked up and saw Blondie looking down at me with a concerned frown. I can't help but smile. I could see more of her tits when she is bending over like this than I do of her frown. I stopped ogling and concentrated on my descent. Then came the tricky bit. As soon as I let go of the tender, I was going to sink like a ton of lead.

The moment I let go, I had to get my left hand firmly on my mask or would be ripped off my face.

Simultaneously, I had to pinch my nose with my right hand to enable me to compensate quickly enough for the rapid pressure change, all the while keeping the crowbar securely in the crook of my elbow. The first 10 metres are crucial, or I would risk bursting my eardrums, and, most likely, my eyes would pop out just for good measure.

And, if that's not all before I fall too far, I would need to extend my body like an aerofoil and use my fins as ailerons so I could glide to my destination. I would have to let go of the tender first because if Lindsay was in front of me, I might not be able to steer out of his way.

I looked over to Lindsay and nodded, then I let go. Fortunately, everything went smoothly. I managed to pull out of my freefall just seconds before the mainmast came into view. Then, I began to glide and steered towards the starboard hull. The end of the crowbar just missed the ship's gunwale by inches.

The moment I could see the safes on the ocean floor, I dropped the crowbar. Nevertheless, I must have held onto it a little longer than I should have, as I still managed to crash into the mud. I composed myself and immediately set about looking for the best way to sling the safes.

A few moments later, Lindsay joined me, and it was immediately apparent that our plan to sling them from underneath was impossible, so bringing the crowbar down was a waste of time. The only option is to wrap the sling around both safes, as close as possible to the hull plate and under the thick legs. The tightening noose of the sling should hold it firmly, but just to be on the safe side, I used the 6mm rope I brought down with me to tie off the lifting point of the sling to a jagged part on top of the hull-plate.

Soon, the safes were slung and ready to connect to the lifting rope and bag. Our fifteen minutes had disappeared as though it only had been one. Lindsay signalled it was time leave by banging his knife onto his steel scuba tank. I watched him spear the crowbar and reo bar upright into the mud so they would be easy for us to find later, and we both swam towards the surface.

Back in the tender, Blondie was laying on the front seat, face covered with her hat, sunbaking, with half a nipple protruding from her skimpy bikini. I rolled my eyes at John, and he just smiled.

When back on the *Scorpion,* I outlined what we had managed to get done to Tony and Garth. Their next job was simple. They only had to take down the lifting bag and secure it to the slings with the 10 metres of rope. As soon as the lifting bag was on the bottom and securely in position, we would be ready for the afternoon's lift.

With the tender loaded, Tony and Garth were off. I hadn't even finished my coffee, and they were back.

'Shit, that was quick. Are you sure you didn't forget something?' I said.

'What are you talking about? We've been gone for 30 minutes,' Tony replied.

'Fuck me, drunk! I must be losing it. How did it go?'

'Piece of piss. It all went smoothly, and everything is in place, ready to lift.'

'Good, I think we might go to the club for lunch and get some local news on the *Santo* incident. What do you reckon?' I said.

'Sounds like a good idea to me.' Tony replied.

* * *

An hour later, we were crossing the road to the Yacht Club. Dave was nowhere in sight, but that was to be expected. Our favourite table on the veranda was vacant, so we made a beeline for that and settled in. Looking at the club's chalkboard menu, we chose our meals and Blondie went to place the orders and pay.

'I think I might go to the bar and see what gossip is out there about Dave's accident,' I said with a grin.

Before I had a chance to get up, Blondie returned with the drinks, 'No need,' she said, pointing to the newspaper on the tray. 'They made the local news. Looks like their anchor dragged into an unexploded WW2 bomb, the poor buggers.'

Sure enough, there it was the headline: 'SALVAGE BARGE ANCHOR EXPLODES WW2 BOMB', and a photo of the *Santo* high and dry.

'Well, that's that!' I said, smiling looking at those around the table. 'How unlucky can you get?'

Lindsay couldn't contain himself. 'Poor cunt,' he blurted out, trying to stop himself from laughing, his crazy chuckle breaking into full-blown laughter. It was contagious, and soon we were all in fits of laughter, dispelling the pent-up tension we all felt, – except for Blondie. It all went over her head.

Back on the *Scorpion,* I asked John to get the tender ready with two manta boards, each with 10 metres of tow rope and a couple of scuba bottles. It was time to find a suitable place to drop the safes.

Because we wanted to work underwater for extended periods so we would not have to decompress, it was essential to keep the depth to around 10 metres. This was also deep enough to keep it hidden from the prying eyes of local fisherman in their canoes, who just might want to fish right where we have dropped the safes. Because the *Scorpion* was a wooden boat, I also needed to make sure that we were out of the direct line of any underwater blast. The shock waves from even a small explosion had the potential to knock the calking from between the planks, and if not discovered in time, could sink us. Times like this, I wish I had a steel boat like Dave's.

There was a small indent a couple hundred yards from where we were anchored, and this looked like it might be the perfect spot. There was no one living nearby, and I didn't think the tender being there would arouse too much curiosity. If anybody did ask, I'd simply say that we were doing some research in the harbour for sea cucumber, the local name for beche-de-mer.

It took just a few minutes for us to reach the entrance to the little indent. Jack was at the bow using the lead-line to check the depth. He sang out, 'About 8.5 metres, boss.' That was an excellent depth to start looking.

Tony and Lindsay, using just masks and snorkels, were keen to ride the manta boards. Meanwhile, I was sitting in the tender with scuba gear on, waiting to jump in as soon as they found a suitable spot. We crisscrossed the little bay a few times. The boys were continually gliding the manta boards below the plankton level, giving them a panoramic view of the ocean floor. Eventually, they signalled John to stop, had a chat while treading water, and seemed to come to some sort of agreement. They then pulled themselves along the towrope back to the tender.

They explained that the bottom was reasonably uniform. There was a bit of wartime junk scattered about but nothing that would worry us. Tony asked John to take us just a bit further into the bay and suggested I should go down and have a look.

I did a quick dive, and they were right. The volcanic dust had compacted to a solid bottom, and it was about 9 metres according to my depth gauge, a good depth for us to do our work. I was happy and made my way back to the surface. We took bearings from shore marks to make sure that we would be able to come back to the exact same spot, and as soon as we returned to the *Scorpion*, John began loading the tender with the diver's equipment and extra scuba tanks. Each set was rigged with belt clips, and he also included 100 ft of 6mm rope. Soon, everything was ready for the 4:30 p.m. dive.

* * *

This was starting to get exciting. In just a few days, without any interruptions, we should see if it was all worth the drama we have had to go through. For this afternoon's dive, Garth and I would go first, each taking an extra three scuba bottles. It would be our job to get the bag off the bottom and hanging safely at the 20-metre mark.

When we arrived at the ocean floor, we found the rope snaked nicely away from the safes to the lifting bag. Everything was in place for us to start pumping air into the bag. Garth moved over to the top corner of the bag and lifted one end to create a small catchment area for the air. Meanwhile, I shoved a scuba bottle as far as I could into the opening and started pumping air into the bag. To encourage the air to continue collecting in the pocket, Garth lifted and shook the top corner to give the air a larger catchment area.

Soon, as more air filled the bag, it began to rise off the ocean floor. It was now time for Garth to join me in emptying the rest of the scuba bottles. This did not take long, and very soon, the bag was on its way upward. We followed it, all the while continuing to empty our scuba bottles until the bag had reached the end of its tether. We were now working at 20 metres. The empty scuba bottles hung from the D- shackles under the bag like teardrops. When the last scuba bottle was empty, it was time for us to head to the surface, taking as many empty bottles with us as we could manage.

The lifting bag was now very solid, but there was still not enough air in it for the load to come off the bottom. It was now Tony and Lindsay's turn to continue pumping air. They would be working at only 20 metres, so they had over an hour of bottom time. They would be able to make several trips back to the tender for fresh tanks without concern for decompression.

While waiting impatiently for the safes to lift off the bottom, I had to ensure that John kept a close eye on the diver's air bubbles bursting on the surface. For as soon as the package came off the bottom, the outgoing tide would start drifting it away from the wreck, and he would have to follow in the tender.

As our store of full scuba bottles began to diminish in the tender, I knew the lift would soon begin. I slipped into the water and snorkelled down. I could see that Lindsay was already sitting on top of the bag so he could start venting air with the blow-off valve. Meanwhile, Tony must have felt the bag rising as he stopped putting air in the bag. I watched him clip the scuba bottle to a D- ring. Bursting for air, I made a quick exit to the surface.

Tony held onto the bottom of the bag for the ride to the surface, exhaling forcibly to minimise air volume in his lungs and reduce the risk of an embolism. He had to maintain his position at the bottom of the bag just in case the inertia caused it to fly out of the water and deflate. If that happened, he had to be in a position to quickly inject more air.

I could see the bag was now well and truly on its way to the surface, and as the air expanded, the speed increased. Lindsay now had the vent wide open, but the expansion of air was greater than his ability to vent it. At about 10 metres from the surface, it was time to jettison from the bag or risk getting a case of embolism and potential death. We watched helplessly as it broke the surface.

This was a tense moment. This was a bloody big bag, designed primarily for heavy, shallow-water lifts, hence its design. It is shaped like a brick with spreader bars at the bottom to keep it square. If over-inflated, it had a habit of flying out of the water like a rocket, and then, like a big bag of shit, sink all the way back to the bottom. This would mean the whole process had to begin over again.

This time, luck was with us. The bag did break the surface, but fortunately, only a little, and Lindsay was able to scramble back onto the top of it and shut off the valve. Meanwhile, Tony squirted more air into the bag, and soon it was happily bouncing on the surface. It was now ready to be towed to shallower water, and the whole process would be repeated the next morning. Thankfully, that would be from a much shallower depth and more manageable.

With the divers in the water watching the progress, John towed the bag in the direction of the little bay. When the load started to drag across the bottom, and he could not make any further headway, it was time to drop everything carefully to the ocean floor. Garth jumped into the water to check the condition of the safes and the surrounding ocean floor. He very quickly popped back to the surface and gave the 'okay' signal. It was now time to vent the air from the bag and drop everything to the ocean floor.

But first, Lindsay tied a buoy line to the bag and swam away from it trailing the line behind him, making sure it would not tangle into anything as the bag fell to the bottom. Meanwhile, I snorkelled over to the bag and opened the valve, and slowly it disappeared below the surface. Garth followed it down to guide it to a good position for tomorrow's lift, then headed back to the surface.

Meanwhile, both John and I took landmark bearings of the location just in case some villager pinched the marker buoy and rope overnight.

Back on the *Scorpion* that afternoon, John had quite a few hours work pumping scuba tanks. Excitement and speculation were mounting, and talk of treasure dominated the dinner conversation. From now on, we would no longer be constrained by the dangers of depth and limited bottom time. We would be able to work day and night, if necessary. Only exhaustion would stop us.

*　　*　　*

Well before breakfast, John and the boys already had everything ready and in the tender, including extra scuba bottles for the lifting bag. Thankfully, the buoy was still visible from the deck of the *Scorpion*. This was a blessing and saved us wasting time searching for the safes with shore marks.

As the second lift was from shallow water, it was relatively straightforward and went off without a hitch. In just 40 minutes, the two safes, complete with the section of the hull, were now dangling some 8 metres below the surface and slowly on their way to the little cove. Ten minutes later, we were at the drop-off spot.

I sent Garth down to ensure that the safes would fall facing the surface. He was physically the strongest member of the crew and the best man to make sure they did.

As soon as everything was ready, Lindsay took his place on the top of the bag and slowly began to vent air. Tony was hanging under the bag with a spare scuba cylinder to slow the descent, or even raise the safes, if necessary. As the hull section landed gently on the ocean floor, it balanced precariously for a moment. Garth was able to exert just enough force to ensure the ship's hull would fall onto the ocean floor, ensuring the safe doors faced towards the surface. It did not take long to unshackle the lifting bag, remove the slings and rope, and bring everything to the surface.

We were now ready to begin cracking the safes.

Chapter 20

The Oxygen Lance (Burning Bar)

The way I saw it, the best way of getting into the safes would be by cutting away a corner section on the top of each safe. But here comes the contentious bit, I believed the only way to do this is with an oxygen lance, more commonly called a burning bar. Using explosives alone, even the incredibly powerful Hydrogel 90 dynamite which we commonly used for cutting steel, would have little effect on such solidly constructed safes. I would have to use so much dynamite to risk sending them and everything in them, to kingdom come! I know this only too well because I've fucked-up before.

I also know from experience that getting in through the front door was virtually impossible, so I'm not even remotely going to go there. The casing is the Achilles' heel, and that's where we need to concentrate. The cabinet on older style, freestanding safes such as this are usually constructed in three layers. They have a thick outer layer of steel, then a fire/heat insulation and the inner shell is typically a thin layer of steel.

My suggestion was to cut away a large corner piece of the outer layer using a burning bar exposing the insulation. Then, use a small amount of explosives to clear away the fire insulation. All that remains then is to cut the thin, inner layer with the burning bar or possibly even with explosives.

There were a lot of disapproving murmurs about using the burning bar. It was not one of our favourite tools, but it had its uses. It's a dangerous and unpredictable piece of equipment, and one with the potential to explode. Fortunately, both Lindsay and I have used them on several occasions, so we could pass the knowledge on to Garth and Tony.

A professional, commercial-quality burning bar is simply a hollow piece of black iron pipe stuffed with clean lengths of iron wire. The iron wire acts as an amalgam to maintain the burning. The iron pipe with the wire, the burning bar, is screwed to a handle, incorporating a simple shut-off valve. This is then connected via an air hose to several large, pure-oxygen cylinders fitted with high-flow regulators on the surface.

Unfortunately, professional burning bars or parts were not available to us in New Guinea, so by necessity, we must, as usual, improvise. Instead of regulation, 'black-iron pipe and wire' which burns cleanly, we are forced to use standard, hot-dipped galvanised water pipe stuffed with galvanised fencing wire. The galvanised pipe and wire make the burning very lively and dangerous – exploding sparklers comes to mind,

To give you an idea of the awesome power these burning bars have, once this monster starts roaring, it will make a 3-metre length of half-inch pipe disappear in about five minutes. That's a burn rate of approximately 600 mm per minute. And they will empty a large oxygen cylinder in under ten minutes. The immense heat generated by the burning bar melts, or more correctly, vaporises, whatever it comes in contact with.

Once ignited, it works equally well above or below water, but much more spectacularly below water. Reluctantly, everyone agreed that the burning bar was probably the best option. Also, it would cause the least damage to the contents of the safes.

John and the local crew made several quick trips to CIG, the local gas supplier, for the large G-size oxygen cylinders. I wasn't keen to take the *Scorpion*. Loading a dozen oxygen cylinders at the wharf might attract undue attention, especially if Dave came to hear about it.

Tony and Garth picked up the galvanised water pipe, fencing wire, and a couple of gate valves from

Steamships Hardware. We now had everything we needed to make a couple of crude burning bars.

* * *

Early in the morning, John and Garth quickly made up ten lengths of the burning bars, four of which were already in the tender. Meanwhile, Tony and the local crew, using the ship's winches, finished loading the large oxygen bottles. The small workshop acetylene-oxy unit was also in the tender. This was necessary to provide the heat to fire up the burning bars. There was now a mountain of equipment in the tender including the scuba bottles, diver's heavy clip-on weights, and jungle boots which were necessary when working on the bottom. It was all part of our standard equipment.

As I said before, we were now free to work underwater all day, as there was no time restriction when diving to 10 metres. It also meant we would have less free time. Working deep with only two short dives a day tends to make you lazy. For me, it also meant that I would have less time to devote to Blondie, and she might get restless being on the *Scorpion* by herself for most of the day. But that was something I could not worry about now. I would just have to see where the chips fall on that score.

The shore marks for the position of the safes was easy to line up. We simply could not risk putting a buoy. That would have been just plain stupid. You never know who might come snooping around. As we started to get close to the position, John slowed down, and Garth got ready with the anchor. John was standing while maneuvering the tender, carefully getting us into position. When he was satisfied, he sang out 'Drop it, Garth.'

I said to Lindsay. 'Grab a mask and check that we're in position.'

Lindsay slipped over the side and was back in a flash. 'Right on the button, skipper,' he said as he spat out the snorkel and swung himself onto the gunwale.

Two lances were quickly screwed together with the burning bars. The threaded end of the burning bar simply screwed onto a standard, single-lever gate valve, which allowed the diver to control the flow of oxygen or shut it off. This was technically the 'lance', the burning bar being the part that was consumed during the cutting process and replaced.

We used standard, half-inch diver's hookah hose to feed the oxygen to the burning bars. Interestingly, Garth had to modify the oxygen gauge. To do this, he had to enlarge the venturi, thereby allowing more oxygen to pass through to the lance, enabling it to work at full capacity.

Everything was ready in the tender. First, a quick dive down to double-check the best way to start the cut. On reaching the bottom and looking down at each safe, there was no question – the best option was to remove the outer top corner of each safe. With the boys looking on, I drew my hand across each safe where I thought might be the best place to cut. There was a nod of approval and thumbs up from everyone, so I gave the signal to surface.

I confirmed with the crew, 'I'm going to start my cut from the centre to the outer edge just above the door and try and remove the corner section in one piece.

'What about the fire retardant? Garth asked.

'I think the lance will have trouble with that. We'll just have to set a small blast once the outer section is off,' I replied.

I was then speaking to them all when I said, 'Okay, get your boots on and let's see if we can't make a hole in those bloody safes. Lindsay and I'll start the first burn.'

I made sure that my boots were securely tightened and clipped two massive teardrop lead weights to my belt. This would give me the weight I needed to allow me to walk along the bottom. I slipped the scuba bottle over my head, tightened the straps, put on my mask, and slipped into the water. I could see Lindsay mucking about with his straps, but I knew he would not be far behind.

John carefully slipped the oxygen supply hose into the water and handed me the lance. Garth was meanwhile busy adjusting a hot flame on the oxy-acetylene torch. When he was ready, it was time to fire-up my burning bar. I was near the back of the tender, and Garth was up the front. He grabbed hold of the burning bar a short distance from the end to steady it and started to heat it up.

Once it was glowing red-hot, he sang out for me to open the oxygen flow. With a bit more prompting from Garth's oxy-acetylene torch, the lance burst into life. And boy, was it bubbling and roaring! To say, 'spitting fire' does not do it justice. The galvanised pipe was burning like an angry sparkler.

No time to waste! At a burn rate of 60 cm a minute, I had to get down as quickly as possible. I'd already lost almost 60 cm of the burning bar before I even got down to the safe. I immediately set about gouging a track across the top, starting from one end and pushing the molten metal away from the groove.

I had to be careful, as the groove tended to re-weld behind me because of the water's quick cooling action. So, it was necessary to dig deep with the burning bar and push the molten metal away. Then, just as I thought I was getting the hang of it, I was down to less than 60 cm of the bar.

It was time to shut off the flow of oxygen and kill the beast. When the fire-spitting, crazy-bubbling lance was quiet, I was able to take a look at what I've achieved. I saw that I'd managed to gouge out a line about 60 cm long down, in most places, to the fire-retardant. Only three more cuts to go and I should be able to lift off the steel plate. At this pace, I would have the outer layer off by tomorrow.

I stop momentarily to see how Lindsay was progressing, then threw the lance over my shoulder and started climbing up the anchor chain to the surface. I passed the lance to John and remained hanging onto the gunwale while he quickly screwed a new burning bar into the lance. Garth once again fired it up, and in a few minutes, my burning bar was once again spitting flame like a fire-breathing dragon. It was quite spectacular to watch.

This time, I first cut diagonally across the front, and for the last few minutes, increased my first cut by about 30 cm. I soon had to shut the flow of oxygen as my bar was getting dangerously short. I watched Lindsay coming down, ready for his second burn, as I once again climbed up the anchor line to the surface.

When Lindsay finished his second cut, we returned to the *Scorpion*. It was time to offload the empty oxygen cylinders and replace them with full ones and four new burning bars for the Lance.

The cutting proceeded at a steady pace, and by the end of the day, there was not much left holding the thick corner pieces in place. There were just a few spots where the molten metal had 're-welded' behind the burning bar as it was pushed forward.

We agreed the best option at this point was probably just to set a small explosive charge and remove the cut section on both safes. A few sticks of

Asahi Sakura 90 plastic pushed into the deepest parts of the groove on each safe and then capped with mounds of clay should do the job.

It did not take long to place the charge on my side, and as soon as I finished, I took my Cordtex tail across to were Lindsay was working and waited for him to finish. When he was done, he handed me his tail. I joined the two ends together with a neat figure-eight bend knot. Meanwhile, Tony was making neat clay mounds over the explosives.

I took an electric detonator out of my pocket, shoved it into the knot, and securely wrapped it in in place with the tail wire. I joined the detonator tail to the 'det-wire' that Tony had brought down, and the explosives were now live and primed to fire. This was very dangerous, and I desperately hope that nobody did anything stupid on the surface.

I quickly searched for a protruding, jagged piece of steel to which I could tie off the 'det-wire'. This was to stop the detonator accidentally pulling out of the Cordtex, and then made my way to the surface.

It is only a small, 2.5-kg blast, but a potent explosion, and we are right over the top of it. So, everyone lifted their bums off the seats, and on command, John detonated the blast. Seconds later, a hard thump on the hull signalled that the explosion has ignited. The next morning, we will see how successful it was. It will be a contest, now, between Lindsay and me, to see who had the best outcome.

* * *

Fridays are always special at the Club, so we gave Cookie the afternoon off and headed over to the Club for dinner. Dave and his crew were already there taking a well-earned rest from their salvage of the *Santo*. We have no choice but to join them. We pulled up a table and some chairs. Everyone shuffled around and got settled.

As usual, Blondie and John were off placing orders and getting drinks. I asked the obvious question, directing it at Dave, 'How's it all going?'

'Not too bad,' he replied.

'Are you going to slip her back in?'

'How did you guess?'

'It's probably a bit harder, but it's the only logical conclusion. The bow is already up in the air, so there's not much lifting to do. The Public Works Department has a shitload of old, WW2 oxygen bottles, and also a lot of round steel lamp poles you can use as rollers. They even have railway lines – everything you need. You only have to blast a short, shallow, 16-metre channel at your stern and borrow a bulldozer to push you in.'

'Well, fuck me! You got that all worked out, haven't you?' He said, cracking a smile.

'Not all my idea. I watched Peter Johnson get the *Jan Dirk* back in the water at Voco Point in Lae last year. Quite successfully, I might add, and she was 34 metres, much bigger than you.'

'I've got two 60-ton bottle jacks onboard with a 15 cm lift. I'll be able to get the stern up without too much trouble. The last thing I'm going to do is blast the channel. I don't want the harbour master breathing down my neck.'

'Yes, funny that, they don't seem to mind demolition work in deep-water, but as soon as you play around in the shallows, they get panicky,' I said, and going on, 'If you ask permission, you can bet your balls it's going to be refused. Better do it on the weekend or late in the afternoon when everyone's gone home.'

'You got that one right. Anyway, we have at least another week before we are ready to do any blasting.'

With dinner over and drinks starting to take effect, it was time to pull the plug and head back to the *Scorpion*. I couldn't risk any loose tongues. Anyway, it was already 10 p.m.

*   *   *

It was a late start for us in the morning, just about everyone except John and the local boys had slept in. As usual, Blondie was also still off with the fairies. John and the boys already had the tender fully loaded with fresh oxy cylinders, burning bars, and scuba bottles.

Scrambled eggs, baked beans and something that was supposed to be bacon, together with a big pot of coffee was waiting for us in the galley. I called out to John before settling into my seat, 'Better also put ten sticks of Sakura 90, and a roll of Cordtex with some instantaneous detonators into the tender as well, John. We might need to set another blast. Also, a large, short-handled sledgehammer.'

'Okay, skipper.'

And with that, he was off to get the explosive from the magazine.

Chapter 21

Garth's Tragic Accident

With breakfast over, we quickly dressed and were ready to dive. Getting dressed to work underwater in the tropics is somewhat different from Australia's colder waters where most divers simply wear a 6 mm wetsuit. On the other hand, we looked nothing like what most people perceive a professional diver should look like, but rather a motley band of pirates.

If not diving in a t-shirt and speedos, I was dressed in jeans, a long-sleeved football jersey, and genuine high, lace-up, army jungle boots. Garth favoured tight-fitting, lightweight Australian Airforce overalls, which he usually stuffed into his laced-up jungle boots. Tony, on the other hand, preferred to wear a robust military shirt, jeans, and jungle boots. Lindsay, the skinny wimp, got cold even in tropical waters and usually wore a colourful, long-sleeve football jersey over high-waisted, neoprene diver's bottoms, thick, football socks and cheap, Chinese-brand jungle boots. I could never understand why he kept buying those cheap boots. The inner sole was cardboard and used to rot away after just a few dives. They were then extremely uncomfortable, hence the thick socks.

When we arrived at the dive site, I was keen to check out the results of the blast before starting work, and so, it seems, was everyone else. With only masks and a snorkel, we were quickly on our way to the bottom. Today, the visibility near the surface was not very good. There was a clearly defined thermocline, but once past that, the safes were clearly visible.

There was no immediate sign of either outer shell. They had simply disappeared. The blast also removed much of the fire retardant, but what remained had become super-hard because of the heat generated by the explosion. There was nothing for it. We had to set another small blast on each safe to remove the last of the fire retardant before starting on the inner shell. Otherwise, the hole would be too small. With our lungs screaming for air, we scrambled to the surface.

We quickly made up a couple of small charges, which Lindsay and I took down and set. The blast went off without incident. There was no use in hanging about, so we headed back to the comfort of the *Scorpion* for an hour or so while the incoming tide moved the dirty water away. The sharks would also have cleaned up the dead fish and be gone.

* * *

It was noon, on a Saturday, a day that will remain indelibly imprinted on my brain forever. Before starting work, I quickly snorkelled to the bottom, visibility was good, and it was immediately obvious the second blast had done its job. I was satisfied we could now begin the last phase of the operation.

Garth and Tony would start the burn. I was confident the wall thickness would not be more than 13 mm. This was an easy burn, and the steel should just melt away like butter. Garth was in position at the gunwale, and Lindsay fired up his lance. As soon as it was spitting fire, he dropped below the surface. Now, it was Tony's time to light up. As soon his lance was belching flame like a roman candle, he too disappeared below the surface.

Lindsay and I prepared to get comfortable and relax for ten minutes or so, but I had no sooner stretched out on the front seat when all hell broke loose. Tony broke the surface, screaming, 'Simon! Simon! Garth's dead! Fuck me! Garth's dead!'

Both Lindsay and I shot upright in a flash. Tony was at that point, still hanging onto the gunwale, rubbing his eyes. I grabbed his arm and dragged him on board. He was shaking like a leaf. 'Calm down. What the fuck are you talking about?'

'Jesus Christ... Garth's dead. Simon, the lance... the lance speared right through him.'

My heart skipped a beat, and I was starting to get seriously worried, but also annoyed. 'For Christ sake, Tony! You're not making sense!'

Lindsay was standing to one side. He took hold of one of Tony's shoulder, shaking him. 'For God's sake, Tony, calm down.' he said quietly, trying to get him to relax.

He was hyperventilating, and now tears were rolling down his cheeks. He was stomping around in one spot with eyes glued to the deck, unable to speak.

'Tony, what the fuck are you talking about?' I demanded in a more forceful tone.

'Garth's dead, Simon. Fuck me...' Slowly, his breathing returned to something like normal as he struggled to compose himself. His hands were still shaking as he spluttered out his grim tale, in between sobs. Slowly, he told his story.

Moments after he'd let go of the gunwale and begun to sink, he was still holding his lance up at about a 45-degree angle. There must have been an accumulation of zinc at the end of the burning bar because it exploded, sending a shower of molten metal in all directions, bits landing in his hair and down his back. A small blob lodged between his thumb and forefinger, burning into his flesh. By impulse, and not thinking of Garth below, he dropped the lance, all the while trying to brush the molten metal off his hand.

The lance, spitting flame, speared down towards the bottom. Garth was hunched over the safe, concentrating on working his burning bar into the metal. He didn't know what hit him as Tony's lance speared through his body, entering just below his shoulder and exited out of his stomach. It was like a red-hot knife through butter. Death was instantaneous.

When Tony reached the bottom, he simply could not believe what had just happened. He was horrified, but fortunately had the presence of mind to switch off both lances before heading to the surface.

This was not good! Instantly, preservation mode sprang into effect. But first, I had to go down and have a look for myself. I still kept thinking, *This can't be happening, this can't be true!* However, even before I reached the bottom, I could see Tony was right. What confronted me was something I would not wish on anyone, nor hope ever to see in my lifetime again.

Garth's lifeless body lay hunched over the safe, with Tony's Lance still protruding from his back. It had burnt a hole 150 mm in diametre clean through his body and buried in the mud. I gently pulled the lance out and handed it to Lindsay, who had just joined me, indicating him to take both lances to the surface.

I removed Garth's heavy weight belt. He was now almost weightless and carefully put him over my shoulder. I walked to the tender's anchor line and climbed hand over hand to the surface. John and Joe were there waiting to drag his body into the dinghy. There was surprisingly little blood for such a large wound. You could easily pass your hand right through his body.

Sitting down, I looked at the crew and said, 'Fuck me. This is bad, really bad. I guess we have two options. We go to the authorities, or simply weigh his body down and drop him in deep water. We can tell Blondie he's staying with a girlfriend. No one onshore will miss him.'

Tony was horrified. 'What the fuck are you talking about, Simon?'

'Just what I said. We can bury him at sea, and carry on as if nothing happened. Or we can notify the authorities and bring the national spotlight down on us, which will probably include an autopsy... and then jail.'

It was a sobering thought, and my logic resonated with Lindsay and John, but Tony would have none of it.

'What about his family? A burial, Simon? You cannot do this.'

'Yes, I can... and the more I think about it, the more I think it's the best option.'

In desperation, Tony appealed to Lindsay and John, 'Please, guys. After all this time we owe Garth more than just feeding him to the sharks.'

Tony's comment hit a soft spot. No, I could not just feed him to the sharks.

Thinking on my feet, I remembered an incident on the *SS President Coolidge,* where a diver was severely injured when a phosphors bomb went off and took off the side of his face. That may be our way out.

I turned to Tony and said, 'Okay, it's on your head, but if you think you can convince the authorities that you were on the *Hakkai Maru,* and you saw Garth pick up a strange-looking cartridge, and it shot out flames. I'll call the harbour master when we are back on the *Scorpion,* and afterwards, we'll take his body shoreside.'

Tony was grasping at straws and readily agreed. He was probably the smartest of us onboard, and I was confident he could carry it off. So, the die was cast, and we headed back to the *Scorpion.*

On seeing the gaping hole in Garth's body, Blondie almost fainted and broke down in sobbing fits. I had Joe take her back to the galley. John and Jack transferred Garth's body to the *Hiptimco* as I went up to the wheelhouse to radio the harbour master on channel 16. I knew, because this was an open channel, soon everyone in Rabaul would know.

I outlined the accident at the *Hakkai Maru* and requested an ambulance at the Yacht Club jetty. John had covered Garth's body with a bedsheet, and soon the five of us were on our way to the jetty.

The ambulance was already waiting for us when we arrived. The driver took one look at Garth and was shocked.

'Jesus Christ! What the hell happened to him?' he said, screwing up his face.

Tony responded in an off-the-cuff manner, 'He picked up some kind of bomb on the *Hakkai,* and it went off.'

'Bloody hell!' was all the driver could say.

A small crowd of curious people had by now arrived as the body was loaded into the ambulance. I turned to Tony, 'You better go with the driver, I'll send Joe back with the *Hiptimco*, and he'll wait for you here.'

Tony nodded in response. He knew there would be many questions for him to answer when they got to Nonga Base Hospital.

With the ambulance on its way, I turned to Lindsay and John. 'What do you reckon? Shall we go back and get those fuckin safes open?'

'Nothing else to do,' was Lindsay's simple reply.

'Okay, then let's get back to the *Scorpion*. John, you and the boys load up as soon as we get back. Lindsay and I'll get cracking on the inner shell.'

Then, without a further word, we were on our way back to the *Scorpion*. It was a silent trip, everyone dealt with their demons quietly and in their own way. As soon as we were back on board, I went up to comfort Blondie. I thought this will cause her to have nightmares for quite a while. It's traumatic enough to see a dead body, let alone one so mutilated.

She lay on the bunk facing the wall, so I cuddled in tight behind her, I could feel her sobbing. She turned to face me, tears in her eyes. 'It's so sad, Simon. Garth's gone. I can't believe it. He was such a beautiful, attentive person.'

Hmmm, I didn't want to shatter her illusion or memory by telling her that his one goal was to get into her pants, so instead said, 'It was a terrible accident, and we are all going to miss him.' I whispered that in her ear as I pulled her close, comforting myself as much as her.

Lindsay calling my name and urging me to get ready, broke the spell. I kissed Blondie on the lips and said, 'Be strong and remember the good times.'

And with that, I left to get ready to work.

Chapter 22

Bullion, Jewellery, and Gold Coins.

Back at the dive site, Jack fired up my lance, and in less than a minute, I was on the bottom. As I suspected, the burning bar easily penetrated the thin shell. Better still, the molten metal had fallen away into the safe, so it did not re-weld as before. It was like poking a pencil into paper.

I saw Lindsay still working away as I made my way to the surface to change burning bars. I passed the Lance to Jack and hopped into the tender. I want to wait and go down with Lindsay after he came up and have a look at what we have managed to achieve. It would also give us a better idea of how much remained to be cut, and where.

Using scuba, both Lindsay and I were on our way down. When I reached the safe, I saw that I had managed to poke quite a lot of holes in the steel, but there was not a clean cut. Moving over to Lindsay's safe, I noticed that he hadn't fared much better. It was the bubbles and sparklers at the end of the burning bar that made it very difficult to see where you were cutting. Once back in the tender, I suggested that we have one more go with the lance. If necessary, we could set a couple of small blasts to crack any last bits that may be holding things together. Lindsay nodded in agreement. I was pleased this might be the last of the lance work.

Soon, we were both back on the bottom with fresh-burning bars. I gouged away blindly at every restriction I felt while trying to keep everything in a straight line. I kept poking away until I was again out of burning bar and then headed back to the surface.

Sitting on the gunwale while taking off my gloves and boots, I turned to John, 'Do you still have the explosives and detonators on-board?'

'No, I took them off yesterday.'

'Okay, we'll just have to go back to the boat. I want to see how Blondie is getting on, anyhow.' I continued while putting on my fins, 'When Lindsay comes up, I'll make a quick snorkel down to have a look at the cut, and then we'll return to the boat.'

'Okay skipper, not a problem.'

As soon as I saw Lindsay's lance break the surface, I was over the side and heading to the bottom. On reaching the safe, I noticed my side still had a few spots that needed cutting, Lindsay's was a bit better but was also still held in place by a couple of unburnt steel strips. I guess four sticks on my side and two on Lindsay's should do it.

*   *   *

Back on the *Scorpion*, John and the boys helped unload the oxygen cylinders and other gear from the tender and then reloaded fresh scuba tanks and explosives. Meanwhile, the rest of us relaxed on the back deck with a coffee and sandwich.

'Let's hope nothing more goes wrong,' I said to no one in particular.

'Let's hope no one else dies!' Blondie snapped, with tears again starting to well in her eyes.

'No, Julie, that was just a horrible, freak accident.' I purposely used her real name to highlight the sincerity of what I said. 'It may not appear like it, and we might clown around a bit, but everything we do is calculated. We are always mindful of the depth we work in and the explosives we use. There is not much that is left to chance.'

John stuck his head around the corner. 'Everything's ready. Do I have time for a cup of tea and a sandwich?'

'Yes, but hurry up,' I said with a grin.

This time, we would use up some Hydrogel 90, a bit fiddly to use, but otherwise a good explosive. On returning to the safes, we went about setting our charges. We pierced each explosive stick and threaded it with the Cordtex primer cord and placed it for maximum effect. With thin steel like this, there was no need to use clay. So with explosives in place, all that was left was to connect the electric detonator to the det-wire and head back up to the surface.

Just as John was about to pop the blast back in the tender, a stupid song sprang into my head. It was one of Elvis's, and it went something like '...this is the moment, I've been waiting for...' over and over again. The suspense was killing me. The crack on the tender signalled the blast had gone off.

I said to Lindsay as I reached for my flippers and mask, 'Fuck this! I'm going down.'

'I'm coming too,' he said as he made a mad grab for his mask and snorkel, trying to keep up with me.

'What about you, John?' I said in jest

'Fuck-off! If you think I'm going down there with the sharks, you're off your head.'

'Pussy!' I yelled as I went over the side. He made a fake lunge at me just as I disappeared.

Visibility was nil. I kept my hand out in front of me to stop from running into anything. Soon, however, I found the safe. Like a blind man, I went about groping for the hole in the safe. I found the door handle and quickly worked up from there and... bingo, there was now a gaping hole in the safe. I stuck my arm in as far as it would go, but all I felt was mud. I was getting hungry for air so made a beeline back to the surface.

I hopped back into the tender. Lindsay was right behind me. I spat the snorkel out of my mouth and said, 'I don't believe it. The fucking thing is full of volcanic mud.'

'So is mine, but I got a couple of these,' Lindsay said, holding two gold coins.

I took one of the coins and inspected it. It was a 20-mark, German, New Guinea gold coin, just beautiful. 'Well, that's a good sign!'

'Didn't have enough breath to dig deeper,' Lindsay said, looking dejected.

There was a feeling of optimism on board, but I was puzzled by the mud. 'How the fuck did the mud get into the bloody safe? The fuckin things were locked and then in a storeroom. This has just got me buggered.'

'John, head back to the boat and throw the three-inch Honda pump into the tender and the fire hose with the big brass nozzle.'

Jack pulled up the anchor, and we were on our way back to the *Scorpion*.

I looked at Lindsay, saying, 'Don't bother getting changed. We'll head straight back.'

Joe and Blondie were there to catch the mooring lines and tie us up.

I turned to Joe. 'Joe, jump down into the hold and pass up the Honda water pump and hose.'

John and Jack jumped on board. Jack went to get a can of petrol, and John helped Joe with the water pump. Ten minutes later, we were on our way back to the safes. I connected the fire hose to the pump and Lindsay threw the hose overboard to allow it to untangle and straighten out.

As we entered the bay John started to slow down, Lindsay began to pull the hose in, while at the same time, letting the loop run out. On John's command, Jack dropped the anchor, and we were ready to get back in the water.

The plan was simply to wash the mud out of each safe. The Honda pump was capable of 600 litres per minute, and it did this with a lot of pressure. If this didn't flush the mud out of the safe, nothing would.

I picked up the heavy brass fire nozzle and jumped over the side. With my extra lead weights, I dropped to the bottom like a stone. Unless Lindsay had a death wish, he'd better wait until I'm in position before starting the pump. I would be flung around the ocean like a wet rag if he decided to play funny buggers.

I was safely on the bottom and in position when the firehose started to stiffen. I could even feel the engine vibrations as it filled with water. Soon, there was a powerful stream of water spewing from the nozzle. I shoved it into the hole and dug my heels deeper into the ocean floor. Leaning forward, I jammed my shoulder against the safe to stop the jet-like action of the water from shooting me in the opposite direction.

Almost instantly, a thick black cloud of fine volcanic mud enveloped me. Every few minutes, I pulled the nozzle out of the safe and waved it around the ocean dispersing the dark cloud of mud. Slowly, the amount of black soot coming out of the safe was less and less, and soon it was just clean water.

Lindsay was standing close by, watching me, waiting for me to finish so he could start cleaning out his safe. I made gestures for him to get into position so I could pass the nozzle. The moment he stuck it into his safe, the whole area was instantly enveloped in a dark cloud of volcanic mud. There was nothing for me to do but head for the surface.

I gave Lindsay five minutes and did a quick snorkel down to see how he was progressing. As I got close, I noticed he was looking up, obviously for me. He gave the cut-throat sign and pointed to the nozzle.

I quickly surfaced. The water pump was making a hell of a racket. I had to shout out loud to get John's attention. I made the cut-throat sign pointing to the water pump. John understood that it meant to shut the motor down. He did that, and then he automatically started to reel in the fire hose. I got Jack to pass me a dive torch from under the seat, and again I disappeared below the surface.

On the way down, I could see Lindsay scrounging around the ocean floor. I was puzzled. *What the fuck is he doing?* I tapped him on the shoulder. He looked up at me with that stupid grin of his, then with head and eye movements, prompted me to look down. My eyes nearly popped out of my head.

Scattered on the ocean floor was a carpet of coins. Most were gold, some silver, and also an assortment of jewellery, including teeth. The power of the water pressure forced out the mud and also many coins and other bits.

At one time, these would have been securely packed in leather bags, but the bags had long since rotted away. I flashed the torch into Lindsay's safe, and it was still packed with coins. This was mind-blowing.

I quickly moved over to the safe I had been working. I was now desperately hoping that this one was where they stored the bullion. With my heart in my mouth, I bent down and stuck the torch into the safe. The unmistakable sparkle of gold bars greeted me. All I could do at that moment was punch the water and shout. 'You fucken beauty!' And yes, you can talk underwater. It's just that no one can understand you.

I quickly leaned over to Lindsay and urged him to drop his trinkets in a pile and have a look in my safe. I handed him the torch and pushed him towards the opening. He stuck his head in and switched on the torch. Moments later, he pulled his head out and looked up at me. His eyes were bulging, and he had that silly grin, but then, it was even bigger than ever. I thought for a moment that his regulator was going to drop from his mouth. He bent down to have a second look as though he could not believe his eyes the first time. Ecstatic, he shook me with one hand and making the thumbs-up sign with the other.

I pointed to his pile of coins and jewellery and swam over to it. With sign language, I asked him to put some in his pocket, indicating we will come down with buckets to pick it up. So, with pockets full, we headed for the surface.

Lindsay still had a grin from ear to ear when we surfaced and burst out in uncontrollable fits of laughter when I told John with utmost sincerity that the safes were empty.

'You're fucken kidding me,' He said depressed and looking disappointed.

'No mate, nothing but mud and paper.'

'Well, I guess that's that... what a bugger,' he said, sitting down, now seriously looking dejected.

Lindsay couldn't contain himself, and with a smirk, dug into his pocket and pulled out half a dozen gold coins.

Talking to John, who was now staring blankly at the decks, he said, 'We did find a lot of this stuff though.'

John looked up at Lindsay and then down to his handful of coins, he remained expressionless and didn't say a word, and then he exploded! 'You fucken cunt!' In that microsecond, he lunged at me with full force, grabbing me in a tight bear hug.

He took me completely by surprise, and before I could react, he burst out laughing and said. 'You really are an arsehole, you know, Simon. You had me going there.'

Lindsay handed John a handful of coins and then brought us back to reality. 'Looks like the *Hiptimco* is coming back,' he said, pointing to the horizon.

'Okay, John,' I said. 'Take us back, I've got some ideas on how best to get the stuff out of the safes, but we have to see what Tony has to say first.' I continued, 'But don't say anything about the gold until we've had a chance to hear the outcome of his trip to the hospital.'

We arrived at the *Scorpion* the same time as Joe and Tony. As usual, they tied up on the port side and we on the starboard.

We were still all shocked by Garth's death, and in varying degrees, it weighed on our minds, but more so, on Tony. I guess that's natural as he was ultimately responsible, so it was something he was just going to have to live with for the rest of his life.

According to Tony, the phosphor munition story seemed to have gone down well, and he didn't expect any problems. I guess that may be partly tributed to a spate of 'accidents' on the *Hakkai*. But there have been numerous munitions accidents in and around Rabaul for years, both in water and above. Many locals like to extract the explosive powder from WW2 bombs and use it to make homemade fish grenades. There have been many accidents because of this throughout the country.

Hopefully, in the authorities' eyes, Garth's episode will just be another unfortunate accident in the country due to WW2 munitions. Tony did provide the police with a statement of the accident, they asked for personal details, next of kin. We never delve much into each other's personal details, so Tony could not say much on that score. He did offer to deliver Garth's passport to the police station. I was confident the police would be able to track Garth's family, most probably via Immigration. One way or another, his remains would find their way home.

'On a brighter note,' I said to John, 'cough up, and show Tony and Blondie.'

'I've no idea of what you're talking about, boss,' he said with all the sincerity he could muster.

'Come on, boofhead. Show them.'

John grinned as he dug into his pocket and slammed the coins onto the table.

Blondie's eyes lit up as she picked up the German New Guinea gold coin. 'Can I have one for a necklace?' she asked as she held it between her breasts, just to demonstrate how good it would look on her.

Everyone was looking, but not so much at the coin. Tony commented, 'That's nice, Blondie.' then looking at me. 'So, you got the safes open?'

'Yes, both of them. One has loose stuff – coins and jewellery – while the other gold bullion.'

'When are we going to load up,' Tony asked.

'It's not that easy. Lindsay flushed a whole lot of the small stuff out of the safe with the pressure hose, so tonight we were hoping to go down with buckets and collect that first.' Looking at Tony, I said, 'Do you feel up to a night dive?'

'I'm good. If I don't hit the water now, I never will!'

'Okay, that's good. Tonight, we'll scrounge around the bottom and pick up as much of the loose stuff as possible. Early tomorrow, we'll move the *Scorpion* over the top of the safes.'

'I want you,' pointing to John, 'and the boys to rig up a heavy side lift when we get back tonight. Right now, go and organise three sets of scuba tanks and three fire buckets with 40-ft lanyards. Also, you better throw a spare plastic storage box in the tender just in case we need it.'

With everyone at the table, I outlined the plan. 'Tomorrow, we'll take the *Scorpion* over the top of the safes. Using the heavy side lift, we'll pick up one end of the safes so all the gold will fall down and out of the holes. We can use the ship's cargo winch with the steel scrap cage to bring up the heavy bullion.' It was time to get back to work.

Chapter 23

The Treasure

I t was almost dark when we returned to the safes, and in the failing light, John was having a little trouble lining up the marks, but eventually, he gave Joe the signal to drop the anchor.

We were all as excited as hell to get into the water, and no sooner had Jack dropped the anchor, we quickly disappeared over the side. Moments later, our powerful torches were making round searchlight patterns on the ocean floor, and each piece of gold sparkled brightly, like fox eyes in a spotlight.

Just like excited children searching for Easter eggs, we rummaged around on the ocean floor, picking up coins and jewellery of every description, even occasionally gold teeth. Once the most visible pieces were safely in our buckets, we started to sift through the upper layer of mud with our fingers revealing even more treasures.

After almost an hour or so of fossicking around in the mud, my bucket was almost a quarter full, and all the obvious pieces were now in our buckets. I decided to call it quits for the night and head to the surface. I gave a quick tug on the line, and my bucket was also on its way up.

I noticed that Tony's bucket was also heading towards the surface. I was keen to show him the bullion in the other safe. I momentarily flashed the torch in his face to get his attention and then signalled for him to come over to me and stick his head into the hole.

His enthusiastic 'thumbs up' showed his pleasure. The safe was some 2 metres deep, and unfortunately, the gold bricks were all jammed together at the bottom end. We would have to wait until the next day to find out how much they each weigh.

Tony and I sat in the tender, waiting for Lindsay to surface. In the torchlight, I fumbled through the items in the buckets. A couple of adorable diamond rings, one with what looked like rubies down the side immediately took my fancy, so I put them down the front of my speedos. I was sure to win a few brownie points from Blondie with those.

I hear John grunting while pulling up Lindsay's bucket, and moments later, Lindsay bounced onto the gunwale and swung on board.

'I reckon there's still a fair bit scattered around down there,' he said. 'Every time I thought "That's it", I'd come across another piece.'

'I believe it, but we have much bigger fish to worry about, and in any case, there's still a shit-load of this small stuff in the safe.' I replied. 'Let's not risk losing the big stuff for nickels and dimes.'

There was general agreement on that score. As we watched, Joe hauled up the anchor. John pulled hard on the starter cord, and the outboard sprang to life. We were on our way back to the *Scorpion*.

* * *

We had just made ourselves comfortable on the afterdeck and about to enjoy a cold beer when Blondie joined us. She saw the three, red, fire buckets on the table and demanded to know, 'What are those filthy buckets doing on the table?'

'John put them there, the idiot,' I casually replied and continued, 'You're standing up. You put them down.'

She raised her eyebrows and gave one of those annoyed, frustrated looks as if to say, 'Who was your maid in your last life?'. She stretched out her hand and took hold of the rim of the bucket closest to her, and nearly tripped-up. She had expected it to be empty and was surprised when she could not lift it. She stepped closer and had a look inside. Her eyes wide and mouth agape, she burst out with, 'Jesus Fucking Christ!'

'There's more where that came from,' I said with a smile as she sat down next to me.

'John, get another bucket, will you?'

When he came back, I spoke to everyone at the table, 'So long as you all agree, I think the best thing to do with this small stuff is to empty the contents of the buckets onto the table and sort it into four roughly equal piles. Everyone will be responsible for looking after their own loot.' I continued, 'Whatever ends up in your bucket will be yours to keep, even if you melt it into ingots, which you may have to do anyway before we get to Australia. What do you think?'

Everyone agreed, so we emptied the three buckets and began to divide the spoils into four piles. Some good-hearted shenanigans were going on, especially with Lindsay and John each pretending to grab the larger, more valuable items. In the end, everyone was happy, as everyone scraped their plunder temporarily into a bucket.

'How's that?' I said as I placed my buckets on the table. 'Now remember, each of you is responsible for their own loot, and it might be an idea to keep it hidden from prying eyes. We have a few old scuba bottles that we can use to keep it safe. No one will look in there.'

'Good idea,' Tony agreed. 'When I get time, I'll take a couple of tanks to Pat's workshop and cut open the base with his lathe. With the boot back on, they'll look normal.'

And with that settled, I grabbed my bucket, and Blondie's hand and I left for the relative privacy of the wheelhouse. We were sitting on the bunk admiring some of the pieces when I remembered the two rings, that were still tucked in my speedos. It was time for a little game.

I got up, stood in front of her, and said. 'Okay time to pull down my speedos.' My dick just happened to be at the right height for a blowjob.

She looked up at me, then to the doorway and whispered, 'Someone might see.'

I thought that's strange. She had never worried about that before. 'Stop mucking about and pull them down!' I said, with my hands on my hips.

Without further ado, she leant back a little as she took hold of the top of my swimmers and pulled them down, inside out. My stiffening member popped out. Instinctively her hand was already heading for my dick when I stopped her and said. 'No, pull them further down.'

The waistband of my speedos was now down near my knees.

'I've got a special present for you,' I said.

'I know.' Her breathing was getting shallower, as her excitement increased. She took a firm hold of my rod.

'No, not that. Have a look lower,' I said, laughing.

She moved my rod to the left and looked down. Then she spotted the rings highlighted in the white lining of the speedos. To my dismay, she let go of me. Her attention was now firmly centred on the rings. She picked them up one at a time and admired them.

The magic of the moment was gone, so I pulled my swimmers up. And just in the nick of time because moments later I heard Joe struggling up the ladder with an old scuba tank.

I turned my attention back to Blondie. She was thrilled with the rings, and they were indeed beautiful. While admiring them, I whispered to her, 'There'll be many more beautiful things coming to the surface tomorrow. You can have your pick of anything you desire.'

She kissed me with a newfound sincerity. Maybe it was a perception of financial security, perhaps she was just grateful, but something was different. My words had somehow resonated with her.

I was about to start loading the trinkets into our bunk's bottom drawer when she got up and turned the lights out.

'Now it is my turn to surprise you,' she said as she stripped naked and picked up a bottle of baby oil.

I was out of my speedos in a second and let her have her way with me. Sometimes a root is more than just a root, and tonight was such a night.

Chapter 24

The Treasure Comes Onboard

I t was 5:00 a.m. in the morning. Joe is standing on the ladder to the bridge, bashing on the wall shouting, 'Get up skipper, time to get up!'

I rolled out of the bunk, and as always, covered Blondie's naked body with the sheet and slipped on my speedos. There was a slight chill in the air that morning, so I grabbed a t-shirt before making my way to the galley. Cookie had a pot of coffee on the table, and breakfast was almost ready.

Everyone was there except Blondie, and of course, Garth. It felt strange, him not being there. Sad, actually, after all those years, but life must go on.

With breakfast over, Tony disappeared down the engine room hatch to start the main engine. Lindsay and Jack headed off to the anchor winch. It had a cranky, two-cylinder Lister diesel that sometimes could be quite tricky to start. I made for the wheelhouse, taking Joe with me to man the helm.

With the anchor safely in the hawsepipe, it was time to get underway. The main engine was running at idle. I slipped her into slow reverse and ordered the helm to full port. I gave her a touch more throttle, and the boat started to swing to starboard. I told Joe to put the helm to full starboard, and I gave her full throttle for a few seconds. The boat now started to spin on her axis, and as soon as I was happy with the direction, I ordered 'amidships', reduced the speed to a couple of knots, and headed to our new anchorage, just a few hundred yards away.

The little cove we were heading for was not well protected, especially during the south-east season. We only planned to be there for a day, and in any case, the weather has been calm for weeks. So I didn't envisage any problems. Again, we would be anchoring close to shore. This time, I would position her over the top of the safes. Once I get the anchor away, I will have the boys take a stern line to the beach and tie it to a coconut tree.

The manoeuvre goes well, and the marks line up for the safe's. I swung the boat around, so the head was facing out to sea and the stern to shore. With the anchor out, Jack jumped into the water for the short swim to shore, taking the stern line with him. Soon we are securely in position.

Tony shut down the main engine, and the boat was once again deadly quiet. Blondie is on deck wearing a long-sleeved shirt of mine over her skimpy bikini, looking magnificent as usual. She came over to me as I made my way to the tender and gave me a big hug and cooed, 'Be careful, please.'

I guess she's beginning to realise just how dangerous our job can be, irrespective of how much we might clown around. John already had a couple of slings and shackles in the tender. Everything was ready for us to take down. The *Scorpion's* heavy side lift falls were also already under the water. I found a small, 3-metre-square canvas tarp, which I planned to put under the hole of the safe with the jewellery. This should stop most of the small stuff from ending up in the mud.

We had to be very careful about placing the slings. It was important they didn't slip. The last thing I wanted at this stage was to have a safe fall on someone, especially me! Fortunately, sections of the hull to which the safes were welded were quite jagged. The force of the explosion had curled the steel outward from the safe, and this provided good anchor points for the sling. The hull section was solid being 25-mm-thick steel, and there was no way this would let go.

The mud on the ocean floor was compacted, but just soft enough for me to force the sling under the hull-plate. This was a webbed sling and had an eye spliced into each end. By passing one end of the sling through the loop, I was effectively making a noose. So, when the lift began, it would tighten like a hangman's noose – the more pressure, the tighter the grip.

I watched Lindsay walking along the bottom towards me, carrying the lifting hook and dragging the davit falls behind him. As he got close, I held open my end of the sling, allowing him to attach the hook with ease. I told him to stay with sign language, while I went to the surface and got John to reel in the slack. He nodded in agreement.

John was standing at the gunwale and watching the falls. On my signal, he told Jack, who was operating the winch, to start reeling in the cable. Soon, the cable had begun to tighten, and as it did, it started to span outward from the boat some 30 degrees. I signalled John to stop and drop back to the bottom. I needed to make sure that everything was okay before too much pressure was on the lift. Lindsay was looking up and signalled okay, so I headed back to the surface. It was time to continue pulling the boat directly over the top of the safes.

I asked John to continue reeling in until the cable until it was vertical and then stop. In a few minutes, the boat had stopped moving sideways, and the falls were now vertical. This meant the *Scorpion* had been dragged directly over to the top of the safes. I called out to Joe to get me a 40-ft length of cord. I needed a signalling line so I could control the lift.

John threw me one end of the signal line. He knew the drill, one tug means stop, two tugs mean up, and three tugs mean lower. Tony had jumped into the water with two sledgehammers and instantly disappeared below the surface. I followed him down with the signal line trailing to the surface.

*   *   *

The moment of truth was at hand. Everyone was in position. I slowly pulled on the signal line until it was tight and then gave two tugs. John replied with two tugs, and I saw the wire rope roll through the block and tighten. I then carefully watched the sling noose tighten around the safe.

At that moment, I was aware that the *Scorpion* was slowly being pulled down. This would continue until such time as the Scorpion's flotation capability exceeded the weight of the safes.

The *Scorpion's* side-life capability was about fifteen to twenty tonnes. I estimated the safes at around five tonnes, so it was an easy lift for the boat and winch. John, however, would still be watching the rigging very carefully as it creaked and groaned.

Ever so slowly, the bottom end of the safes began to come off the ocean floor. They were soon at about 45 degrees, and smaller bits of jewellery and coins were starting to spill onto the canvas. I signalled John to stop.

I was a bit wary about putting my head up into the bullion safe. I didn't fancy being hit in the head with a ten-kilo-or-so gold bar. So, I asked Tony to climb onto the top of the safe and give it a bash. The sound of him slamming the sledgehammer into the side of the safe echoed like a gunshot through the water. After the second hit, we were rewarded with a few bars falling out of the opening.

I called the boys away from the safe and made the signal that I would increase the lift. I pulled the signal line until the slack was gone, and once again gave two sharp pulls. Almost immediately, the bottom of the safe began to rise further. This time, I took it to almost vertical before I signalled John to stop. I thought to myself, *If it doesn't work now, it never will.*

Again, Tony climbed back onto the top of the bullion safe and gave it a hard smack with the sledgehammer – nothing. Then, a second hit, and again, the sound reverberated underwater. Seconds later, we were rewarded with a loud tumbling of metal in the safe.

Tony then maneuvered over to the top of the coin safe and gave it an almighty smack. Again, he was rewarded with tumbling coins and jewellery. Then again, another smack and more fall out. I signalled Tony to hit it again, and another bang reverberated through the water. But not much fell out this time.

I pointed to Lindsay, making the sign to look in the safe. He pulled out his small emergency torch, brushed a heap of coins onto the canvas until he had enough space to stick his head into the hole. He turned upside down and shined the torch up into the safe. Backing out, he made the okay signal, and I took it to mean that everything worthwhile had slipped out of the open end.

I got everybody's attention by banging my knife onto my steel scuba tank and pointed to the surface, and up we went. First, I had to get John to secure the lift. We don't want anything to slip or move.

I pointed to John. 'Tell Joe to get three buckets ready for the small stuff. Put Cookie to work on one of them. And you and Jack crank up the winch and swing the cargo boom over the side with the steel basket.'

The fire buckets were on their way to the bottom, and the basket for the heavy bullion was also in the water. A quick drink of cordial, and it was time for us to get back to work.

Tony and I concentrated on loading the bullion into the wire basket. It was heavy work, and soon I found myself switching to reserve. I let Tony know I was almost out of air. He gave the okay signal in acknowledgement and indicated that he was also getting low.

He would come up with the basket, making sure it didn't catch on the safe while on its way to the surface. As soon as I reached the tender gunwale, I spat out my regulator and sang out to John, 'Okay John, take her up slowly and get the gold bars straight into the hold. Stack them in a pile and cover it. Then send the basket back down.'

I climbed into the tender for a fresh scuba bottle. I watched the basket come out of the water and disappear into the hold just as Tony joined me. He quickly ditched his scuba tank. 'Not much left down there from what I can see,' he said in a mock-dejected tone.

'I'll be glad when it's all on board, and we get back to our anchorage. It looks like one more dive will do it. I wonder how Lindsay is getting on,' I replied.'

At that very moment, Lindsay popped his head out of the water and made his way to the ladder. He was still halfway up the ladder when he said, 'I think that's about it from my safe.'

'We'll take a couple of torches down just to make sure,' I said, as I lifted the lid of the seat and rummaged around for two torches.

Lindsay looked up at Joe and Cookie and gave the signal to start lifting. 'Slowly, slowly,' he sang out. Then looking at me, he said, 'It's only about half full.'

'Better than nothing!' I replied as two of the buckets came onboard. Joe immediately began lifting the third. Directing my attention to Cookie, I said,

'Cookie, empty one bucket into another and send it back down.'

Meanwhile, Tony and Lindsay had already begun to change dive bottles when John appeared on deck. Leaning on the gunwale, he said, 'Okay, boss. All unloaded and stacked in the hold.'

'Okay, get that bloody cage back in the water and on the bottom,' I replied.

Lindsay and Tony were already bobbing on the surface, waiting for John to drop the cage. I handed them a torch each, and moments later, only their bubbles were left bursting on the surface. Then I too dropped over the side and disappeared below.

The last of the bullion lying at the safe base was then quickly loaded into the cage. I found two more stray ones still stuck in the corner near the opening. I scraped them out, and they too were soon stacked in the cage. A further check confirmed that the safe was now empty. A sift through the mud also failed to find anything more.

Tony made a flying visit to the surface to tell John to reel the cage in while I sent it on its way. Tony quickly re-joined us, and we then all concentrated on the safe with the jewellery and other bits. I took the torch from Tony and stuck my head in the hole. I looked up towards what was once the bottom, and nothing there. I looked up and down each side, also nothing. Looking to the left of the hole, I saw quite a bit still stuck in the corner and started to scrape it out with my hands. A few minutes later, another inspection confirmed the safe was now empty.

Lindsay carefully scooped everything that he could find into the bucket and then made signs that he wanted to continue looking around on the ocean floor. Tony and I started picking up the tools and took them with us to the surface.

John and Jack disappeared down the hold to stack the last of the bullion. Five minutes later, Lindsay surfaced and asked Joe to pull the bucket up and announced nothing left below.

So that was that, no reason to stay here any longer. Tony and I got out of our dive gear and climbed aboard the *Scorpion*. Tony went straight down to the engine room and cranked up the main engine while I headed to the bridge.

As soon as John reappeared out of the hold, I had him drop the side lift letting the safe fall to the seabed. Lindsay was still suited up and waiting in the tender. He then went down to unhook the slings. They would come up with the side lift. Soon there was nothing left on the bottom but a couple of empty safes. I had to have a bit of a chuckle to myself, thinking what someone finding the safes would be thinking. I could visualise them scratching their heads.

It did not take long to tidy up the decks, and soon, when the stern line was back onboard and anchor on its way up, we made way back to our safe little cove. All we had to do now was to count and weigh the gold and get it away from prying eyes.

And for that, we had the perfect place, our secret explosive magazine. Sometime before I purchased the *Scorpion,* the owners had converted her from a coastal cargo vessel to a prawn trawler in Cairns. They installed heavy-duty trawler winches and masts, and she was also fitted with extra-long-range fuel tanks.

The largest of these was amidships, directly in front of the engine room bulkhead. This tank ran from port to starboard and the full height of the hold. It was approximately 4.3 metres long, 1.6 metres high, and 90 cm wide. From inside the ship's hold, there were no openings or inspection holes.

We always had problems with over-zealous port authorities whenever we wanted to come alongside a wharf. We were known as a salvage vessel, and authorities naturally assumed we would have explosives on board. There were a whole lot of stupid rules and regulations that we were required to abide by. The most frustrating was we could not come alongside when another vessel was at the wharf. We were also supposed to run up a red flag and a whole host of dumb, time-wasting, stupid rules. This pissed me off, so I looked for an answer, and the most obvious answer was this particular unused fuel tank. I checked the width and height. It looked more than adequate for an explosive magazine.

And most importantly, as I said before, there was no opening or inspection plate in the fuel tank when viewed from the hold. This was crucial because there was no chance of a diligent customs officer or official asking us to open the inspection cover to look inside.

The engine room bulkhead was timber, and thankfully, the planks ran vertically. There was a lot of bilge plumbing and valves situated low against the bulkhead, just above the keel, but this was not high enough to worry us. There was also a lot of electrical stuff to the port and starboard. But right smack amidships, there was an open space just large enough for us to cut a hole big enough for a man to pass through.

It was the perfect entrance. We carefully cut the timber bulkhead using jigsaws to give us access to the tank. We then fashioned a door from the bulkhead timber that could easily be lifted out and put back in. Then, with an angle grinder and some thin cutting blades, we opened a hole in the fuel tank 77 cm wide by 120 cm tall. We then fashioned also a door from the piece that we had cut out.

The fuel tank was laboriously cleaned and washed out with degreaser, a dirty job, and I'm bloody glad I had a crew to do it. Once clean, the tank was lined with thin plywood. I didn't want sparks setting off the nitro-glycerine explosives. And bingo! We had the perfect, invisible explosive magazine.

When standing inside the ship's hold, it was impossible to imagine that the tank was anything but a fuel tank. There were no inspection holes, so no way to enter the tank from there. And from the engine room side, with the bulkhead door in place, it was impossible to imagine that a door or opening existed.

Now, because the authorities are not totally stupid and everyone knew we were a salvage vessel, it just followed that explosives would be on board from time to time. So, we had a small, dummy explosive magazine built on the foredeck. However, this was mainly used to store rope and buoys.

The magazine already had the silver ingots neatly stacked on the floor with ten boxes of explosives sitting on top of them. I had the crew move the dynamite further into the tank and away from the opening making space for the gold.

Meanwhile, we weighed and counted the ingots. We ended up with fifteen 12-kg ingots. We also managed another three buckets of the small stuff. With the gold counted, the crew loaded it on top of the silver in the magazine. The explosives were then reloaded on top of the gold. With everything safe and secure, we could now start to relax. We might even give Dave a hand to get the *Santo* back in the water, but then again, maybe not!

The only thing that was now left to put this salvage project to bed was to finish cleaning up around the *Hakkai*. We still had the tools we used when moving the safes littering the ocean floor. There was also a small matter of the booby traps that needed disarming and removal.

All evidence that the booby traps ever existed had to be wiped clean.

Chapter 25

Celebrations and Tidying Up Loose Ends

It was a standing joke among us that the local divers would be a lot more careful when visiting the *Hakkai* for quite some time, especially after the last couple of incidences, and in particular, Garth's unfortunate accident which also was attributed to the wreck. The crew were making jokes at the local divers expense, when I interrupted their merriment and said, 'How about we leave cleaning up the *Hakkai* until tomorrow morning? This evening, I'm going to treat you all to the Rabaul Steakhouse, I think we all deserve a meal at the best eating-house in Rabaul!' My announcement was met with a good deal of enthusiasm.

It's hard to imagine that a chef to royalty and who has also cooked for President Nixon could end up in a backwater like Rabaul, but Joe Cook and his wife Marcella had built up a solid reputation for the finest food in town. So tonight, we would all spruce up and celebrate. Blondie would be beautiful as usual, but especially so tonight showing off her new diamond rings and gold necklace. Unfortunately, the chain and pendant also brought undue attention to her rather low-cut dress and ample breasts, but that was Blondie!

A shave, clean shirt, shorts, and sandshoes were the order of the day for the guys. Wearing a shirt and shoes was considered 'dressed' in Rabaul. Thongs and t-shirt were definitely casual.

It was a fun night, and the cocktails flowed freely. Tony ordered oysters, something I simply could not stomach. He made a song and dance about it. While at the bar, he had noticed some Middle Eastern type guys enjoying snails and dared me to order some. I was 'snookered'. I had never eaten escargot, but it had to be better than oysters, so I ambled over to the loudmouth Muslims and had a peek to see what the snails looked like. Well, at least they were cooked and looked well-done, so I took the plunge.

To my surprise, the garlic-butter escargot was actually quite good. I enjoyed them. Now, thanks to Tony, I had found something a bit more sophisticated than the usual prawn cocktail entrée to impress friends. Joe's steakhouse lived up to its reputation. I had yet to figure out how the hell he was able to make the steak so tender. The art of aging meat was not something I was aware of yet. But, like all things good the evening did not come cheap.

All too soon, it was time to leave. John was starting to slur his words and dribble, a sure sign he was reaching his alcohol limit. It was time to get him out of there before he got totally out of control. It was midnight before we were back on board the *Scorpion*.

The deep, alcohol-induced sleep ensured that it was a late start the next day for us all. With her insatiable sex drive, Blondie insisted on being looked after in the mornings, which usually meant that I was the last to make it to the galley. Today, the fresh stains on my Speedos explained why, and of course, someone had to notice.

Lindsay, the idiot, could not help himself and blurted out loud, 'Pissed yourself?'

What could I say but, 'Shut up, arsehole,' as I rubbed my speedos in an effort dry it, but I only managed to spread the 'love juice' around further. 'Fuck it,' I said to no one in particular as I sat down.

There was a generally good mood at the table, mainly because this latest project not only was almost at an end, but it had also been stunningly successful – except of course for the tragic loss of Garth. With breakfast over, I asked John to get the tender and dive gear ready and also gather up a couple of small lifting bags.

The dive plan was simple, Lindsay would go down and remove the booby traps, battery, det-wire, and mercury switches. Tony and I would do the deep stuff and pick up the tools, including the heavy crowbar that was hopefully still standing in the mud.

* * *

The freefall to the wreck was as magical as ever. One can never get tired of diving this magnificent ship. On the bottom, we quickly collected the tools and shackles. I tied off a small lifting bag to the crowbar and the iron rod and sent a puff of air into the bag. I took stock of my surroundings, and then filled the bag with air and took an express ride to the surface, venting air to ensure it didn't rise too fast.

I was first to surface, but some distance from the tender, fortunately, John spotted the bright orange lifting bag and paddled over to me, lifting everything onboard. Just then, Tony's bag appeared not far away, and soon his stuff was also safely in the tender.

John paddled back to the *Hakkai* buoy, and we settled down to wait for Lindsay. Ten minutes later, he surfaced with the explosives, battery and mercury switches. He had crunched the old 'det-wire' into a ball and jettisoned it over the side of the *Hakkai* where it became just another bit of ocean junk.

It was 12:30 p.m. when we got back to the *Scorpion*. We were now at loose ends, and for all intents and purposes, finished in Rabaul. The work had not been altogether hard. We have worked physically much harder on many other wrecks, but it was the mental strain that took its toll, the strain of knowing that at any moment, the real reason for our being here would be discovered and we would lose everything.

* * *

With the salvage now finished, I thought it might be a good idea to take a few days off and enjoy Rabaul. Everyone deserved a break, including the local crew. Lindsay and John were happy to pub-crawl and spend time with girlfriends. Tony was keen to explore some newly found Japanese caves.

I paid the local boys, including a bonus, and sent them shoreside, Cookie included. Over the weeks, Lindsay and John had made friends with many single, and some not-so-single, ladies. However, they preferred the nurses who were always quick to jump into bed, so they were happy to spend some free time onshore.

On the other hand, I had Blondie to keep me company and was happy to stay onboard and putter around a bit and just relax. Sooner or later, one of the crew would be back to babysit the *Scorpion*.

* * *

Blondie and I were each stretched out on a bench at the back deck, relaxing with a glass of wine, when I heard the drone of an outboard slowly getting louder and louder. I thought nothing of it. Every day, many tinnies or speedboats would go racing by. When suddenly it went quiet, and a few seconds later the tone changed to roar, obviously in reverse, then came a loud crash alongside the *Scorpion*.

We both jumped up to find Dave and Johnno standing in their work tender holding onto the gunwale.

'Jump on board,' I offered. 'To what do we owe the pleasure?'

'Thanks, but don't have time,' Dave replied, 'I want to know if you can give us a tow to Pat's wharf. All things being equal, we're ready to go back into the water tomorrow morning.'

'Not a problem, just give me a call on channel 16 when you're ready,' I replied. 'What's wrong with your engines?'

'The blast lifted my main fuel tank off its mountings and ripped the connection lines out of the tank.' Dave went on, 'I had 2,000 fucking litres of diesel floating around in the engine room. Fortunately, we were able to save most of it some 44-gallon drums.'

'Jesus! That's no good. Just give me a shout tomorrow, and we'll get you to Pat's. Not a problem.'

'I'll give you a call,' he said with a smile, and with that, they shoved off and were on their way back to the *Santo*.

The rest of the day was uneventful. I took the opportunity to tidy up the bridge. Blondie was content to lie in the sun as usual and re-read her girlie magazines for the third or fourth time. She was still in a very attentive mood, and around lunchtime, she poked her head into the bridge to announce that she would make lunch today.

'What would you like me to make for lunch?' she purred.

I was engrossed in sorting the navigation charts into some sort of order for our proposed trip to Cairns, so I wasn't paying too much attention. I simply replied, 'I think there's still some fish in the fridge that you can fry. That and some rice would be good.'

And with that, she shimmied down the ladder. Watching her disappear, I was amazed at how confident she was getting around the boat, and it made me smile.

Soon, I'd finished the jobs I set out to do. When I looked up at the ship's clock, I was surprised to see it was already 1:00 p.m. Strange, I hadn't heard from Blondie, so I make my way down to the galley.

Some things stay with you forever. For me, one of them was the sight of her standing by the stove in the hot galley, her long blonde hair tied in a big knot, wearing only a skimpy bikini and in her bare feet, with a pot that I presume had rice in it madly boiling away at the back of the stove. A wooden spoon in her hand stirring something that resembled vomit in a large fry pan.

On the sideboard, I saw two empty cans of a Chinese-brand tuna and an empty can of corn kernels, which I presumed were the contents of the frypan. Blondie looked up at me with those beautiful brown eyes and a huge smile, obviously pleased with her progress.

I asked her, 'What are you making?' With as straight a face as I could muster.

'Fried fish with corn and rice,' she said with a huge grin.

'And in the pot?'

'That's the rice, of course!' she replied, in a tone to suggest I'd asked a stupid question, which is probably exactly what I'd just done.

With the rice pot madly bubbling away, I suggested that it might be cooked, to which she responded in a very matter-of-fact way that she had watched her mother cook potatoes and rice would be no different. I thought it best to keep my mouth shut and not spoil her efforts to please me, and just wait to see the end result.

Having worked on small ships for more years then I care to remember, I've had to eat some pretty shitty meals – pan-fried spam and scrambled turtle eggs come to mind. This, I told myself, could be no worse. I left the galley space and sat down at the table to await my fate.

I watched Blondie switch off the stove and start dishing up the fish concoction. Then she dug the spoon into the gluggy rice but was having trouble getting it out of the pot. When she eventually had it on the spoon, even with all the frantic shaking, it wouldn't drop off onto the plate, but she was smart enough to use a knife to scrape it off the spoon and onto the plate.

Eventually, with the gluggy rice and fish concoction on the plate, she stepped out of the galley, smiling and proud of her achievement as she put the dishes on the table. She came back out with two wine glasses and cutlery.

'Don't start yet until I get the wine.' she commanded.

I just sat there, staring at the meal. I did not say a word. Moments later, she was back with a bottle of white wine. 'Open it, please,' she said as she passed the bottle and opener across the table.

I pulled the cork and poured two glasses, sliding hers across the table. I lifted my glass across to her in a salute, and in all sincerity said, 'To us!'

'To us!' she replied, beaming with pride.

Without the slightest hint of apprehension, I dug my fork into the sludge in front of me, stalling for time, I picked up the wineglass again and watched Blondie's reaction as she took her first mouthful.

It was like watching the sun dipping on the horizon. One moment she was glowing, beaming with pride, and the next an expression that can best be described as 'disgust'.

'Nice?' I asked as I put my glass down and picked up the fork.

'That fish is fuckin horrible!' she said, leaning over the side and splitting it into the ocean.

In reality, it was, what it was, fried, tinned tuna. It was edible but horrible. These cheap brands sold by the Chinese trade stores were about as bad as it got, and definitely an acquired taste. When I'd said to Blondie, fish, I meant the fresh fish in the fridge. I've just never heard of anybody frying tinned tuna.

To make her feel better, I said, 'It's not that bad. It's an acquired taste. The local boys like it, but I'm not fond of it either. We have some fresh fish in the fridge. Maybe we should quickly fry up a couple of pieces in butter. You'll like that.'

'Thank you. I would like that,' she mumbled with disappointment written all over her face.

'Come on, give me a hand. Empty the frypan over the side and feed the fish. Give it a bit of a clean while I prepare the fish.' I said in a cheerful tone, trying to make her feel better.

Soon, we had fresh fish sizzling in the pan. It was nice doing something together as simple as frying fish. I could sense that Blondie was content. For her, the dismal failure with the tinned fish wasn't her fault, and we were doing something as a couple.

We had delicious pan-fried coral trout fillets in garlic butter with some freshly cooked rice and a bottle of wine. The wine was enough to send us back to our bunks for a fun, bedtime workout and a snooze.

Chapter 26

Towing the Santo

In the morning at breakfast, I told the boys that Dave had asked for a tow to Pat's wharf today. This did not sit well with Lindsay or John. Both had arranged dates with their girlfriends. Tony wasn't impressed either. He had planned to investigate a newly discovered Japanese cave near the German residency. He was a very avid souvenir hunter.

I thought about it for a moment and decided that all this was not a problem. I suggested they go shoreside. Joe and Jack were onboard and more than capable of helping me with the tow.

* * *

It was not until midday that the ship's radio crackled to life.

'*Scorpion … Scorpion,* This is salvage vessel *Santo.* Do you read?' Dave's voice rang out loud and clear.

'Hi, *Santo*. This is *Scorpion*. We read you loud and clear,' I replied.

'We'll be in the water in half an hour. You may want to mosey over now,' Dave suggested.

'Okay, I'll be there in fifteen minutes. Rather than tow you, it might be better if I rope you alongside. Get some fenders ready.'

'Will do. *Santo* over and out.'

I blasted the horn to wake up the boys. They came scampering out of the forecastle like stunned jackrabbits. 'Get the anchor up!' I ordered as I made my way to the engine room. The engine faithfully sprang to life, and I quickly headed back up to the bridge.

Joe turned from watching the anchor come up and gave the okay signal as he switched off the winch motor. I popped the *Scorpion* into gear, and we were on our way. Meanwhile, the boys prepared the towing lines on the front deck and the stern. Soon, everything was ready for us to move the *Santo*.

As we approached the little bay at Matupit, I could see the channel that Dave had dredged directly aft of the barge and that the *Santo* was almost afloat. His loading ramp was down, and the bulldozers used it as their point of contact for the push. This gave them the extra distance they needed to ensure that he would be afloat before the dozers stopped pushing so they would not risk getting bogged at the water's edge.

We drifted some 20 metres aft of his stern. It was too shallow for us to get closer with our 2-metre draft. Dave sent out his tender with the towline, which was quickly fastened to our stern bollard. I slowly increased power until the line was taut, and then I gave her full power. Moments later, by the yelling and commotion on the *Santo,* I knew that they were fully afloat. I reduced power and concentrated on towing her into deeper water. I knew that right now Dave would be down in the engine room frantically checking the bilges for leaks.

As soon as we were clear of the bay, we released the towline, which Dave's boys quickly reeled in. I then manoeuvred alongside and securely tied up to the *Santo* for the short trip to Pat's jetty.

Dave had previously arranged with Pat that he would use the short, end-face of the jetty. This way, he would not be obstructing the main working area. The water at that point was shallow, so it was rarely used, but it was ideal for a small, 20-metre barge like the *Santo* which had a very shallow draft.

As we got closer, I could see, several small boats were doubled-up to the main face of the jetty. This was great and made it much easier for me to drop the *Santo* off. I was able to simply manoeuvre his bow to the stern of the outside boat and cast him off, from there he could easily rope himself to his berth. The whole exercise went off without a hitch, and when finished, I set a course for the Yacht Club anchorage.

My local crew were happy to relax onboard, so Blondie and I took advantage of this and spent most of the day ashore. We had lunch at the very popular Chung Ching Chinese restaurant on Ah Chee Avenue, in Malay town. This was a nice change from Cookie's cooking and the usual fish and chips or roast at the Yacht Club. We spent the rest of the day buying personal provisions for the planned trip to Australia.

It was quite surreal sitting on the dimly lit back deck of the *Scorpion* late in the evening, the music from the Yacht Club drifting eerily across the water and the lights from ships at anchor and at the main ship's wharf shimmering across the calm water of the harbour. It was going to be bloody difficult to leave all this behind.

Cookie had dug up some crackers and cheese, cold beer – well, almost cold – for the boys and me, and a glass of wine for Blondie.

It was now time to make plans on how best we might be able to get rid of the gold and silver.

Chapter 27

The Proposed Trip to Australia

Speaking to everyone, I said, 'We need to start thinking about our trip south and the splitting-up of the loot. I want no arguments, and I expect everyone to be 100% agreeable.

'What are you proposing?' Tony asked, his face turning a bit serious.

'Very simple. We stick to our standard agreement – 20% to the boat and the remaining 80% split equally among the four of us. That would give each of us personally, 20%. I don't give a shit about the small stuff in the buckets, but if anyone insists, we can count it, or we all simply keep what's in our bucket now and call it a "lucky-draw".'

Tony put his beer down and said, 'I think I speak for everyone Simon. We've spoken about this a couple of times, and we all agree that's the way to go.'

There was a nodding of heads and murmurs of agreement at the table.

Lindsay screwed up his face and said, 'We've talked about this, and we all think that what's in the buckets is probably going to be more trouble to get rid of than it's worth.'

'No not really, Lindsay,' I said. 'I agree most of the silver coins are worth bugger all, but there is some valuable shit amongst that stuff, especially the old German coins. Some of them are going to be very valuable. I just don't want any arguments later on down the track, that's all.'

Tony interjected, 'I agree with Lindsay. The small stuff's probably going to be a pain in the arse to get rid of. Whatever silver coins I have I'm going to give to the kids as play money. They're simply not worth melting down.'

'What about you, John?' I asked, and all eyes focused on him.

John looked startled. His eyes darted from person to person like a jackrabbit waiting to be shot. He was not used to making decisions. He was simply good at taking orders.

'I'm good! I'm good!' he blurted aloud, waving his arms around.

'Okay, we're all in agreement,' I said. 'And just so that you're all 100% clear, I'll look after Blondie out of my share.'

'Deals done!' Tony said emphatically, and we shook hands to seal it.

I was pleased that the divers did not argue about the 20% share to the boat. It did cost an arm and a leg to keep going. I was glad that everyone was happy.

Fortunately, our local crew did not fully appreciate the value of the bullion. Sure, they knew it was more valuable than our usual haul of copper and brass. But to them, it was just another metal salvage. In any case, I would make sure that they were more than happy with the bonus they received.

* * *

'Okay, now that we've got the disbursement out of the way, we have to think about preparing for the trip to Australia,' I said.

'What's so difficult about that?' John said, looking startled as if he had missed something.

'Well, first of all, we have to remelt the gold bullion, including the coins. we cannot leave the Japanese markings on the bullion, or it will instantly be confiscated when we try to sell it.'

'Fuck off! Are you serious?' John replied.

'Yes, mate. You're going to have to be careful when getting rid of the gold. I've even been thinking of getting a prospector's licence, melting down the coins. and stuff it all into water to make it look like alluvial gold, and then selling small amounts at a time.'

John was not the brightest cherry on the tree, and he was also the weakest link in the chain. Discretion was of utmost importance, and that was not one of John's strong points, especially when he was drunk.

To safeguard our money, we were going to have to keep a close eye on him. I also suspected it was going to fall on my shoulders to cash in his share. On the other hand, Tony and Lindsay were old hands at stuff like this and well aware of the risks involved.

'There are just too many prying eyes in Rabaul, and it would be impossible to re-melt the gold here. So, I suggest we do that in Samarai before heading off to Australia.

'Oh, that's fantastic! Will we be going to Townsville?' Blondie asked with a huge smile as she hugged my arm and kissed me on the cheek.

'No, I don't think so. Probably Cairns and later take the train to Sydney,' I said, looking down the front of her flimsy top. I had to tear my gaze away from her breasts. I noticed the boys were sort of sheepishly trying not to stare at Blondie's revealing state of dress.

I grinned and almost burst out laughing at their apparent unease. To help break the spell, I said, 'I've been giving our next move quite some thought. Firstly, I think we should get ready to leave Rabaul in the next couple of days, so let's plan for Sunday morning. That way you guys will have Saturday night to party.'

I turned to Tony, 'Dip the tanks and see how much fuel we have left on board and make sure that we have enough to get us to Cairns. Call the Shell depot on 16 and arrange for us to come alongside the fuel wharf tomorrow.'

'Not a problem. I'll do that first thing in the morning.'

I directed my attention to John and Lindsay. 'Talk to Cookie and find out what we are running low of and get enough provisions to last at least three to four weeks. Also, make sure you get at least six extra bags of rice. I want to give each of the boys a bag or two when they leave. We can top up anything we run out of, including fresh bread, at Samarai before we make the dash south to Australia.'

I went on, 'I suggest we make a beeline straight for Samarai. Everyone knows us there, and no one will pay any attention if we're anchored up in a quiet cove somewhere. We will then have a chance to fix the gold in peace.' I went on, 'And at least in Samarai we will have the benefit of at least some kind of civilisation, and you guys will still have your share of women to keep you happy.'

'Sounds good to me,' Lindsay said.

The others nodded in agreement. Only Blondie piped up with a pouty mouth. 'Samaria's boring, how long are we going to be there?'

'Not long. I guess about a week or so,' I replied, stroking her leg.

There was a good mood at the table, and I think everyone was relieved that we could now see the light at the end of the tunnel. From the conception of the project, everything except for Garth's unfortunate accident had fallen into place beautifully. The incident with Dave and the *Santo* was just an unscheduled necessity. Overall, it had been pretty much a routine project.

'Where do you think we should clear customs in Australia?' Lindsay asked.

'Thursday Island.'

'Oh, fuck off,' was Tony's immediate reply. 'Why that shit hole?'

'Now you sound like Blondie,' I exclaimed and went on. 'Because the customs officers there are bloody slack. They're more interested in drinking piss than they are checking boats. Yes, I know it will take us a little longer to get to Cairns, but it's the safest option. Also, it's usually a calm ride inside the reef. Once we've cleared customs on Thursday Island, we'll be free to go wherever we like, whenever we like. No questions asked.'

'Thursday Island sucks, but I think you are right, Simon. We have too much at stake, and it's better to be safe than sorry,' Tony said and then went on. 'And the way we converted the fuel tank, I don't think anyone will look in there, especially not at Thursday Island.'

'Okay, it's all set then. Tomorrow morning, Tony, you organise the fuel. Lindsay, you and John take the *Hiptimco* and go to Steamships or Burns Philip and organise the provisions. You better take Cookie with you.'

'What about me?' Blondie asked. 'I need to get some things as well.'

'You can come with me. While you're looking for your stuff, I'll see if I can find something we can use to make the moulds for the gold. We'll take the tender. That way we can take our time.'

*　*　*

The next day there was excitement in the air. After a leisurely breakfast, Tony arranged for us to come alongside the fuel wharf at 4:30 p.m. The boys and Cookie left in the *Hiptimco* and headed off to a landing close near Steamships' workshop.

Blondie ended up buying a mountain of stuff from the chemist shop and beauty parlour and getting her out of Dowling's Newsagency was a real challenge. Only I seem to have failed. I was unable to find anything that I could quickly and easily convert into a mould.

In the afternoon, we moved the *Scorpion* across to the fuel wharf. The fuelling progressed smoothly and quickly. We also picked up a couple of 200-litre drums of petrol and a couple of small drums of oil for the main engine. We were back at the Yacht Club anchorage in time for dinner.

In the morning, after checking the ship's stores with Cookie, we found a few things were missing from the list, so I sent the boys shoreside again to pick them up. This pissed them off a bit, as it would cut into their free time with the nurses. As we were still thinking along the lines of melting the gold into new moulds, I also asked the boys to keep an eye open for anything that we might be able to use.

We still had not heard anything from the authorities about Garth's accident - not from the police, the hospital, not even a word from his family. I couldn't leave Rabaul without knowing that everything had been taken care off, so Blondie and I took a taxi to the Nonga Base hospital. That was where they took his body. I made enquiries at the counter, and the nurse directed us to a Dr Simson who had been responsible for his case.

The doctor was sympathetic and went into a lengthy explanation of how munitions accidents were not uncommon in Rabaul. In fact, there had been a few underwater accidents lately. This type of accident was also prevalent with the local population who liked to extract the gun powder from unexploded bombs. We already knew this, but simply had to let the doctor have his say and pretend ignorance.

To him, Garth's injuries were self-evident. He had handled an unstable World War 2 phosphorous projectile, and it had detonated, subsequently burning right through his body. A coroner's inquest was not required. Garth's parents were duly notified, and they requested his body be cremated, and the ashes returned to them in Australia.

So, that was that. Memories recounting the years of stupid things we'd done and the fun we had flashed through my mind, and I couldn't control the sadness that welled up inside of me nor the tears in my eyes. But my feelings must fall far short of what Tony was experiencing and would do so for the rest of his life.

* * *

It was Saturday, and everything was ready for our departure. The boat was fuelled up, provisions on board, and best of all, Tony had been to Louis Chan's bakery on Ah Chee Avenue where, by chance, he spotted some small, half-loaf bread-baking tins. Louis had no use for these and gave him six. They looked like they might be perfect for the smelting job.

This was to be our last night in Rabaul, so it was dinner for all at the Yacht Club. Dave was there as usual with two of his crew, so we pulled up a couple of extra chairs and joined them.

'How are the repairs coming on?' I asked in an offhand fashion.

'Getting there,' he replied in a tone that demonstrated he was not happy and went on. 'We thought we were finished when the engineer noticed the rear engine mounts on both engines had fractured.'

'When do you think you'll be ready to start work?'

'We've already started. I've got Johnno and Rickets working the *Italia Maru* while I concentrate on the *Santo*. The boys are just about ready to bag the condenser to the surface and tow it to Pat's wharf. That will help pay for the repairs.'

'I'm sure you'll have a much better boat after all of this,' I said as seriously as I could. 'I guess you know we're off tomorrow, heading back to Samarai.'

'Yes, I figured that when I saw you refuel. Are you going to take Blondie with you? I'll be happy to look after her for you.'

Blondie pretended shock and horror and put her arm around me, 'I'm staying right here, thank you,' She purred.

The night wore on, and soon it was time to head back to the *Scorpion* and a good night's sleep.

* * *

As usual, the scream of the main engine revving up and down as Tony checked things out woke me up. It took a few moments to focus on my watch. Bloody hell! It was 6:00 a.m. I'd slept in. I looked across at Blondie, and she was still dead to the world and naked after last night's romp. I closed the curtain to the bunk as I got up.

Just then, Joe stuck his head into the wheelhouse, first glancing towards my bunk to ensure he was not going to be embarrassed before coming in and taking the wheel. I could hear the anchor winch clunking away, so I know everyone was ready but me.

Looking down from the wheelhouse bridge wing, I could see the tender was securely strapped across the ship's hold. I shouted down to Cookie to get me a coffee, and looking aft, I saw Lindsay tying-off the *Hiptimco*, which we would be towing.

It seems like we are almost ready to 'rock 'n roll'.

Chapter 28

Back to Samarai

As soon as the anchor was securely onboard, I moved to the wheelhouse door. Joe was at the helm, and I asked him to put it to full port. I then slowly increased the engine revolutions. As the boat started to turn, I asked him to slowly bring the rudder back to amidships. We were now heading for the harbour entrance. As long as we didn't run into any heavy weather, we'd be back in Samarai in two days.

Soon, our mindset once again accepted the monotonous but reassuring drone of the main engine. Everyone on board except Blondie got back to a routine of two hours on and six hours off.

Slowly but surely, the miles slipped under our keel, and New Britain disappeared from view. The next day, Woodlark Island was abeam on the port side, and then Normanby Island was to our starboard. Five hours later, we were preparing to enter the narrow China Strait. Our final destination, Samaria, was now only an hour away.

With the predominant south-east trade winds, I chose to return to a quiet little cove with the grandiose name of Logepwata Bay on Rogea Island. There were other far better all-weather, protected anchorages I could have chosen, but this was a quiet area and not often visited – and it was also just under 2 nautical miles from Samarai.

We dropped the anchor in 3 metres of water very close to shore. Tony shut down the main engine, and the boys immediately lowered the tender into the water and brought the *Hiptimco* alongside. It had been quite choppy crossing the Straits, but here, tucked up in our little cove, there was barely a ripple on the surface. It was time now to de-stress and relax for the rest of the day. Tomorrow we could talk about what to do with the gold.

The weather, it seemed, had not changed much since we left a couple of months ago. The south-east trade winds were still blowing, the clouds were still swirling overhead, and the treetops high on the hill stilled swayed in the wind.

Blondie and I were lazing around, reading and unwinding in our bunk, when the roar of the main engine destroyed the quiet. I thought to myself, *That's strange. What the hell is Tony up to?* I could hear the engine being revved up and down a few times and then stopped. A few moments later, Tony popped his head out of the engine room and called me to come down.

'What's the problem?' I asked.

'I think we've got a head gasket gone,' he said. 'She's been using a bit of water on the trip down, and that's strange because this engine has never used much water.'

'What makes you think it's a head gasket?'

'There are air bubbles in the heat exchanger. That's a sure sign of either head gasket or a cracked head.'

'Fuck off! That means we are going to have to pull the heads off?' I asked.

'Yep, nothing for it. We can't go on like this. It'll only get worse, and we don't want to blow a piston.'

'Bloody hell. I guess the only consolation is that it has happened now and not on the way to Thursday Island.' I continued, 'I guess you'll have to pull both heads off. It's no good doing just one.'

'Yeah, it'd be stupid to do just one.'

'I'll order a gasket set tomorrow from Port Moresby, and you can get started. The engine room will be cool by then.'

'Not a problem,' Tony replied

'We should be okay here, but I think we'd better get ourselves into a more secure, all-weather anchorage just in case the wind changes. I'll take the *Hiptimco* and go over to Kwato and see if we can't tie up to their jetty for a week or so. It's also a bit closer to Samarai.'

'That's not a bad idea. We are a bit exposed here if the weather changes direction,' Tony agreed.

*　*　*

I left the boys to do the usual tidy-up after an ocean voyage when things usually are thrown around the boat. Lindsay and Blondie joined me for the trip to Kwato Mission. I was keen to show her the beautiful church that Charles Able, the missionary, had built on the hill there.

Kwato was famous in the early 1920s for its mission work and the training of locals in the art of boatbuilding. Unfortunately, today, however, it was a far cry from the early pioneering days. The boat work nowadays was very spasmodic, but the legacy still existed throughout the district. The mission, its workshops, the church, and the small community still survived. I did not envisage any issues using the jetty. It's rarely used nowadays. We'd been there on several occasions in the past, but not for any length of time. Anyway, a small donation always goes a long way.

We spent a pleasant hour with our local guide who was keen to explain the function and history of the various buildings and points of interest, including the church. With permission to use the jetty for as long as necessary, we returned to the *Scorpion* and immediately made the short run to Kwato.

The mission jetty was a very safe, all-weather mooring. The work on the main engine might take up to a fortnight, and one can never tell what the weather will do in that time. The issue with time wasn't the work, that was just heavy and dirty, but relatively simple. It was getting the parts from Moresby that was the problem.

Chapter 29

A Trip to Newcastle

N ow that the *Scorpion* was securely tied to the mission jetty and engines once again shut down, and it was peaceful and quiet, I called the crew to the back deck. I had a proposition to put to them.

With up to two dead weeks looming, I suggested it might be a good idea if Blondie and I went to Brisbane. It would allow me to talk in private and confidence with our scrap metal representative, Ray Burgers, and see what sort of deal he can do with the silver. I was also keen to visit a bullion dealer friend of mine in Newcastle about the gold.

I did not want to talk to them over the phone or via telegram. One of my previous divers, was a tech expert and had worked for Plessey in PNG, he mentioned many times that all international phone calls from the country were recorded and monitored. I wasn't sure which words would trigger an investigation, but I would bet my bottom dollar that 'gold' or 'silver' was among them. The only way was to talk privately, face-to-face.

Also, I hadn't seen my parents for several years. It would give me the chance to catch up with them and show off my new girlfriend. Blondie just so happened to stem from Swansea, a suburb of Newcastle. That was only some 80 km from Nelson Bay, so she would also be able to catch up and spend a little time with her mother and sister.

I'd been racking my brain the last couple of weeks on how best to sell the gold. Yes, I could dribble it out as I planned and say it came from a gold lease. But first, I had a school friend I was keen to talk to, Brendan Katz. We used to go out whoring in Newcastle. He and his father were licensed gold dealers in Newcastle, and by all accounts, they did not ask too many questions. It would be interesting to see what he could do for us.

Tony brightened up and said it might also be an ideal opportunity for his wife to visit Samarai and the boat. He had told her so much about it, and she was overdue for a holiday.

I had no issue with this, in fact, I thought it was a bloody good idea. It would keep him happy and working. I even offered him my bunk. It was near impossible to fuck on the crew bunks! Tony got all excited about the idea, which had me stumped, but I guess he was in love. I always thought of Maureen as a bit of a boring person. Her job as a customs agent was almost as dull as being an accountant, and that fact gives testament to her demeanour.

Lindsay and John, on the other hand, were perfectly happy to be in Samarai. They had no shortage of willing young ladies, White or local, to keep them satisfied.

In the morning, Tony and I went across to Steamships. Tony went to the post office to call Maureen, and I booked our tickets on the *Blue Peter* for the trip to Rabi Jetty and airline tickets from Gurney airfield to Port Moresby and onward to Brisbane.

I sent a telex to Ray Burgers, giving him our flight details and arrival time in Brisbane and asked him to arrange a pickup. I bought a small suitcase, not for me, but I'm sure Blondie couldn't travel without her clothes, makeup, and all the other hundreds of bits and pieces that women can't do without.

We were enjoying a cold beer in the Samarai Club when a boy from the post office delivered a telex message from Ray. It read 'Will meet you on arrival Brisbane. Stop. Regards, Ray.' So far, so good. With the die-cast, Blondie packed the suitcase, and we spent the rest of the day relaxing.

In the morning, Tony took us across to Samurai, where the *Blue Peter* was waiting for passengers. There were only the two of us on board, so hopefully, the bus would also be at Rabi Jetty to take us to the old World War II airstrip at Gurney.

It took four bloody hours for us to get to Rabi jetty, and it was not a comfortable bus that was waiting for passengers. It was a bloody, small truck with wooden benches down each side of the tray, side-saddle style. The ride at breakneck speed on the corrugated and pothole-studded track was an experience in itself. By the time we got to Gurney, my skinny arse felt like it had a thrashing by a cricket bat. Blondie fared a little better with her nicely padded rear end. To make matters worse, the truck stopped only long enough to drop us and our luggage off and then, without a word from the driver, disappeared.

*   *   *

Waiting in the middle of the jungle at a remote airfield for the plane to arrive was quite an experience. The terminal consisted of nothing more than a small, crudely put together corrugated tin shed, little more than a lean-to with three walls. A couple of logs nearby in the shade of a large tree served as the 'departure lounge'. To call it primitive is an understatement.

Fortunately, there was one other person already waiting for the plane, so at least we were not alone. A half an hour later, I was beginning to wonder if this wasn't a set-up, and we were soon going to be mugged.

Then, in the background, I could hear the drone of a light aircraft engine, but it sounded different. Soon, a weird-looking, small plane with a propeller in the front, another in the back, and two tails came into view. It quickly landed and rolled noisily down the Marsden matting runway.

No passengers were getting off, just a small amount of freight was unloaded, which the pilot unceremoniously dumped in the tin shed. I guess that was to keep it out of the rain. There was no mucking about. The pilot quickly loaded our luggage, then asked for our tickets and invited us to climb aboard. He followed, locking the door behind him. A few minutes later, we were taxiing down the runway, and then we were off. It was quite memorable listening to the tyres sing while taking off from the Marsden strip.

Landing at Port Moresby was a similar experience with the Marsden matting giving a high-pitched hum as the plane landed and rolled down the runway on the steel matting. At least Port Moresby had something resembling an airport terminal. It was small and untidy, but it had four walls, toilets, and even ceiling fans.

It was a bit unnerving sitting in the terminal building when just a few metres away hundreds of virtually naked New Guinea highlanders were hanging onto the chain-wire fence. All were blankly staring at the passengers and aircraft as they come and went. It must have been a surreal experience for them.

* * *

The trip from Port Moresby to Brisbane was a luxury in comparison to the Gurney flight. The old Ansett Douglas C-47-DL had a modern interior, comfortable seats, and was reasonably quiet. Smoking was allowed, and soon it was impossible to escape the cigarette smoke, but the cigars were the worse. Even if you did not smoke, you did now.

First stop, Cairns – another primitive airport terminal, not much better than Port Moresby. Luckily, we did not have to wait for long, and our flight to Brisbane was ready. Now it got really fancy, a Boeing 707! Some three hours later, we arrived in Brisbane. Thankfully, Ray was waiting for us at the luggage collection area.

Ray Burgers was the Brisbane metal merchant's travelling sales representative. His specialty was the Pacific region. I first met him in Rabaul in 1967 when he tried to get me to sell to Brisbane and not the Sydney branch. He loved the Pacific and travelled extensively building up a very loyal customer base, especially in New Guinea, the Solomon's, and Vanuatu.

Ray was not fond of the office environment and insisted on taking us to a Chinese restaurant. So as soon as we were comfortably seated, and the food orders were taken, and we were able to relax with a glass of cold beer, I got straight to the point. I said, 'Ray, I've got about 850 kg of scrap silver. What can you do for me?'

'Bloody hell! Where did you get all that from?' Then he quickly added, 'No, no, no! I don't want to know. We have bought scrap silver from other guys in the past, so I don't think there will be a problem.' He went on, 'I'll have to call the boss.'

'Can you call him now and give me a price?' I asked and went on, 'I also need to know what the best way for me is to get the silver past customs, both in PNG and Australia'

'For customs, just box it up and simply mark it as "photo-grade scrap silver".'

'This is all in neat, 5 kg ingots, 170 of them, and they're stamped and graded.'

'Bloody hell! Japanese?' Ray asked. He went on, 'You're going to have to deface them if they are Japanese. Just hit them with an oxy torch and melt anything on the face.'

'That's a bloody good idea. Why on earth didn't I think of that?' I replied.

* * *

After dinner, Ray used the restaurant phone to call his boss at home. It was not long, and he was back. They would pay us $47.25 per kilo, with 80% on receipt of shipping documents and the balance within 30 days.

That would give us, upfront, $30,000, I was happy with that. We shook on the deal, and that was that. I would get the crew to talk to the Kwato mission and have them make up 12, long, narrow boxes to hold ten ingots each.

It now occurred to me that I hadn't booked accommodations for the night, but it wasn't a problem. Ray was obliging. He had a spare bedroom and offered for us to stay with him for the night, and he would get us to the airport in the morning.

*   *   *

It was 8:30 a.m. when Ray's shiny HR Holden pulled up in front of the Brisbane Ansett terminal. I purchased the tickets at the airport, for the two-hour flight to Sydney.

On arrival in Sydney, we took a taxi to Central Station to catch the train to Newcastle. It always amazes me that commercial aircraft don't use the enormous Williamtown RAAF base, just 30 minutes from Nelson Bay.

After a boring three-hour train ride, stopping at... I don't know how many stations... we arrived at Newcastle mid-afternoon. The first thing was to hire a car for the week, and the best and cheapest was Budget Rent-a-Car. It is hard to believe it took us almost a full day to get from Brisbane to Nelson Bay! It was 5:00 p.m. before we arrived at my parent's house.

As we pulled up to the front of the house, I could see the upstairs curtains part and Mom curious to see who was parking on her front lawn. However, as soon as I got out of the car, she waved excitedly. Mom gave me a big hug and kiss at the top of the stairs. I introduced Blondie with her real name, Julie. She looked her up and down then smiled and gave her a big hug.

Mom had a thousand questions, which were all to be repeated when Dad returned from his favourite pastime, fishing. That evening, Mom cooked Dad's fresh fish for dinner in a delightful mustard sauce. We washed it down with Dad's favourite beer, Toohey's Old Dark Ale. Hmmm, a refreshing XXXX Gold would have been better. The next day, we would do it all again at Blondie's place.

*   *   *

It was a pleasant drive to Swansea. I noticed that Blondie was more conservatively dressed this morning. I was going to comment but thought better of it. It's no good poking the bear in the eye with a blunt stick. She'd already warned me not to say anything about the 'pirating'. I was smart enough to get the message.

Julie's mother was a gorgeous looking woman with a pleasant demeanour. I also met her younger sister, another stunner. I could see where Blondie got her good looks. Unfortunately, her father passed away some time ago from a massive heart attack, and her mother had not remarried.

Soon, it was close to 2:00 p.m., and it was time to go. I was keen to meet up with Brendan. The 20-minute drive should ensure he was back at his desk after lunch. We said our goodbyes, promising to return.

Chapter 30

The Gold Buyers

Brendan's office was on the second floor in a building on the corner of Hunter and Brown Streets. Finding the office was not a problem, as I'd been there a few times. However, finding a car park in the city was a different matter. Driving around and around in circles was seriously pissing me off. And when we eventually did manage to find a park, it was quite a distance away from Brendan's office.

Soon we were in a rickety old elevator, which was groaning and creaking as we made our way to his office on the 3rd floor. The building resembled something out of the 1920s. I'm buggered if I know what Brendan and his dad, Adam, do all day. The building was as quiet as a morgue. There were very few people on the street and even less in this crappy old building. Looking down the corridor from the elevator, I could see a small sign, 'Katz and Son', on top, and below, 'Licensed Gold Buyers'. The frosted glass on the upper part of the door had the same emblazoned in gold leaf.

The office had not changed from the last time I was there. It was still old fashioned, 'staid' would be a more apt description. After introducing Blondie and a few pleasantries, I asked them if they were in a position to buy some gold. They smiled at each other and nodded in agreement.

'What have you got?' Brendan asked.

'I've got a shitload of these,' I said, pulling a handful of gold coins out of Blondie's handbag and casually letting them fall on the desk. Like little gnomes, their eyes lit up. Adam picked one up and scrutinized it.

'How much have you got?' Adam asked.

'In gold, about 180 kg in total. There are a lot of coins and other bits and pieces like jewellery, gold teeth, and such.'

'Bloody hell! Bring it in!'

'Can't. It's all still in New Guinea. We're planning to bring it down with the boat. The bullion is too heavy.'

'You've got bullion?' There was surprise and concern in Brendan's voice 'What weight?'

'All around 12 kg each brick. What's the problem?'

'Fuck! It's illegal to own bullion in Australia. We could probably risk taking two or three bars off your hands and slowly sell it off to the jewellers, but that's it.'

'What the hell are you talking about... "It's illegal"?' I said, stunned at the comment.

'You didn't know? Bloody hell. It's illegal to own bullion in Australia. In America, it's worse, It's illegal to own any gold except for jewellery, including gold coins. If you have bullion, the government will simply take it off you, and if you can't prove where you got it from, will probably throw you in jail to boot.'

I was dumbfounded, to me, gold was simply gold, irrespective of how it was packaged. I was momentarily lost for words. My mind raced ahead at a million paces.

'I've got too much to spend time slowly turning it into jewellery. What the hell am I going to do now?'

'Shame you're not in England,' Adam replied.

'What is that supposed to mean?' I asked, puzzled by the statement.

'England has no restriction on the ownership of gold,' was Adam's matter-of-fact reply, as if everyone knew that.

My brain was working overtime, and as I'm not totally stupid, as Blondie likes to suggest from time to time. There and then it hit me – England! That must also then mean the same for English territories. Immediately, the Solomon Islands and Fiji sprang to mind. More thinking out aloud than talking to anyone I said, 'I wonder if that includes the Solomon Islands and Fiji, being British colonies.'

'I have a contact in Fiji that might be able to help you,' Adam said as he picked up his phone index. 'Here it is, Adam Fat. He's a nice guy and apparently buys a lot of gold from locals.' He scribbled down the details and handed them to me.

'Do you want to sell the coins?' Adam asked, pointing to the coins on the table.

'How much?'

Brendan scooped them up and dropped them on the scale. 'Hmmm, just on 18 oz. How does $600 sound, okay?'

'Yes, that'll do. However, I do think the coins have more value as coins rather than just the gold value, but $600 is fine.'

Brendan smiled in a sort of uneasy way as he handed me the notes. I knew the coins were worth more, but I did not have the time to muck about trying to sell them individually. I stuffed the bills into my pocket, and after a little more small talk, we shook hands and were on our way back to Nelson Bay.

* * *

The first thing I did when we arrived home was send a radio message to the boat. It was the morning and afternoon ritual on all small ships and out-stations (such as plantations) in New Guinea to listen to the Port Moresby ships' radio schedule on 4165 every morning and evening for the all-important weather forecast and messages. Once the weather forecast was over, they would then broadcast messages to ships.

I had to get hold of Tony and stop him from melting down small items, as some of the coins were now more valuable in the long run

My message to Tony was: To the MV *Scorpion*, callsign ATZ-232. 'For attention: Tony. Stop. Urgent do not. Stop. Repeat, do not melt the stuff in scuba tanks. Stop. For lead bars in fuel tank simply heat the face to melt the crest. Stop. Simon.'

The next morning there was a knock on the door. The postman had a telex for me from Tony. The message read: 'Not melting lead in scuba bottles. Stop. Understood. Stop, Shall only heat face of the lead in tank. Stop. Tony.'

A quick trip to the post office and a reply to Tony: To the MV Scorpion, callsign ATZ-232. For attention: Tony. 'Back on deck next week. Stop. Will confirm date and time. Stop. Simon.'

It was time to make a telephone call to this Mr Adam Fat in Fiji. I rang the number, and a well-spoken voice answered. I broached the subject by telling him that Adam Katz in Newcastle suggested that he be interested in buying some gold. He seemed a little hesitant to talk on the phone but asked how many, I told him I had fifteen ingots, 12 kg each.

There was a nervous silence, then he asked, 'Are we talking pure gold?'

'Yes, all stamped 995.0.'

'What do you expect to get for it?' he asked.

To which I simply answered, 'As much as possible.'

After a minute's silence, he came back. 'I can probably take ten off your hands. I also have a relative in the Solomon's who is buying quite a bit of gold from the locals. He might be able to take the other five. I can pay you $25 an ounce.'

It was the usual Chinese game. Now my turn to cough and splutter. 'Sorry, can't do $25. If you can get your relative to take the other five, I can live with $30 an ounce.'

'I'll call Leong in Honiara, but $30 an ounce, that's delivered to me in Fiji, right?'

'Not a problem. We've got a 20-metre boat and can easily do the run to the Solomon's and then down to Fiji.' I gave him my Newcastle phone number and told him I would be waiting for his call.'

In the morning, I received Adam's call to say that his cousin Leon Chow in Honiara agreed to take five ingots at $30 per ounce. His cousin taking five was good news, but I'm not totally stupid. I am not steaming all the way to Fiji just to get shafted.

I insisted that if Leon was happy with the product in the Solomon's, he would put 50% of the purchase price, which was $70,000, into my Australian account before we left Honiara with the balance paid in cash, Australian money, on delivery to Suva in Fiji.

I suspected that cash would be Adam's preferred method of payment anyway. It was also the best option for the boys and me. There were no legal issues with carrying large sums of cash, so no explaining to do.

Just thirty minutes later, I received another phone call from Adam. 'I have had second thoughts,' he said, continuing, 'If I'm going to pay 50% up-front, I want my man to inspect the product and accompany you to Fiji.'

I thought about it for a minute and agreed. Having another person on board was not an issue. However, I did insist that payment to our bank account would take place as soon as his representative was happy with the product. I would not leave PNG until the money had dropped into my account, to which he agreed.

This gold-salvage project sounded so exciting initially, but it was turning out to be a pain in the arse. I was beginning to think we would have been better off working a couple of steamships, which would have returned around two hundred tons of copper, and nearly the same money without all this bullshit.

It had been an eventful and enlightening ten days, not altogether good news, but in the end, a good outcome. It was time to start making plans to fly back to Samarai. A quick trip to the local travel agent and I had two tickets to Moresby safely stored in my briefcase. Blondie's mother insisted we come over for dinner and spend the night in Swansea before continuing to Sydney.

*   *   *

Dinner with Blondie's mum was a pleasant affair, and the wine flowed freely. Towards the end of the night, Blondie's mother was getting as raunchy as her daughter. I think, like her daughter; she would have been good fun in bed, especially with the right amount of alcohol. Later that evening after my shower, I was sitting on the edge of Blondie's bed looking around the room when I spotted a sizeable, Asian book on the bookshelf. I picked it up and was surprised to see it was the *Kama Sutra*. I couldn't believe it. I said to Blondie. 'Is this yours or your mum's?'

'Sometimes you're so stupid! Mine, of course,' was her sharp reply. 'I'll have you know this is not a dirty picture book about sex. It teaches you everything you need to know from flirting to foreplay, and yes, sex positions. It also teaches you to respect physical intimacy.'

I was taken aback by the seriousness of her outburst. And bugger me, where does this 'sometimes you're so stupid' come from? But I was beginning to understand why sex was so easy and natural to her. She had very few, if any, hang-ups.

'Maybe I should show you some more tricks I've learnt,' she said, giving me a coy smile.

I'm not sure if it was the wine or the prospect of some exciting or forbidden sex that changed her demeanour, but she seemed suddenly more playful and mischievous, 'Close your eyes and open a page, any page,' she demanded.

Sensing she was looking to play a game or two, I gladly obliged. With eyes closed, I fumbled through the pages and stopped. Blondie burst out laughing. 'The Congress of a Crow', She said.

At first, I had no idea what the hell she was talking about. Looking at the picture, I saw a man and women lying on their side in a 69 position. The sparkle in her eyes told me she was delighted with this. It seemed like I was not the only one who would get their rocks off tonight.

Chapter 31

Back to Samarai

The two-hour drive to the airport was uneventful. I dropped the car off at Budget and proceeded to the check-in at Ansett Airlines for the direct flight to Port Moresby. Customs was a breeze, and soon we were sitting in the lounge having a coffee waiting to board.

The flight to Port Moresby, apart from the infernal smokers, was comfortable and pleasant enough. Blondie was very attentive and clingy, maybe because she thought I was flirting with the pretty hosties –but I wasn't. I was just polite.

Port Moresby is a shithole at the best of times, hot as hell, a dry oppressive heat. The plane pulled off the runway onto the apron, and the engines shut down. The front cabin door opened, and a person from the agriculture department came in. He closed the door behind him and proceeded to walk up and then down the aisle, all the while spraying the cabin with a can of poison in each hand.

We then had to endure some five minutes for the poison to take effect. I presume it was intended for whatever bugs had joined us for the trip north. In the meantime, the aircraft turned into a sweltering, hot aluminium sauna. When the hostess finally opened the cabin doors, even the oppressive heat of Port Moresby was welcome.

The walk across the concrete apron to the small wooden terminal building was enough to have me dripping with sweat. My shirt was soaking wet and stuck to my body. The leather belt holding up my jeans had become a dam for the accumulated sweat.

Looking across at Blondie, she wasn't faring much better. She looked like she'd been in a 'wet t-shirt' competition. I had a bit of a chuckle. She had beautiful breasts, and her firm nipples were now seriously poking through her wet t-shirt, leaving nothing to the imagination. She noticed me looking and raised her eyebrows. Smiling as she patted them down, but it didn't help much.

*　*　*

Seven hours after leaving Moresby, we came alongside the jetty at Samarai. It had been a gruelling two hours bouncing around the sky in a small six-seater, an hour wait at Gurney, and then a four-hour trip in the *Blue Peter*. We were both truly buggered. Thankfully, Lindsay and Tony were there faithfully waiting to pick us up at the Samarai jetty.

It was good to be back, but soon I would have to tell the boys about the issue with the gold bullion. I wondered how it would be received.

The crew had moved the boat from Kwato to the SDA mission wharf at Gesila Island. It seems that both Lindsay and John had found a couple of pretty local girls who live in the village across from the mission.

They justified the move because it was closer to Samarai. Also, Gesila Island was not very high, and this allowed for a gentle breeze at the jetty, making it more comfortable, especially in a boat that was not air-conditioned. It was a very calm mooring, I had to admit. Although Kwato was a very safe all-weather anchorage, but with no breeze, it could get a bit stifling. And they were right; it was pleasant here.

*   *   *

I'd finished breakfast and was enjoying the quiet and the view across Kuiaro Bay, when one by one, like lost sheep, the crew, still bleary-eyed and half asleep, came to the breakfast table. The conversation centred on my trip and also their experiences while we were in Australia. I waited until they had finished breakfast and were onto their coffee, and everyone was a bit more alert. It was time to break the bad news. I did not quite know how best to approach it, so I simply told it how it was.

'Listen, guys, seriously – I've got some good news and bad news. Which do you want first?'

'Give us the bad news first,' Tony said, looking me straight in the eyes.

'No, I'll give you the good news first. The bad news won't seem so bad after that. Oh, before I go on, I notice that you've got the silver all boxed up. Any spare blocks left? I wouldn't mind one for a doorstop.'

Lindsay laughed. 'Yes, there are three left.'

'Good looks like one of you guys is going to miss out on the block because I'm keeping one for a doorstop.'

There was a bit of good-natured laughter. Tony piped up, 'I'm going to have another tea. Anyone else for anything?'

'Yes, make that a pot of tea,' I said.

Blondie butted in as she got up from the table, 'You guys keep talking. I'll make the tea.'

'Okay, the good news is that we've got a good price for the silver, and the metal merchants will clear it into Australia as scrap-photo silver. Better still, they will pay us 80% on receipt of the shipping documents. Anyone know when the next Bank Boat is due?'

Everyone was happy with the silver deal, but no one knew when the next Burns Philip ship was due, these are operated by the Bank line and referred to locally as 'Bank Boats'.

'I'll go and see the Burns Philp shipping agent tomorrow and find out.'

'The other good news is I found a buyer for the gold, but they are not paying the full price, and we have to deliver it.'

As I gazed at the crew around the table, all I could see was a whole lot of blank faces. I guessed they were puzzled with the 'we have to deliver it' statement. At this point, everyone was still under the impression we were going to Australia, so what's the problem? It was time to wake them up with the bad news.

Before I could continue, Tony butted in, 'What are they paying.'

'The going rate today is around $35 per ounce. I've been able to get them to agree to pay $30 cash. Also, they will pay 50% upfront here in Samarai.'

'That's not too bad,' Tony replied.

'Yes, but here's the catch. We have to deliver it to Fiji, and we also have to take a minder with us.'

Lindsay was first to respond. 'Why the fuck, Fiji?'

It was time for the punchline, 'Well, I was getting to that. The really bad news is, it's illegal to own gold bullion in Australia!'

I waited a few moments for that to sink in.

Lindsay shook his head as though he had not heard right and was first the pipe up. 'What the fuck do you mean 'It's illegal to own gold'? With particular emphasis on the word 'illegal'.

'You weren't listening, boofhead. I said it was illegal to own <u>bullion</u>. You can own jewellery, and you can own gold coins, have gold teeth, but you can't own gold <u>bullion</u>. It has something to do with the value of the Australian dollar being tied to the amount of gold that the country has in reserve, so only the government can own gold bullion. If they find our gold bricks, they'll simply take them all from us and throw us in jail.'

'I'll be fucked! Are you serious?' Tony said.

'Yes, mate. I was dumbfounded as well.'

I went into some degree explaining my conversation with Brendan and his father and my subsequent calls to Adam Fat in Fiji and the agreed outcome. There were some sad looks, but I got the impression they knew we were 'snookered'.

'Look on the bright side,' I said. 'We all get a trip to Fiji, and that should be fun.' Hoping that would cheer them up. I continued, 'We should get a message in a few days giving us the minder's ETA. In the meantime, we need to make sure that we're ready for the trip. I've already bought charts in Newcastle and also a radio with a direction finder.'

'"Radio with a direction finder", what the hell are you going to do with that?' Lindsay said with a smirk as if I was an idiot.

Sometimes I think he is as dumb as dogshit. 'To pick up the Nandi aircraft beacon once we leave the Solomon's, of course. This is a long, open-ocean voyage of at least six days steaming and only a couple of small islands between Honiara and Suva. Given the need for compass corrections, I don't want to get lost!'

'We're going to need a shit-load of fuel,' Tony interrupted.

'Not a problem. We can carry over 10,000 litres, and I guess we will use about 5,000 litres for the trip to Suva. At five cents a litre, it's bugger all.'

'Now, forget about all that. If we agree that we will make the trip to Suva, we better start getting the boat ready and fuelled up. How did you go with the cylinder-head job, Tony?'

'A piece of piss. The head was only cracked in one place, between the valve seats on number-two piston. It was barely 13 mm long. All I had to do was to stitch it.

'Stich it?' I asked puzzled.

'It's a simple repair. You drill a small, 3 mm hole close to where the crack starts, thread it, and screw in a stud. You cut the stud flush with the cylinder head and then drill the next hole so that it overlaps half of the first stud like a half-moon. Then you just continue doing that to the end of the crack,' Tony replied, with a lot of much-animated sign language.' He went on, 'I've run the engine for several hours and also checked it after we moved to Gesila Island. No sign of a leak.'

'That's excellent. Now make a list of anything you might need for ten days of steaming – oil, grease etc. And dip the tanks and see exactly how much fuel we currently have on board, so I know how much to order.'

* * *

There were a hundred and one things to organise. First was to arrange the shipping of the silver to Brisbane. All I had to have to receive 80% of the payment was supply the scrap merchant with the shipping documents. The rest would be taken care of by the shipping company and stevedores. I didn't give a shit how long it took to get south.

I now had to find a safe and secure place to store the *Hiptimco*. Dusty Miller, the manager of Steamships, came to the rescue. There was a lock-up yard behind Steamships' cargo shed that we were free to use for as long as needed.

Now, there was also the issue of the local crew. Unfortunately, none had passports or travel documents, so they would have to take their leave of us there. I had to go to the bank and arrange their pay and bonus. Cookie would leave us here in Samarai, and we would drop Joe and Jack off at Wari on our way to Honiara. Without my local crew to help make up the roster at the helm, it will mean a lot more work for the rest of us.

* * *

It was time to remove the Emperor's imperial crest from the top of the ingots before Adam Fats representative arrived. That would not take long as we only had to melt the imperial crest back into the metal. Tony has already had a lot of practice with the silver.

The imperial chrysanthemum crest on the top of the ingot was the only identifying feature that could get us into any serious trouble. The crest appeared as though it was stamped with a branding iron while the gold was still soft as it was quite deep into the metal. However, the weight and purity were, in all probability, stamped later. It was in large numbers just under the crest, but not anywhere near as deep.

Tony lit up the oxy torch and with practised ease began to melt the first crest back into the gold bar. Soon, all that remained was a puddle of concentric rings. One by one, each Japanese imperial bar of gold became nothing more than a nondescript gold brick, however, still stamped with .9950.

By the evening, everything in the *Scorpion* was ready for the trip to Fiji. She was fuelled up, food stores organised, and I had paid off the crew, including an extra two months' pay plus a healthy bonus. All we were waiting for then was Adam Fat's man to arrive.

It was quite strange, actually, but there was a mood of excitement on board, and we were all eager and looking forward to what amounted to a new adventure. In essence, there was no extra money for the effort, but this was a new exciting challenge.

Chapter 32

Sam Chow

In the morning, a telegram arrived to say that a Sam Chow would be arriving the following day. I had thought about sending the *Hiptimco* to pick him up at the Rabi jetty. She could make the trip in less than two hours, but I thought it might be more memorable for him to experience the four-hour cruise on the *Blue Peter*.

I checked with Steamships, and the *Blue Peter* was due to arrive Samarai around midday, so just before noon, we left the comfort of the Samurai Club and strolled down to the jetty. Still, no *Blue Peter*, but looking up the channel, a small speck was conspicuous on the horizon. This had to be her fighting against the incoming tide.

I could see no sense in us hanging around the hot stifling wharf for another half hour. The promise of a dollar to a young local lad playing at the water's edge to call us when the *Blue Peter* arrived was all the excuse we needed to return to the comfort of the club for a few more cold beers and a game of darts.

A half an hour or so later, the young fellow's head appeared at the window shouting. 'Mr Simon! Mr Simon! *Blue Peter* is here!' He snatched the dollar I thrust at him and disappeared down the street.

It's only a short walk to the Steamships' jetty, so we didn't rush and finished the last of our drinks before leisurely making our way to the jetty. The whole saga of getting from Port Moresby to Samurai can be quite stressful. I did not want Sam to worry unnecessarily, thinking that nobody was there to meet him.

Just as we were leaving the club, we spotted a half a dozen people making their way towards Bill's Guest House. Most were already sweating profusely and complaining, lugging their heavy bags. Little did they know they would soon have 500 or so painful steps to climb before reaching their destination.

We made our way down the alley between Steamships and the custom shed. As we rounded the corner, we could see a forlorn figure sitting on his suitcase on Steamships' jetty. There was a visible sign of relief on his face as we turned off the track and onto the jetty and started walking towards him.

He stood up. 'Hello, you must be Sam,' I said in a cheerful voice as I stuck out my hand to greet him.

'Yes, yes, I'm Sam. Are you, Mr Simon?' he asked.

'Yes, mate, I'm Simon. Forget the "Mr" bit, and this is Julie and John.'

Sam shook hands with everybody and picked up his rather large suitcase. It must have been heavy because he was struggling. I looked at John and pointed to the bag. Without a word, he took it from Sam and threw it onto his shoulder as if it was empty.

Sam was only a little guy. He must have been all of 167 cm tall and 55 kg dripping wet. He was a handsome guy, in an Asian sort of way.

'Come on. It's time to get you to the *Scorpion* and settled in,' I said as I pointed to the tender which was tied to the main ship's wharf.

During the short but choppy trip across the China Straight, it was apparent that Sam was not much of a sailor. I had a chuckle to myself. He had no idea of what was in store for him.

By the smile on his face, I think he was relieved when he saw the *Scorpion*. I introduced him to the rest of the crew. Both the port and starboard cabins had three-tier bunks. John and Lindsay were in the port cabin, and Tony was in the starboard cabin. It was closest to the engine room entrance. With Garth gone, Tony had the cabin to himself, so it was obvious he was going to have to share with Tony.

I asked Tony to get Sam settled into the cabin, and also advised Sam to get his daily needs out of the suitcase and then store it in the hold. He could go down anytime to get anything that he might need. There simply wasn't enough room in the cabin for a suitcase. That's the reason sailors have duffle bags.

It was getting late, so there was no sense in Sam checking the gold this afternoon. That could wait until the morning. Strangely, I was tired and also had pains in my shoulders. I was looking forward to a short nap before dinner. So, I excused myself and went to the wheelhouse to lay down and relax.

*   *   *

I awoke with a start. Joe was banging on the wheelhouse deck shouting, 'Wake-up, boss. Cookie has dinner ready.'

I felt like shit. I was sweating like a pig, and every bone in my body was aching. I immediately recognised it as malaria. I guess I'd have to go back on the quinine. Bugger!

After some idle chatter, while waiting for Cookie to get dinner on the table, we got to learn a little more about Sam, and one thing for sure he had a passion for whiskey the bottle he had brought with him was already almost half empty. It turned out that he was born and bred in Fiji, hence, the good English. Judging by the look on his face, I don't think he was impressed with Cookie's spaghetti Bolognese.

I thought it was an opportune time to take the mickey out of him, as he was not aware that Cookie would not be on the trip. 'Great, isn't it? We get this five days a week.'

Lindsay and John looked up with a start, raising their eyebrows. Sam looked at me with disbelief etched into his face. 'No, no. I cook. My uncle has a restaurant in Suva. I work for him in the kitchen on the weekends.'

I'm not about to look at a gift horse in the mouth, so Tony was our substitute cook as he didn't have a roster on the helm, but he was a terrible cook. It was usually mashed potatoes and gravy, which was served with everything – snags, bully beef, even fish.

'Not a problem, Sam. You can be the cook. If nothing else, it will stop you from getting bored on the trip. After you check out the gold tomorrow, you can have a look at what's in the pantry and go to Steamships with John and buy whatever you think you might need.'

It was still early, but I felt like shit, so I excused myself and got up to leave. I looked over to Blondie and said, 'You coming?'

'No, I think I'll stay awhile. I'll be up shortly,' she said, tearing her gaze away from Sam.

And with that, I left. Another two quinine tablets and I was out like a light. I awoke with a start, smothered in Blondie's long hair. She was on her stomach with a leg thrown over my belly. I never felt her climbing over me or heard her coming to bed, but I did feel better this morning. I will have to continue to take the quinine each morning for another week or two.

Surprise, surprise! It looked like everyone was up. Joe was in the forecastle painting, Cookie was preparing bacon and eggs, and even Sam was up.

'How do you feel this morning, Sam?'

'I feel good, thank you. Can we check the gold after breakfast?'

'Not a problem,' I replied. 'We've got it all ready for you in the compressor room.'

Breakfast proceeded with the usual chatter, a few diving stories, and when it was over, it was time to show Sam what we had. The boys had already removed the gold from the explosive magazine. The last thing I wanted was Sam to know our secret 'hidey-hole'. It was now in the forward cabin that housed the dive compressor and equipment. The gold was neatly stacked against the bulkhead and covered with a blanket. Everything was ready for Sam's inspection.

I showed him into the compressor room and pointed to the sheet that was covering the gold. 'It's under the sheet,' I said casually.

Sam pulled the sheet off, and for a moment, I thought he was going to have a heart attack. He staggered back, looked at me like a stunned mullet, and then back to the pile of gold. I don't think he ever saw so much gold in one place at one time.

He sat on his haunches and stroked the gold, as tenderly as one might stroke a pussy. Slowly, he regained his composure and looked up at me and said, 'This is real?'

'Of course, it's bloody real. Anyway, that's what you're here to prove,' I said, shaking my head at such a stupid comment.

I glanced over to Tony, who was sitting on the scupper-board in the doorway. He had a grin from ear to ear and looked like he was going to crack up laughing at any moment. Sam opened his bag of tricks and set a collection of small bottles on the deck.

He randomly picked up an ingot and set it down on a sheet of plastic, which he had previously neatly unfolded. He then chose a small bottle from his selection from which he carefully sucked up some liquid with an eyedropper. He scratched a deep score into the gold brick with a penknife into which he very carefully put several, equally spaced drops of this liquid. When it finished bubbling, he then dug into the bag and pulled out a huge magnet and began to slide it over the top of the ingot. He turned around and looked at me and said, 'Yes, definitely pure gold and no steel bar inside, but I'll have to check every gold bar and weigh it.'

'Not a problem. Go right ahead. Take your time. Tony and Lindsay will be here to help you if you need it.'

I was not going to hang around for an hour while he checked each block, but nor did I have any issues with him doing so. I understood he had to be a hundred per cent satisfied. I now had to concentrate on getting the customs clearance to allow us to depart Samarai for Suva, Fiji.

It was almost an hour later when Tony finally poked his head into the wheelhouse to say that Sam had finished checking the gold and that he was ready to go to Samarai and send the telegram to Adam giving the okay to proceed.

Chapter 33

Samarai to Jomard Passage

Tony and I were enjoying a coffee on the back deck and just generally chatting about the trip to Fiji when it occurred to me that we should be having this conversation with the whole crew.

I said to him. 'Tony, before Sam goes shore-side for the stores and to send the telegram to Adam Fat, I think I should outline the voyage to Fiji to everyone. Tell Sam and the boys to get to the back deck.'

'Okay, Simon, I'll round them up.' He said, getting up and disappearing down the passageway.

Soon with everyone, including Blondie comfortable at the table, I began to outline the trip. 'Firstly, I think it's best if we stick to daylight steaming as far as Rossel Island anyway. It's just too tricky steaming 24-hours non-stop in these poorly charted waters.'

There was a murmur of agreement, though Sam looked a little worried. I continued. 'Our first stop will be Wari island. There, we'll drop Joe and Jack and spend the night. We will leave early the next morning for Jomard Passage. I know a safe and calm anchorage close to Jomard. Then, it's off to Snake Passage on the northern side of Misima. It's the most fantastic experience, and I'm sure everyone will enjoy it. Also, there are good anchorages at both ends. From there, it's an easy seven-hour trip to the Jinjo Mission at Rossel.'

Both Tony and Lindsay had done the trip with me out to Pocklington Reef a couple of times, so they were aware of the issues. The voyage inside the reef as far as Rossel is usually quite pleasant. However, the sea can get very uncomfortable out from Rossel, especially if the south-east trade winds pick up.

There were no questions, so I continued. 'Rossel to Honiara is approximately 360 nautical miles. That's only 42 hours steaming. If it gets really bad out there, Pocklington Reef is only 12 hours out from Rossel, and I know of a high-tide passage into the lagoon at the eastern end. We can hole up there for a couple of days, or even weeks, if necessary. The lagoon is a fantastic anchorage.'

'I like Pocklington. It's very mysterious sort of place,' Tony said. 'If we stop there, I'd like to take the magnetometer and continue sounding for shipwrecks.'

'So, would I, but we need to concentrate on getting rid of our cargo,' I replied and continued. 'I know time is not a great issue, but if we have good weather, we must take advantage of it. We can easily do the crossing to Honiara in just under two days.'

Blondie was looking worried. She had not done any serious ocean crossings. I quietly wondered how she was going to react to the next part of the trip.

I looked at everyone in turn and said with as straight a face as I could manage, trying not to laugh, 'Okay, the last part of the journey is just a little bit longer. Honiara to Suva is approximately 1,200 nautical miles. If we have no issues, we should be able to do the run in six to six and a half days, non-stop steaming.'

Looking around the table, the only two people showing any sign of concern were Sam and Blondie. I now had to put their minds at ease.

'Look,' I said, 'it's a fairly straight run from Honiara to Suva. A quick, calm trip down San Christabel, where we can stop if the weather looks like it's getting dirty. We'll change course a little to take us close to the Santa Cruz Islands then another slight course change to Tikopia Island. If there are any issues with the boat or motor, we can stop there. From there, it is only 680 nautical miles, or just three and a half days to Suva.'

John put his two cents worth in, with a big smile. 'A piece of piss.'

His comment was welcome as it broke the ice. I looked at Tony and said, 'Let's hope that engine repair of yours holds up, or we are going to be in deep shit.'

'Don't you worry about the engine,' Tony replied. 'You just worry about getting us to Suva without hitting anything.

Tony's comments prompted some lively remarks about a few previous reefs I'd managed to run over and about being a member of the so-called 'Overlander's Club.'

I took them all on the chin and changed the subject by switching my attention to Sam and said, 'After you finish sending your message to Adam, go shopping with John and Lindsay. If you're going to be the cook, you better make sure you get enough supplies for the next two weeks.'

Turning my attention to John and Lindsay, 'You guys take Sam to Samarai this afternoon and help him get the supplies, and anything else you think we might need. Anything we run out of or fresh product we can get in Honiara. Let's plan to leave tomorrow morning if everything is ready.'

'On second thought, let's all go to the club for lunch, after which we can buy the ship's supplies and get our personal bits and pieces at the same time.'

I was glad that it was all settled, and we would soon be on our way. I was actually looking forward to the adventure. Before leaving Samarai, I wanted to check and make sure that the *Hiptimco* was securely tied to the trailer, and the tarpaulin was nice and tight. I didn't want it coming off during a storm.

The required customs and immigration clearance allowing us to depart New Guinea was a mere formality. Finally, yet importantly, I wanted to say goodbye to Dusty Miller at Steamships, his help and friendship over the years has been enormous. Now, with everything taken care of, it was time to load the tender onto the hatch and secure everything for an early morning departure.

That evening, I spent some time convincing Blondie that this was going to be an exciting trip, and she would get to see places and experience things that most can only dream of. As she cuddled up and started fondling me, I wasn't sure if she was in a sexy mood or just trying to take her mind off the trip. But I didn't care, so long as she didn't stop!

The truth was the trip as far as Rossel and on to Honiara was nothing less than 'Adventures in Paradise'. If everything went well after leaving Honiara and we had a relatively smooth run, it might just get a bit boring.

*   *   *

It was still dark when the scream of the Caterpillar diesel woke me. Tony must have shit the bed. I looked at my watch, and it was 5:50 a.m. I could smell the coffee brewing even above the diesel fumes spewing out of the funnel. So, I guess, Cookie must be close to having his last breakfast ready. Reluctantly, it was time for me to get up.

The local crew had already finished breakfast, and I could see that they have already removed most of the mooring lines and were just waiting for the word to cast off the last lines. Well, they were just going to have to wait. If I could not have sex, then at least I was going to have breakfast.

Baked beans, scrambled eggs, bacon and toast! Cookie had outdone himself that morning. Being this was the last meal he'd fix for us, I guess he wanted it to be memorable. I suppose it's a little like restaurants – if you have a great dessert, you'll generally forget the lousy entrée.

I said to Cookie, 'Do you want me to drop you at the Samarai wharf?'

'Yes, boss. Will I see you again?' he asked.

'Yes. We'll be back in a few months, and if you don't already have a job, you will have one with me.'

'Thanks, boss. I'd like that.'

I finished my coffee and went up to the bridge. I called out to the boys, 'Cast off forward and aft. Leave the forward spring. I want to kick the arse out.'

With all the lines off except the spring, I gave a touch ahead to kick out my stern, and then put her into slow reverse. I watched Joe flick off the spring and pull it in. I spun the boat on her axis and set a course for Samarai wharf.

The tide was running flat out, at least four knots at the main wharf, so I headed for the sea-bath swimming enclosure on the island's western tip that doubled as a small-ship jetty. With his meagre possessions stuffed into his pillowcase, Cookie was standing on the sponson, ready to jump off. I took the nose right up the jetty so he could simply step off. The moment he was on the jetty, I punched her into reverse and cranked up the engine revolutions, quickly backing away. With a wave goodbye and a toot of the horn, we were on our way to Wari Island.

It was almost midday as Bell Rock slipped past our starboard side. That meant that it was now only half an hour to the narrow west passage into Wari lagoon. Soon, the massive Cliff Rock was abeam, home to thousands of pigeons and terns. I liked to get quite close and fire my cut down .303-calibre pistol. It is always a thrill to watch thousands of birds take to the air.

The western entrance and passage to the lagoon is narrow and unmarked. In some places, coral bommies were just a couple of feet from the hull. Fortunately, I knew the passage and anchorage well, having been in and out of there more times than I can remember.

Once inside, I carefully navigated to the small anchorage. On my demand, the chain rattled through the hawsepipe as the anchor made its short trip to the bottom. The tropical island scenery was spellbinding, especially for Sam and Blondie. But, if they thought this was good, there would be better to come.

Soon, the tender was in the water and all ready to go, I was keen to show Blondie around the village. First, I had to get her to dress a little more modestly. In the island society, she was allowed to show a bit of tit, but no thigh! Fortunately, she agreed to wear a sarong, more commonly known in PNG as a 'lap-lap.'

The stroll through the village to the local jetty on the eastern side was enjoyable. The people were proud of their island, the houses and yards were neat and tidy, and the village's central pathway was lined with giant clamshells and shaded by large trees. Blondie, with her long blond hair, was the centre of attraction. Children and adults flocked to touch her hair and stare. Very few had ever seen anyone with such long blond hair.

When we returned to the landing, the tender was alongside the *Scorpion*. I suspected that Joe and Jack had taken their families out to show them around the boat. It would be a big deal for them.

It was a hot and muggy day, so while waiting for them to return shoreside, Blondie and I took the opportunity to cool off in the lagoon. The water was refreshing, and soon after splashing around in the shallow water, it became evident that Blondie wanted to play. First, she tried to duck me under the water without much success. When that didn't work, she became a little more frisky, trying to pull down my speedos. I grabbed her head and pushed her head down to my crutch. Thrashing about, she instinctively grabbed me by the balls and squeezed. I quickly let her go.

She surfaced coughing and sputtering. There was hatred in her eyes as she tried to slap me. I easily blocked her wild swing and laughing, I grabbed her waist and pulled her close so that I could kiss her. At first, she tried to avoid me but quickly mellowed, and the scowl was replaced with a smile.

She tightly wrapped her legs around my waist as she leaned back, letting her hair fall into the water, straightening it as she swung back. I could see by the look in her eyes and the curl on her lips that she was getting frisky. My speedos were still around my knees.

'Put it in,' she whispered as she wriggled her bum to help me enter, there was an urgency in her voice.

I was just about to enter her when a dozen kids came running to the water's edge, yelling and whooping, stumbling and falling as they raced into the water at full flight to join us.

'I'll get you later,' she said with a smile.

'Promise?' I replied.

She smiled as she let go and dropped into chest-deep water. Quickly, my speedos were back where they belonged, and a gaggle of kids were in the water with us. We played for a while. They enjoyed being picked up and thrown into the deeper water.

I picked up a little guy and threw him further than the rest, a second later a shark fin appeared not far away on the surface.

'Look!' I said to Blondie, 'A shark!' I was momentarily stunned, being defenceless I didn't quite know what I could do.

There was terror etched in her face as she struggled to make the shore. I looked at the kids, seemingly oblivious the shark, still playing in the water. I reached out and grabbed the little boy I'd thrown and pulled him to me. I pointed to the now two sharks that were only some 6 metres away, he just laughed and wanted me to throw him again!

From the safety of the shore, Blondie was trying to encourage the kids to come out of the water, but they would have none of it. They just continued to play as if nothing was wrong. I picked up the young fellow and threw him, but this time towards the shallow water as I waded to shore.

We sat down in the shade of a candlenut tree, watching the kids play. We were astounded just how accustomed and at home they were in the water. Even circling sharks were of no concern to them. They truly understood their environment.

Just then, I saw movement on the deck, so I stood up and waved. Jack waved back, and soon the tender and its passengers were on their way back to the shore. The rest of the crew, including Sam, were still somewhere on the island. It was better the tender stayed shoreside, so Jack took us back to the *Scorpion*.

* * *

I woke with a start. It seemed this was becoming a bad habit. It was just on 6:00 a.m., and the screaming Caterpillar turbocharger shattered the deadly quiet. I was sure Tony got some perverse pleasure out of doing this. On top of that, there was the clunking of the winch and cargo boom as John lifted the tender out of the water.

I made my way to the galley, and Sam had prepared his first breakfast – scrambled eggs, toast, and baked beans. So far, so good. I grabbed my coffee and headed back up to the bridge. It was a tricky job turning the *Scorpion* in such a narrow channel, and it was important I knew the moment the anchor came off the bottom.

I listened to the rhythmic clunkidy-clunk of the anchor chain as it passed through the hawsepipe. Suddenly, Lindsay shouted, 'She's off the bottom!'

There was little to no wind, so turning in this confined space should not be a problem, then suddenly, I see Joe is still onboard. What the hell is he doing here? The current was running out of the channel, probably around two knots, so my steering was limited. The ship's speed had to be greater than the current flow, or there is no steerage. There are several large coral bommies that I needed to be careful of, which limited how close I could take the boat to the beach to drop Joe off.

I had no option but to turn the ship's head into the current. This way, I could slow to a virtual stop, and with the current running past the rudder, maintain my position. With a smile and a wave, Joe dove into the water and started swimming towards the beach.

I used the current to my advantage and let it help me turn. The coral bommies slipped past the hull.

'Shit, Simon! That was close,' Blondie exclaimed.

I laughed and concentrated on getting us out of the channel. On rounding Wari Island, I set a course for Panawan Island, which is close to Jomard. Our expected arrival was 4:30 p.m.

Without my Wari Island crew onboard, John, Lindsay, and I would work to a strict roster of two hours at the helm and six hours off for the entire trip. Tony's main responsibility was the engine room. However, he would relieve me at the helm from time to time, as I was on call 24/7, and sometimes I needed to concentrate on navigating.

Since leaving Wari, we had been skirting long patches of reef and uninhabited islets along the Sunken Barrier. All just begging to be explored, both above and below the water. Soon, the reef encircling Bramble Haven lagoon was on our starboard and not far to go. Panawan Island was already visible on the horizon, and we should be there in under an hour.

I had anchored in the calm shallow waters of Panawan Island many times. It was the perfect anchorage when working the Jomard wrecks, especially during the south-east trade winds.

At the turn of the century, Panawan was popular with the beche-de-mer, the sea-slug, fishermen. In the 1920s, it was the headquarters for a unique copra plantation. The plantation consisted of approximately fifteen small islands, all situated on the sunken Papuan Barrier. Each little island had been laboriously planted with coconut trees, and many of the original trees still exist today.

The plantation house on Panawan had long since disappeared, though the front steps and other concrete foundations still existed. Some fruit trees had also managed to survive. Of particular interest to me when visiting the island was, what is called in New Guinea, the 'German Grapefruit', otherwise known as 'Pomelos'. Also the starfruit, (Carambola) a five-cornered fruit which had survived on the island. Fresh fruit was always a welcome addition to our diet.

The crew would have the rest of the afternoon to explore the island and see what it had to offer, and we would also take the opportunity to top up with coconuts. Homemade coconut chips were easy to make and always welcome, especially when at the helm.

On approaching Panawan, John already had the tender in the slings, and Lindsay had the anchor in position and ready to drop. I slowly nudged the *Scorpion* towards the beach until I felt the keel riding on the sand. Lindsay dropped the anchor in two feet of water, and I immediately backed off. He then allowed the chain to roll out until I gave him the signal to lock it off. With that, we were secured. The southeast trade winds should keep us hanging off the beach. Two minutes later, the tender was in the water, and John starts getting things ready.

One of the benefits of being the boss was I could relax and goof off. I told the boys to explore the island and see what fruit they can find and load up with coconuts. While Blondie and I went to the southern tip to sunbake and relax.

It was only 300 yards or so to the exposed, south-easterly tip of the island, with its beautiful white sand beach and refreshing breeze—a great place to picnic and relax. Blondie had packed beach towels, some nibblies, and vodka. All I had to do was provide the young coconuts, and on the smaller new growth palm trees, that was easy.

After a quick dip in the ocean to cool off and while Blondie relaxed on the beach, I quickly found and cut down a couple of fresh, green coconuts. Soon the refreshing, but extra strong alcoholic drinks, worked their magic, and Blondie was getting very affectionate. It did not take long for her to hop on top of me, riding me cowboy style. All the action in the tropical heat ensured that the sweat ran down both of us in rivers.

Combined with the coconut oil that Blondie used for tanning, ensured it was an enjoyable, slippery experience, especially with her on top. A refreshing skinny-dip afterwards was just amazing. A nude romp on a deserted beach with a stunning blonde – what more can a guy ask for? It was a memorable way to spend a few hours.

* * *

It was almost 6:00 p.m. when we finally got back to the *Scorpion*. The tender was already tied alongside, so I assumed all the boys were back. The outgoing current had swung the *Scorpion* broadside to the beach. The tender was now just some 3 metres from shore. Blondie was happy to wade out and swim the last few feet to the tender. I took her beach bag, and being tall, was able to wade all the way. The boys had obviously been busy shoreside. I noticed a huge pile of coconuts stacked at the forepeak.

John poked his head around the corner. 'Got some nice grapefruit and bananas. They're in the compressor room.'

'Excellent! Where's Tony?' I replied.

'In the engine room, checking oil and shit.'

I stuck my head through the engine room hatch and shouted, 'Hey, Tony. You in there?'

'Yep, what's up?'

'We've got a long trip tomorrow. Can you crank up at 5:00 a.m.?'

'With pleasure,' he said, looking up from the bottom of the ladder with a huge smile.

Sam was living up to his promise. Dinner was excellent – fresh mackerel steaks marinated in a sauce of some kind and tasty fried rice. Even Blondie was impressed. I could see by the coy smile on Sam's face, that Blondie's approval seemed to embarrass him, but also pleased him.

Chapter 34

Jomard Passage to Rossel Island

True to his word, Tony cranked up the main engine just before 5:00 a.m. ensuring everyone except Blondie was out of bed. The tender had been locked down on the hatch the evening before, so all that was left now was to bring the anchor on board, and we were on our way.

We cleared Panawan, hugging the reef as far as the Jomard Passage entrance, then I increased the engine revolutions to bring my speed up to nine knots. My charts to Louisiade Lagoon were from the 1888 original RN Admiralty survey, and much was still shown as unsurveyed. There were only some minor corrections for mariners recorded at the bottom of the chart. Not very reassuring.

For the first six hours, we held a direct course to Panawina Island. This part of the trip was reasonably safe. Also, I had done this stretch a couple of times before. But after Panawina we would need to keep a sharp lookout. The hours melted away and we passed a succession of small islands. Soon Panawina was abeam. The passage between Wanim Island and Pana Tinani was now visible. From there, the next two hours steaming would get tricky, and careful navigation was required. Someone was always up the mast keeping a lookout for coral bommies.

Once we entered the Gold Rush Channel, navigation was more relaxed. We were now only a mile or so from Snake Passage's entrance, locally called Yuma Passage. All too soon, we were looking for a suitable coral bommie to which we could tie-up.

Anchoring close to the reef in a channel with a strong current was not an option, so the boys rigged a mooring rope with a 6-metre length of chain. Lindsay volunteered to go down and wrap the chain around the base of the bommie and tie it off with a shackle. Once that was done, we would be going nowhere and being close-hauled, we were safe to swing 360 degrees.

John had just finished tying off the mooring line when Lindsay popped to the surface, yelling, 'Quick! Get me a gun and an onion bag!'

'What the fuck's up?' I said, concerned there was some danger.

'Crayfish, hundreds of them!'

I virtually jumped down off the bridge and raced into the compressor room to get my mask and snorkel. Tony was right behind me still covered in oil and grease having scurried out of the engine room like a jackrabbit. John, in the meantime, had thrown Lindsay a speargun and an onion bag. Soon, we were all in the water.

It looks like we've stumbled upon an annual lobster march, all merrily on their way to the spawning ground. There were feelers everywhere. The water was crystal clear. I could clearly see Lindsay on the bottom some 10 metres below, spearing one after another. Unfortunately, we didn't have a good working freezer on board, so there was little sense in taking more than we could eat in a day or two. I got one on my hand spear, swam back to the *Scorpion* and handed it to John who ripped it off.

I did not bother to spear any more crayfish. Instead, kept my eyes open for coral trout. I was just happy to be in the water. I watched Tony for a while. He had three on his spear and was now swimming back to the boat. Lindsay was still on the bottom. He looked up and lifted his bag to show me his catch. I motioned that he stop and surface. He made the okay signal and slowly began to make his way up. It looked like we would have lobster for breakfast, lunch, and dinner!

Sam had outdone himself for dinner that night. He had kept the lobster bodies and cooked them up to make bisque. The tails he sliced down the middle and simply cooked in garlic butter and served with leftover fried rice. His uncle had taught him well. This boy was good!

* * *

It was 6:00 a.m., and Lindsay was again in the water, this time un-shackling the mooring line. As soon as he was back on board, I took the *Scorpion* into Snake Passage. This was a four nautical mile, narrow passage that snaked its way through Rawa Reef north of Sudest Island, also called Tagula Island. It is the easiest and also most exciting way to get to Rossel Island.

Today everyone would be in for a treat, especially John, Sam, and Blondie. It's a wonderful experience cruising up this channel. The water is as smooth as a baby's bum and crystal clear. One can see all manner of sea creatures, including sharks and shovelnose rays, swimming along the bottom. However, the helmsman needs to be on the ball, but everyone else can enjoy the cruise. Half an hour later, we had reached the exit, and it started to get a little choppy. But the seas were head-on so did not feel too bad.

An hour and a half later, we were cruising along the outer reef on the northern side of Rossel Lagoon. Unfortunately, the lagoon was mostly uncharted and full of bommies. It was much safer and quicker to stay on the calm, northern side of the reef. If the wind picked up and it got rough, I could always pull into Relief Opening and navigate the bommies to Jingo

Mission. Otherwise, I would continue on the outer reef to Heron Opening.

From the seaward side, Rossel Island looked mysterious and dangerous. At one time, it was the most feared Island in Papua. Cannibalism was rife, and many stranded seafarers perished. The most famous, or more correctly, infamous, was the French ship the *St Paul*, where some 310 passengers were massacred and eaten. Some, after having been penned up like animals with their arms and legs broken to stop them from escaping into the bush. Then, mercilessly, had their limbs hacked off while alive to satisfy the natives craving for meat.

I mentioned this as we are now steaming past the wreck of the *St Paul*, and in a few minutes, upon entering Heron Opening, we would pass a little islet to our starboard which was until recently known as 'Cannibal Island'.

I planned to anchor there and travel the short distance to Jinjo in the tender. But, on entering Heron, I just wasn't happy with the exposed anchorage. The south-east wind was a bit brisk, so I decided instead to go the short distance further south and navigate the narrow reef entrance to Jingo Mission.

A half an hour later, we were tied up to the small mission jetty, the jungle coming right to the water's edge. It was amazing. Looking shoreside, you would never know that anything existed there, never mind a sizable mission. The only clue was the small jetty and a narrow track leading into the jungle. Having been to Jinjo once before, I was keen to show Blondie and the others the marvellous Shangri-La that the fathers had created for themselves there.

After a short walk up the hill through the dense jungle path, it eventually opened up to a large clearing with sparkling white buildings surrounded by manicured lawns and gardens. We approached a nun, who was on her knees, weeding the garden. I asked her if Father Earl was still there. She stood up and smiled at us. I took a mental note of how pretty she looked, and with a slight Irish accent, she said he was, and asked us to follow her. Without a further word, she led us to a beautiful, white-timber building on stilts. As she walked up the stairs, she asked us to wait at the bottom.

Father Earl was an imposing figure as he emerged from the doorway. He was a huge man, and he looked even more imposing standing at the top of the stairs clutching a Bible in the crook of his left arm. I briefly wondered if it was stuck there.

He beamed a huge smile as he walked down the stairs with the little nun following and said, 'Well hello. We don't get many visitors here. How can we help you?'

I found the courage to speak as he towered above me. 'We are on our way to Honiara and waiting on the weather for the run across the Solomon Sea. I was wondering if you guys might be interested in swapping some bread for fresh fish?' I continued, 'We might even go diving for a few lobsters.'

He laughed in his loud booming voice. 'A bottle of rum might be a better swap!'

'Sorry, can't help you there. No one onboard drinks rum,' I replied, shrugging my shoulders.

'What kind of sailors are you, with no Rum?' He boomed in a jovial way in his loud, authoritative voice. 'Then I guess a lobster or two will be in order. Come by in the morning, and we'll have a couple of loaves for you.'

'Can you make that four?' I asked sheepishly.

He laughed, 'Four, it is.'

Father Earl oozed authority. It was easy to see how he kept his flock in line. This man alone with three nuns... Boy! I would like to be a fly on the wall when the sun goes down.

Back on the *Scorpion,* Lindsay and John got the tender in the water and loaded it with line fishing and spearfishing gear including a couple of dive torches. Tony and John would troll along the reef's edge for fish, while Lindsay and I would snorkel for lobster. Sam and Blondie would remain onboard and prepare dinner.

It was just on dark as we got underway. By the time Lindsay and I got into the water, the sun was already below the horizon, a good time to look for lobster. Painted lobster come up from the deep at night to feed and picking them up is dead easy. Hit them with the spotlight, and they freeze like foxes. Simply pick them up and pop them into the onion bag, where they instinctively huddle at the bottom.

What we were not prepared for some half-hour into the dive were the sharks. The shark numbers here were the equivalent of what cars are to Pitt Street in Sydney, seemingly hundreds. And every single one of them was interested in our bag of lobsters. When we could no longer keep track of the sharks, Lindsay, the wimp, made the sign for 'Let's fuck off out of here!', so we retreat to the crown of the reef. As they say, discretion is the better part of valour, so I agreed.

We were still not out of danger. The water over the top of the reef was up to our waists, and there were shark fins circling on the surface everywhere. Fortunately, John and Tony spotted our signals, and soon, the lobsters and we were safely in the tender.

Interestingly, the lobster will survive for quite a few days if kept in a dark, cool, and wet place. Hessian copra bags were ideal for this. Back on the *Scorpion,* we tied the bags to the gunwale near the anchor winch and ran the deck hose over them. That should keep them happy until the morning. John cleaned the fish, and they went into the fridge.

Dinner was ready, lobster again, but this time with a cheese sauce and sweet potato, Sam had begged from a local lad. We were being seriously spoilt. Blondie was not her usual talkative self, almost reserved I would say, but I thought nothing of it. The beer and whiskey flowed as we spoke of the next part of the trip, and soon it was time to retire.

Back in the wheelhouse, I had just enough beer to get a glow-up and watching Blondie get undressed was enough to make me horney. Blondie was never one to refuse sex and always ready to suggest positions, but tonight she seemed a little hesitant. I didn't want to pressure her and put it down to anxiety regarding the next part of the trip. Not a problem. I can wait until the morning. She's always turned on and demanding then.

* * *

We agreed to spend the day at Jinjo and leave at midnight, Pocklington Reef was almost 100 nautical miles east of Jinjo. That meant 12 hours steaming, and I wanted to arrive there during daylight hours just in case the sea was rough, and we needed to find an anchorage.

Early in the morning, Tony and John delivered the fish and crayfish to the mission, and as promised, came back with four loaves of tantalising, fresh, hot bread. The smell was to die for. One loaf was devoured at breakfast as soon as it hit the table. Some eat it with butter and jam, John spread his Vegemite, and Blondie ate it with baked beans. It's amazing that such a simple thing as fresh bread can give so much pleasure.

The tender was securely tied down on the front hatch and the anchor roped down, derricks secured. Everything on the boat, including the ship's hold and cabins, were locked down tight. I calculated that the bulk of the sea should be on our starboard forequarter, and that would make for a reasonably comfortable trip. If it changed to beam-on, we would be in for two very uncomfortable days.

At midnight on the dot, Tony cranked up the engine, and as soon as Lindsay cast off the last mooring line, we cautiously made our way. Very slowly and carefully, I navigated the narrow passage in the dim moonlight. Lindsay was up the mast with a spotlight marking the reef's edge, and John with a powerful dive torch at the bow looking out for bommies.

The first 270 metres ran parallel to the shore and was quite narrow. Once we reached the channel proper and turned to port, heading out to the outer reef, navigation was much easier as the channel widened.

Twenty minutes after leaving the jetty, we were clear of the reef and into the open sea. I changed course for Pocklington Reef, and we were now well and truly on our way. We had plenty of fuel onboard, so I brought the engine revs up to give us about nine knots. At that speed, we would be there around 9:00 a.m.

Before the advent of GPS, currents and leeway in an open ocean, especially at night, were the dread of sea captains. You might still be steaming your set course, but you never knew how far to port or starboard the wind or current had drifted you. Yes, you can watch your wake or drop a bottle and see which direction it drifts, but all this was crude guesswork.

So far, the sea has been kind to us, and we appeared to be making good time. At 8:30 a.m., I sent Lindsay up the mast. If he did not spot the reef by 9:00 a.m., we would have no idea of where we were. The only option then would be to continue on our current course and hope for the best.

Then, I heard Lindsay shout, 'I see a ship off our starboard bow!'

I struggled to see anything. I took my binoculars and scanned the horizon – nothing.

'Whereabouts?' I sang out.

Lindsay pointed just off our starboard bow. Then I remembered a Japanese mother ship had grounded on the western edge a year ago. Speaking to Lindsay, I said, 'That might be the Longliner mothership wrecked on the reef.'

He nodded in agreement. I slightly changed course to take us more directly to the ship. A few minutes later, I could make out the blimp on the horizon. It was probably about four miles away, about half an hour steaming. If that ship didn't shift position, then it was definitely the wreck. If it did, we were in trouble.

The northern side of Pocklington reef is almost a sheer drop off, and along the entire eighteen-mile reef there are only a couple of places very close to the reef edge where one can get a precarious anchor. At the spot where the Longliner is grounded, the lagoon was just over a mile wide.

Lindsay sang out loudly, 'I see the reef. Change course a little to starboard.'

I slowly swung the head to starboard until Lindsay called out, 'That's it. That will do for now.'

I replied, 'Let me know when we get abeam, and I'll take us a hundred yards or so off the reef.'

'Okay, skipper.'

Five minutes later, Lindsay shouted, 'Almost abeam.'

I changed course until I could see the reef from the bridge and then ran parallel to it, creeping closer until we were just some 30 metres or so off the edge. It was now very calm, and we could look forward to a couple of hours of smooth sailing.

*　*　*

Pocklington Reef is one of those mysterious reefs that rise out of nowhere, almost smack bang in the centre of a major shipping lane. This reef has been the death-knell for many sailing ships over the last two hundred years. Also, many steamships in the modern era have come to grief here. This is where you can look for treasure and expect to find it.

The edge of the reef was clearly defined. It must have been low tide as the reef was almost 1 metre out of the water, and there was a seemingly never-ending waterfall as the water from inside cascaded over the edge. I would have liked to have investigated the Japanese mothership, but I had to be sensible and take advantage of the current calm weather and continue to Honiara – but there was always the trip back.

It was 11:00 a.m., and I could now see the reef folding away to the starboard. In a few minutes, we would again be in the open sea and at the mercy of the south-east swell. If everything went according to plan, I estimated that our ETA Cape Esperance, at Guadalcanal Island, would be around midnight.

Once again, we slipped into our monotonous routine and were subject to the incessant drone of the main engine. I lay in my bunk, thinking just how reliant we were on that motor. Any one of a thousand things could go wrong, and we would be dead in the water, but it never happened. It was just amazing.

Blondie came to bed around 9:00 p.m. just having showered. Her still-damp hair dragging over my face as she climbed over me to get against the bulkhead, she smelt very nice. I pulled the curtain closed, cuddled up to her and fell asleep.

It was midnight when John woke me. He was worried because we should be able to see the Cape Esperance lighthouse by now. I had to be extra careful here because there were outlying, fringing reefs. I grabbed the binoculars and climbed up the foremast to increase my field of view. Ten minutes later, off the starboard forequarter, I could just faintly see the flash of the light on the horizon. It disappeared, I counted to ten, and there it was again, the unmistakable flash of the Esperance lighthouse, one flash every ten seconds.

I was very familiar with the flash of Cape Esperance lighthouse and had a bit of a smile as I recalled working the huge, 2,135-ton Japanese submarine, the *I-1*, on the reef just out from Paru village in Kamimbo Bay. Now that was an exciting job.

The ocean currents had drifted us a few miles to port. From this point, I could now safely change course to a mile or so off the lighthouse. Ten minutes later, Savo Island was just visible off our port side bow in the dim moonlight. I was now able to get an accurate fix on our position. Soon we would round the cape, and I could safely change course and steam close to shore, all the way down to Honiara. Our ETA at Honiara was now 3:00 a.m.

Chapter 35

Arrival Honiara

We arrived just as predicted, right on time. The pratique-mooring buoy was clearly marked on the chart, and we easily found the buoy and quickly tied up to it. I displayed the yellow pratique flag from the poop deck, and that was that. Meanwhile, Tony shut down the main engine, and once again, there was a deafening silence. We then had to wait until morning for an officer from the agricultural department and customs to come and inspect the boat. Once we received the Pratique Certificate, which is a bill of health, we would be free to go alongside the small ship's wharf.

But this was Honiara. It was already midday, and we were still cooling our heals with no sign of anyone. Honiara is nothing more than a small, country town, with a total population of around 10,000 people. As far as I could see, things here would not be much different to New Guinea. I was getting seriously pissed off, so I instructed John and Lindsay to get the tender into the water and had Tony take me shoreside. I was going to find someone, anyone, to get the clearance procedure underway.

Tony remained in the tender, and I was standing on the wharf, looking around. There was no security hut, so the cargo shed was the place to start looking. I got that right and very quickly found the customs office. It was stuck in the corner of the main cargo shed close to one of the large sliding doors. I approached a guy sitting behind a desk, smartly dressed in a crisp, white uniform and introduced myself. I explained that we were on the pratique buoy and asked if he could find someone to give us clearance.

He was very apologetic and explained that they didn't have a dinghy. He said it would be much easier if I just bring just the boat alongside the coastal wharf. Hmmm, not strictly according to the rules, but who am I to argue? He said he would arrange to get the officer from the agriculture department to come down, and together they would fix us up. Simple as that.

With the *Scorpion* alongside the coastal wharf, the customs and health officer arrived and unceremoniously stamped my transit papers and everyone's passports. In John's case, they stamped his Seamen's record book. The customs officer had a quick look around, once satisfied they both left.

Sam was now free to leave the boat, find a payphone, and call Leon Chow. John had already brought up Leon's two boxes and put them in the compressor room. One box contained three gold bars and the other two. He removed the screws from the lids, so everything was now ready for Leon to inspect.

Tony was in the process of filling the water tanks when an old, dilapidated utility pulled up and an elderly Chinaman stepped out of the car and hobbled towards the boat. Sam jumped onto the wharf to meet the old gentleman. They exchanged a few words and Sam pointed at me standing on the bridge.

I swung down from the bridge to the main deck and went to the bulwarks to take Leon's hand and help him onboard. After introductions, we chatted briefly, and he said, 'You have some gold for me?'

'Yes, that is, if you've got some money for me. Come this way, please,' I replied as I lead the way to the compressor room.

'John, get Mr Chow a stool, please.' John nodded and came back in a few seconds with a small stool.

I placed the stool down in front of the two boxes and motioned for Leon to sit down as I went on my haunches and removed the lids from the boxes. There was a smile on his face as I pulled out a 12 kg bar and handed it to him.

The weight surprised him, and he nearly dropped it. He looked at Sam. 'You checked these?'

'Yes sir, I checked and weighed every bar.'

'Good, put the lid back on and get them into the car. I have to give Mr Simon some money.'

I gave John the signal to lock up the boxes as Leon handed me a wad of cash.

'$67,000,' he said. 'As agreed, all in Australian money.'

'If you don't mind, we will count it here. It's too public on the afterdeck,' I said.

I handed a wad of cash to both Lindsay and Tony, and together we quickly counted the three lots and tallied it together. It was $67,000 on the dot. John and Sam picked up the boxes of gold and carried them to Leon's car. We watched him drive off and headed to the afterdeck to celebrate with a beer.

Sam asked if he could have a look around Honiara for a few hours. We wouldn't be leaving until the next morning, so I had no issue with that.

'I'll hire a taxi, and maybe Blondie would like to come along for the ride,' he said, looking at her then me for approval. Like a little child, she begged, 'Please, Simon, please. Can I? we might never get back here.'

I had a lot to do if we were going to get away tomorrow, so I agreed, but said, 'Be careful.' Blondie squealed with joy as she hugged me and then raced up to the cabin to get ready.

Sam left to find a cab and was back relatively quickly, but he still had a ten-minute wait before Blondie was ready. And when she appeared, boy she looked red-hot! I was almost jealous, but I noticed she was wearing knickers, so I guess she had nothing but sightseeing in mind.

* * *

It was mid-afternoon before I had the customs transfer documents, which allowed us to leave the port. We also took on board a thousand litres of fuel, just in case of emergency. Meanwhile, Lindsay and John had been to the supermarket for supplies.

It was late afternoon, around 5:30 p.m. We were relaxing on the back deck with a fast-disappearing bottle of Vodka and discussing the day's events and the next part of the voyage when a taxi pulled up close to the edge of the jetty.

Blondie stepped out, holding a plastic shopping bag. It looked like it contained takeaway tubs. She came close to the edge of the jetty and knelt down, steadying herself with one hand on the wooden kerbing block. She had to reach over quite a way to pass the bag down to Lindsay, who was sitting on the wharf side of the boat. Not a good idea, as she leant forward, both boobs smartly popped out, dangling in plain sight. There was nothing she could do until Lindsay grabbed the bag. He burst out laughing as

Blondie promptly fixed herself and gave a sexy nod of the head and coy smile.

Sam missed all this, had his back turned while he was paying the cab driver. He looked a little perplexed, having no idea of why everyone was giggling. He also had a bag of takeaway cartons, so it looked like dinner was taken care of tonight.

Blondie was not one to be embarrassed, and after a quick fresh-up, she joined us at the table. Sam's selection of Chinese was fantastic. We had a pleasant dinner and drank and talked late into the evening.

Chapter 36

Honiara to Suva

It was another early start, and at 6:00 a.m., we cast off for the final leg of our journey to Suva. Honiara quickly disappeared from view as we cruised down the Guadalcanal coast. The first 14 hours steaming down the 'slot' past Malaita and on to Ulawa, the seas were quite calm. The weather reports were promising, but anything could happen with the weather in six days.

We settled into our routines at the helm and eating, resting, and sleeping. Hour after hour, the miles slowly slipped under our keel, and before we realised it, two days had disappeared as though they had never existed. Early in the morning, the approach to the Santa Cruz Islands brought us back to reality.

Once abeam of Santa Cruz Island, also called Ndeni Island, I made a small course adjustment to take us close to Tikopia. This would be our last opportunity for shelter if anything went wrong. Also, from there, I should be able to tune my range finder into the Nadi aircraft beacon frequency. Then, I would not have to worry about leeway or chart-deviation calculations, I could just follow the radio beeps.

In just a few hours we would be steaming close to Vinikolo island. This is where La Perouse came to grief sometime in 1785 when the French ships *Boussole* and *Astrolabe* slammed into one of the reefs around here. It would be fun to look for them, but we are on a mission – maybe on the way back.

Day three, and Tikopia was on the horizon, dead ahead. I purposefully took us within half a mile of its southern coast. The closer we got, the more mysterious the island appeared. From seaward, it looked like a collapsed volcano with a large lagoon. I climbed up the mast to get a better view, but I could not see an opening to the lagoon. If there was ever a pirate's lair, then this was it.

Everyone was on the bridge-deck watching Tikopia slip past our stern. There were only six hundred and fifty nautical miles to go. It was time to change course to 125°. Fiji, here we come.

As the day progressed, it became more and more overcast, and there were rainstorms in the distance. Things were looking somewhat ominous. However, the sea remained relatively calm. Day turned into night, and in the morning, nothing much changed. It was still overcast with occasional squalls in the distance.

Throughout most of the day and night, I was busy. I was navigating, on watch, or at the helm. Blondie was left with little to do for most of the day. For her, this was now becoming boring. Likewise, Sam had little to do other than his duty in the galley, and she had begun helping him at every possible opportunity. It was natural that they would end up spending more and more time together. He even tried to teach her backgammon. Ha! Good luck with that!

I was too busy to notice that sparks were beginning to fly between them. Although Tony did try to warn me in a roundabout fashion, sadly, it all went over my head.

We were now only a couple of hundred miles away from Fiji, so I started to look for the Nadi beacon, and there it was – the reassuring dash-dot, dash-dot, repeating over and over. The direction finder showed that we had drifted to starboard, so a course change of 20° to port brought us back on course.

Late in the evening on the next day, we caught a glimpse of the Fiji mountain ranges in the far distance. Now, there were only thirteen hours to go. At around 10:00 p.m., I crawled into my bunk. Being careless, I woke Blondie. She turned to face me and kissed me tenderly on the lips. She was shivering. 'Fuck me. Fuck me hard, Simon.' she whispered.

We had the most fantastic session. This was animalistic sex in its rawest form, and then, in the end, a tenderness I had not experienced with Blondie before. She held me close for a long time before we both drifted off to sleep.

Chapter 37

Suva and the Sale of the Gold

John woke me. Suva harbour was less than an hour away. I got up and replaced the cruising chart with the Fiji Harbour chart. I'd already found and marked the pratique buoys. Lindsay climbed onto the poop deck and hoisted the yellow pratique flag, and then took the wheel, sending John to wake Tony and get the mooring line ready.

Cruising through the narrow reef passage into the harbour was a thrill, and once inside, the water was dead calm. Soon, the yellow pratique buoy was visible in the distance. I reduced speed, and ten minutes later, we were securely tied to the buoy. All we had to do now was wait for customs and health to come and do the formalities.

Clearing customs in Fiji proved to be a far cry from Honiara. At 9:30 a.m., a launch came alongside with the customs, immigration, and health officials. Tony ushered them to the back deck where I had all the ship's documentation and crew details ready on the table. The immigration officer stayed with me, while the health and customs officers went with Tony to inspect the boat for contraband.

My ship's documentation and transfer papers were found to be in order, and the passports and John's Seaman's record book were duly stamped and signed. Customs and immigration also gave us a bill of good health, we were now cleared to land. It was all very efficient and over in thirty minutes. As the officials left, Sam joined them for the trip shoreside. All that was left for us to do now was leave the pratique buoy and join the yachts at anchor in the harbour. The boys already had the tender into the water, and as soon as our business with Adam Fat, was concluded, we would be free to party on shore.

* * *

It was almost 11:00 a.m. when we spotted a speedboat heading our way. As it got closer, I recognised Sam sitting at the back. By the time we got to the front deck, they were already bobbing alongside. We made fast their lines and helped them come on board. Sam politely introduced us to Adam and Michael. Adam smiled as he shot out his hand. His handshake was strong and firm. I instantly took a liking to the guy, and I didn't even know him. I was quite surprised. Adam was not at all what I expected. He was one of those debonair men that oozed sophistication. He was charming and friendly. I think he was also a man used to dealing with people and getting his way.

I asked them to come to the back deck and make themselves comfortable, while the boys went down to the explosive magazine and brought up the bullion. While we were waiting, Adam politely asked, 'How was the trip to Fiji?'

'We had an excellent trip, Adam. No issues at all.'

'I've been looking for a coaster. Would you consider selling?'

I was taken aback. 'I've never thought about it. Maybe we can talk about it in a day or so.'

'That's fine. Once we have finished the business with the gold, I'd like to have a look around, if you don't mind.'

'No, not at all. You're more than welcome to bring a shipwright or engineer on board if you wish.'

'Good,' Was his simple reply, just as Lindsay brought the first box and put it on the table. The Kwato mission had really done an excellent job of these. There was even a rope handle at each end. I had a Phillips screwdriver ready and quickly opened the first box.

Adam lifted a 12 kg gold brick from the box. His eyes never left it for a second. I do not think any other race on the planet has an appreciation of gold equal to the Chinese. The look on Adams's face was one of sheer ecstasy. It was as though he had a sexual experience.

The rest of the boxes were soon all on-deck, and John quickly removed the lids. Adam looked serious as he turned his attention to Sam and asked if he had checked every ingot, to which Sam replied that he had.

Adam smiled and asked Michael to open the small suitcase, 'Here's $67,000 in Australian money,' he said.

The money was in $20 Australian notes. I spoke to Adam, 'This is going to take a little while to count. Maybe you would like to look over the boat with John and Sam.

Blondie had been very quiet and withdrawn all day. She looked at me and asked, 'Can I go with them?'

'Yes, of course,' I replied, thinking, *What a stupid question.*

I pulled out the first wad of $20 and started counting. Lindsay and Tony also went to work counting. True to his word, with the tally finished we came to the same amount – $67,000. I picked up the briefcase and headed to the bridge. Adam was just stepping out of the wheelhouse when I got there. I threw the suitcase onto the bunk and turned to Adam.

'Well, what do you think?'

'It's a practical little boat. I like it. Sam was also impressed with it on the trip here.'

'I'll think about your offer, but there were a few places we are keen to stop off at on our way back,' I said.

'We can talk about it later. I would like to invite you all to my favourite restaurant tonight. It's on me. What do you say?'

'That would be very nice, thank you.'

He pointed to some fuel tanks onshore, 'See the fuel tanks? Just to the left of them is the coastal wharf. Right next to that, I have a small jetty. Be there by 6:00 p.m., and Sam will be waiting to drive you to the restaurant.'

'Sounds good to me. See you then.'

The boys loaded the five boxes into the speedboat, and Adam and his guys were on their way. I quickly went up to the bridge and grabbed the binoculars so I could watch precisely where they went. I didn't want to screw up and go to the wrong jetty.

Back to the galley, it was time to have some lunch and celebrate. I had been seriously mulling over Adams offer and wanted to swing it past the guys. Except for Tony, who had a wife and life, the boat was the boy's home as much as it was mine. However, everyone understood that it was over at the end of a project unless there was some follow-up deal.

With the boys all on the back deck, it was also an ideal time to talk about money. I picked up my beer, and I said, 'I haven't worked it out exactly, but I estimate we will each earn about $40,000 from the gold alone, never mind the scrap and silver. That will probably amount to another $10,000 each.'

There was a nodding of heads, so I continued.

'Tomorrow, if you're all happy, we'll share the cash that's stashed under my bunk equally with no deductions. That will give us about $33,000 each, in round figures.'

I waited for that to sink in and added. 'I know this has been a shit job. But don't forget there's still the money that Adam put into the account in Samarai. I reckon that will be another $16,000 to each of your bank accounts when I return to Australia.'

'I'm all good with that, and so is everyone else,' Tony said, speaking for the crew.

'All's good, then. I'll work it all out tomorrow or the day after. I have to send a telex to the scrap merchant and find the total amount they owe us before I can do the tally.'

'Where's Blondie?' I asked, looking around.

'Probably enjoying her favourite pastime, sunbaking on the top deck,' Lindsay said with a smirk.

'Well, I had better go and see.'

Climbing the ladder to the top deck, I could see she was not sunbaking. I stuck my head into the cabin and found her lying on the bed and not looking her usual self.

'What's, wrong?'

'Nothing,' She mumbled with her head buried in the pillow.

'Looks like you need cheering up,' I said as I lay beside her. She turned onto her side, facing me, and hugged me tightly. I could just make out the beginning of a smile as I kissed her neck.

'Please, cheer me up,' she whispered as she wriggled closer.

I pulled down my speedos. They were now tight under my balls, pushing them up. I pulled down her panties and found the baby oil. I squeezed a generous amount on her pussy and began to massage her gently. Soon she was moaning and squirming. It was time to enter.

'Oh, God, that's beautiful! Fuck me! Oh, fuck me hard! Oh, God! How am I going to live without this?' Her utterings were meaningless to me. I was in my own heaven.

I lost track of time; it was irrelevant. Blondie's appetite for sex was insatiable. Exhausted, I fell asleep, still deep inside her. A knock on the cabin door startled me. It took a moment for my brain to orientate.

'Got to start getting ready to go shoreside,' John said in a loud voice.

I shook off the cobwebs and forced myself awake. I gently shook Blondie to wake her. I know she would need some time for make-up and such. We both went down together, Blondie to the shower, for me it was the usual bucket-wash on the front deck. By 5:30 p.m., we were all ready to go. I watched Blondie slide down the ladder. She turned, and I noted just how beautiful she looked, accentuated by the jewellery I had given her. But something was different. Her tits were more erect. Then it struck me, she was wearing a bra. I never knew she even owned one!

It was only a short distance to Adam's jetty, and as we approached, I could see Sam waving. As we came alongside, Tony threw him the headline, and he tied us off. John scrambled up like a monkey, while Sam held out his hand to Blondie and helped her up and then gave her a quick hug. I thought, *What the fuck?* Then, quickly put it out of my mind.

Sam explained that we would be going to the new Travelodge Hotel on the waterfront, not far away and an excellent restaurant. Sam was lucky he had a Ford Falcon with a front bench seat because we were all 'skinny buggers' except for John. Otherwise, we would not all fit into the car. Even so, it was a squeezy ride.

Sam parked close to the main entrance and led the way into the restaurant. He wasn't kidding when he said it was an excellent restaurant. This was way out of our class. I was going to have to watch John. He did not even know in which hand to hold a knife and fork.

Adam and his wife and Michael were seated on a lounge near the bar. He introduced us to his wife, Tracey, and I was surprised when he went on to say that we had already met his two boys. Not once did Sam even hint that it was his father who was buying the gold.

Adam called over the waiter and asked him to take our order. After some small talk, I said to Adam, 'I don't want to talk shop, but I've considered your proposal, and I'm prepared to sell the *Scorpion*. But I want to keep the dive gear and compressor.'

'How much are you thinking?'

'Close to what I paid, $40,000, and considering it's here in Fiji, that must make it a bargain for you.'

'I'll think about it and get back to you tomorrow.'

'Not a problem.'

Looking at the menu was daunting. There were selections I've never heard of. Adam suggested I try the Duck a l'Orange. That seemed good enough for me. John looked quizzingly at me with a tilt of his head. I whispered, 'Just order a steak. Then, you can't go wrong.'

For someone not used to fine dining, dinner was a fantastic experience, and this was something I could easily get used to. The conversation was also interesting. Adam mentioned some of the difficulties of living in a small country with a diverse, ethnic population. He was also worried about the upcoming independence. We kept our host amused with stories of life in New Guinea and diving experiences.

With the dinner plates cleared from the table, it was time to study the dessert menu. Crepes Suzette sounded interesting. I pointed it out to Blondie, and she agreed. With the order taken, Blondie excused herself to go to the ladies room, and Sam also left for the gents.

Some fifteen minutes later, the desserts arrived at the table, but neither Blondie nor Sam had returned. Looking a bit sheepish, Michael stood up and offered to find them, just when they were spotted walking towards the restaurant. They appeared to be in earnest conversation, almost arguing.

Sam apologised and said they had strolled past the pool to the water's edge and lost track of time. Desert was delicious, and we retired back to the comfort of the lounge for coffee and drinks. After the first round of drinks, Adam and his wife excused themselves, saying it was time for them to retire, but the bar tab was open.

After a couple more rounds, the conversation was interesting and lively when suddenly Blondie turned to me and asked in a demanding but pensive tone to come for a walk. Once we were out of the restaurant, she put her arm in the crook of mine, strange she was shivering yet it was not cold. We walked in silence past the pool towards the sea wall.

She smiled and pointed to a bench that was overlooking the harbour. We sat down. She was still tightly holding onto my arm. Something was seriously troubling her. I was beginning to think she might be pregnant. I turned to face her and asked, 'Okay, what's the problem?'

She looked me in the eye. 'I'm so sorry, Simon. I'm so sorry, I don't know how to tell you.'

'It can't be that bad, surely.'

She put her head on my shoulder and in a teary voice, she replied, 'I love you, Simon. I really do, but I'm not in love with you. Oh, God, I've had the best time ever. I'm so sorry, but I'm not coming back to the boat.'

Being stupid, as she so often reminded me, I did not fully comprehend exactly what that meant. 'What do you mean? You want to stay shoreside for the night?'

She burst into tears, shaking your head. 'No, no, no... I mean I'm not coming back to the boat, ever. I'm staying in Suva with Sam. I love him, Simon. I'm truly in love with him.'

It took microsecond for what she had just said to sink in. My head was spinning, and it felt as though my chest would explode. For a moment, I was speechless.

'You can't be serious! I thought we had a fantastic relationship. I've never felt this close to any woman in my life before!'

'We've had a lot of fun, and the best sex ever, but I'm genuinely in love. I can't fight it. I've tried. My God, how I've tried!'

My breathing was returning to normal, but I could now feel the resentment welling up inside me, betrayal and then jealousy. I jumped up and paced back forth in front of her, momentarily wanting to hurt her. I wanted to hurt somebody.

'Please, Simon It just happened. For God's sake!' she cried. 'I haven't even had sex with him yet.'

'Fucken bullshit!' I shouted in disbelief. In my twisted mind, why else would this sex goddess be leaving me except for someone better in bed?

'Honestly, no sex, I just fell in love with the person. You have to believe me. I don't know how, and I don't know why. It just happened.'

The emotional shock was starting to subside, and common sense was kicking in. I had been in this situation once before when I did all the begging and pleading, which was ultimately all to no avail, and I did nothing more than make a fool of myself.

I sat down and put my arm around her and held her tight. 'I may never have said it, but I do love you, Julie. I really want you to stay.'

'You don't understand, Simon,' she said in between tears. 'You're a pirate, an adventurer. You'll always be an adventurer. No matter how much I crave you in bed, I need security. I want a home. I want a husband at home with me. I want a family, and Sam can give me what you cannot, security.'

The tears welled up in my eyes. I was hurt, and it was not just pride. Somehow, in my befuddled mind, I understood. I pulled her close and kissed her as I never kissed her before – a sincere emotional kiss mingled with our tears. It was a beautiful moment.

The spell was broken by Tony heading our way, singing out, 'What are you guys doing out here?'

'Fuck off, and bring a couple of drinks. I'll have a double scotch on the rocks and Blondie will have a double vodka.'

That gave us a couple of moments to both compose ourselves and wipe away our tears. We sat in silence holding hands like lovers, looking over the Suva Harbour. Any other time, it would have been a beautiful romantic interlude.

The sound of voices told me that more people than just Tony were making their way past the pool. Tony handed us our drinks. I took a long reflective drink and let the calming sensation wash over me. Blondie had also composed herself and looking into her eyes, I said, 'I think we have an announcement to make.'

She wiped a tear and nodded in silence. I took another drink and got up from the bench and looked at Sam, and then said in a calm voice, 'You may want to sit down,' pointing to the bench.

Taking a deep breath and with as much courage as I could muster, I looked at the crew and said, 'Guys, I'm sorry to say I've got some bad news. Blondie is leaving us today. She'll be staying in Fiji to make a new life with Sam.'

The response was not exactly what I expected. They all sort of looked at each other with raised eyebrows, a type of, 'I told you so' look. It didn't look like anyone was that surprised.

'We are truly going to miss you, Blondie,' Tony said in earnest. 'You did bring some joy and class to the boat.'

There was a murmur of agreement as everyone tried to make an awkward moment as comfortable as possible, for everyone, but especially for me.

Blondie stood up and with tears rolling down her cheek and hugged everyone briefly in turn. She turned to me and held me tight and whispered in my ear., 'I'm going to miss you, Simon. Thank you.'

'I'll never forget Julie McVey. I'll never forget you,' I said in a low voice as I gently moved her away from me.

Sam had shuffled up behind Blondie, and as soon as she was free of me, and without saying a word, he leaned over and shook my hand. He then put his arm around her and immediately led her away. Watching her walk down past the pool at the Travelodge in

Suva was to be my last but lasting memory of Blondie. I was never to see or hear from her again.

I turned to the boys and Michael. 'We have a bar tab, so let's have a few stiff ones before we go back to the boat. I assume you are taking us back to the jetty, Michael?'

'Yes, Mr Simon,' Michael replied.

It was evident from the conversation at the bar the boys had suspected something was happening between Blondie and Sam, but like most men in my situation, I was blind to the signs. The truth is, I would not have believed it even if someone had said something. I had used the sex as a barometer for the success of our relationship, never thinking that Blondie, like I guess most women, wanted more.

* * *

It was midnight before we returned to the *Scorpion*, and it was all somehow different now. 'Empty' is the best way to describe it. I know I was being irrational, but I now sincerely hoped that Adam would buy the boat.

In the morning apart from a splitting headache, I was emotionally a little better. Calculating the split of the proceeds gave me something to do other than pining for Blondie. It was pleasant on the afterdeck. The boys were enjoying putting their money into bundles of $10,000. I paid the crew for the full amount received for the gold, including the money that Adam had put into my account in Samarai.

I still had no idea of what the scrap merchant owed us for the silver and scrap copper that we had sent from Samarai. We had $134,000 on hand. I agreed to pay the boys $40,000 each now, leaving me $14,000 cash. I would reconcile the rest when I got back to Australia. I estimated after deducting the boat share, I would still owe them about $12,000 each.

The crew were happy, and so was I. Their share of the money was now their responsibility, so they had better not lose it! With that settled, it was time to become better acquainted with Suva. With pockets full of money, we hired a taxi to explore this modern city of some 100,000 people.

One thing for sure was that Suva had a dazzling array of pubs, clubs, and restaurants. It was busy and vibrant for tourists like us, and it appeared friendly and safe. The diversity was staggering – Indian street vendors were selling strange sweets that they deep-fried, and there was the Hare Krishna restaurant, now this was something new. We had no idea it was vegetarian, but the food was divine, especially the yogurt. There was a bit of political stuff going on, something to do with independence. But this was no concern of ours. We were simply looking for a good time.

The boys were keen to find a massage parlour and the taxi driver was only too happy to oblige, but the pain of separation was still too raw for me to indulge in prostitutes at this time. After dropping Lindsay and John off at a massage parlour, the driver took us to the iconic Grand Pacific Hotel on Victoria Parade. It looked a little tired now, but it was easy to imagine the splendour that it once had. I thought this would make an elegant casino. Our taxi driver guide took us across the road, and we strolled the grounds of the Fiji Parliament, another spectacular building.

When crossing the road, I noticed that the Travelodge was next door to the Grand Pacific, so I paid the driver off, and we walked the short distance to the bar. It was nice to get into the air-conditioning and sit down with a cold beer.

I was still not over the shock of losing Blondie and confided so in Tony. He listened to my ramblings with patience. When I had finished, he said, 'I don't know how you didn't spot the signs, Simon. They'd been away with the fairies ever since we left Rossel Island. I did try and mention something to you once, but it just went over your head. And if we had pressed the issue, you probably still wouldn't have believed us.'

'Well, I guess you are right about that, but I should not have given in so easily and fought to keep her.'

'Mate, it would have done you no good, seriously. She stayed with you for the adventure, but she fell in love with someone else. I know it is a stupid thing to say, but as the saying goes: There are plenty more fish in the sea.'

'That's easy for you to say, Tony. Blondie was uncomplicated, had no baggage, beautiful from head to toe, and the best root ever. It's going to take someone exceptional to fill her shoes.' Tony must have known he was fighting a losing battle and changed the subject.

* * *

Soon it was close to 5:00 p.m. and time to get back to the *Scorpion*. When we arrived at the jetty, John and Lindsay were patiently sitting on the curbing block waiting for us.

'Adam has been looking for you. He said for you to go to the little office over there and give him a call. Here's his number,' Lindsay said, handing me a scrap of paper and pointing to a small shed.

I found a security guard, and he let me into a small office. I dialled the number, and soon, a voice answered, 'Adam Fat here, how can I help you?'

'It's Simon, Adam. You left a message for me to call.'

'Yes, it's about the *Scorpion*. You suggested $40,000 might buy it.'

'That's what I said.'

'How does $38,000 sound to you?'

'With recent developments, that I'm sure you're aware of, I'm keen to get away from here as soon as possible. So, I guess $38,000 sounds good to me, but I keep the dive gear and compressor.

'That's fine with me. We can meet up tomorrow at 10:00 a.m. and cement the deal. I can pay the funds straight into your account.'

So, that was that. On the one hand, I was sad, but on the other, I was glad that this chapter in my life would soon be over.

* * *

Next morning on the dot, I was on the jetty at 10:00 a.m., as arranged. Adam handed me a simple contract for the sale and purchase of the boat. The nut and bolts were simple, he would be responsible for any import duties or taxes. And importantly, the deal was based on 'as-is, where-is, with all faults, if any'. It was a straightforward chattel sales agreement

We went to Adam's bank in the city where we signed the contract in the manager's office and arranged the transfer of funds to my account. We had a coffee giving ample time for the funds to transfer. From the comfort of the bank manager's office, I rang my bank in Nelson Bay and confirmed the funds had arrived.

Tongue in cheek, I said to Adam, 'Well, it looks like it's your lucky day. For a bargain price, you've got a great boat and a beautiful daughter-in-law.'

He just smiled and shook my hand. Adam asked me to bring the boat alongside after lunch, and his guys would help us unload the diving gear that we intended to ship to Australia. He gave me the name and address of a forwarding agent that he used regularly and assured me that they would look after us.

We bought the *Scorpion* alongside and immediately started unloading the compressor and the most valuable diving equipment and stacking it all onto pallets. Using Adam's strapping machine, we securely tied everything down. The crew packed their gear into dive bags, and each kept two scuba cylinders.

We decided to spend the night on the *Scorpion* and move to the Grand Pacific hotel the morning. To an extent, I think everyone was a little sad that it was going to be our last night on board. We have all had many adventures on the *Scorpion*, and she has proved to be an excellent dive boat.

I had another restless night, but it was getting easier. By mid-morning, the forwarding agents had completed all the necessary documentation, and our equipment was loaded onto trucks and whisked away. This also included both John's and my gold coins and jewellery, which we concealed in the two, 72-cubic-foot steel scuba bottles.

The neck of the bottles was too small to accept coins, so Tony removed the tanks tight-fitting boot and cut a hole in the bottom. We wrapped the jewellery in two separate pillowcases and placed them inside the bottles. The steel base was replaced and spot-welded, it was then ground smooth. A quick coat of fibreglass resin, a clean-up which included painting the bottle, was done before we replaced the boot. All this work was invisible except for the most thorough scrutiny.

We were all done and ready to go. I had one more quiet stroll around the boat, with good memories flooding in, and the best of which were of the girl I'd just lost.

We booked into the Grand Pacific for two days, but the old grey mare was not what she used to be. We were in the 'new' section, probably built in the 1950s. The rooms were large, but the paint was peeling, the box air-conditioning was noisy, but the bed was divine. At least it was to me, especially after the sponge mattress on the boat.

That afternoon, we arranged our flights. Lindsay was heading home to New Zealand for a spell and the rest of us to Sydney. Tony would travel onto Rabaul, and John and I would head to Nelson Bay, NSW. So, the die was cast.

We did several pub-crawls of the city's nightclubs, and everywhere we went, I secretly hoped to catch just a glimpse of Blondie, but it was not to be.

The taxi took us to the Suva Airport for the short flight to Nadi International Airport. I was concerned that this piss-ant little plane would not be able to take us and all our scuba gear.

Leaving Suva was unceremonious. No one was here to see us off. Not Adam, not Sam, and sadly not even Blondie.

As we circled Suva, I looked out of the window trying to spot the *Scorpion*. An uncontrollable sadness swept over me, and tears rolled down my cheeks. I made a solemn promise should I ever fall into another meaningful relationship, I would try and be a better and more caring person.

Epilogue

Gold Price and Australian Gold-ownership Restrictions

Ahh, but to have a crystal ball... By late 1969, the price of gold had dropped to $35 an ounce. By 1973, it had risen to $106 an ounce. After the Banking Act was relaxed in 1976, the price of gold rocketed to $600 an ounce.

It was 30 January 1976 when the Australian government relaxed. Still, it did not fully repeal, Part IV of the Banking Act of 1959, which restricted residents the freedom to own, buy, and sell gold bullion.

Julie McVey (Blondie)

Watching Julie walking away with Sam, head bowed in the twilight past the Travelodge pool, is the lasting memory I have of her. That night was also the last time I ever saw or heard from her. She simply disappeared. (Authors note; I looked for her and the *Scorpion* in the early '80s when I worked out of the Australian High Commission, Suva. I did learn that the

Scorpion had ended up on a reef in 1972. I could find nothing about the Fat family and not a single word about Julie McVey)

Lindsay Hill

Lindsay went back to New Zealand to spend some time with his family. Somehow, he fell in with a yachty and ended up in Santo, Vanuatu where he jumped ship to work with Barry April and his crew on the *Pacific Dolphin*. Barry was working the *SS President Coolidge* at the time. Barry was a shrewd operator and ruthless competitor.

Tony Thomas

Tony returned to domestic life in Rabaul with Maureen. He picked up a position as workshop manager for a prominent Rabaul logging company. Tony also invested heavily in the property market, mainly in and around the Redland Bay area of Brisbane. The next time I heard from him was when he called me to say a Japanese submarine had been found in Three Islands Harbour, New Hanover.

John Clark

John, on the other hand, had nowhere to go, so I invited him to come and stay with us at Nelson Bay. John moved into a caravan at the back of our property and was very happy there. He bought a new Ford Mustang, a Harley Davidson, and many other expensive toys, including hunting rifles, knives, watches, and such. He would come back to New Guinea with me to work the submarine.

Simon Jaeger

I hung onto most of my cash. I did, however, buy a new, two-door VG Valiant 770 and also invested in a residential property close to Newcastle University.

The Suva experience had, to an extent, crushed my confidence with women, so I felt compelled to prove myself. I began to spend three or four days a week visiting night clubs in Newcastle and Sydney in search of women.

It was exhausting, I was sleeping all day, and out most of the night. It had its rewards, and there were many conquests, most of which I took to the nearest hotel for the night. None, however, measured up to Blondie.

In Newcastle, a new up-market nightclub opened called the Jolly Roger, and it quickly became the place to be seen. One night at 'JRs' I spotted two scantily dressed, gorgeous young women. The petite blond with teased hair down past her waist was spectacular, and I couldn't help but stare.

Over the coming days, every night at the club, I watched one guy after another get a frosty reception and rejected by the girls. I was beginning to wonder what the hell was wrong with these women. Were they gay? One night, the place was packed, and the blond and her girlfriend were there again. I was leaning against the wall watching the band when I noticed the blond get up and make her way through the crowd towards me. She stopped in front of me and looked me in the eyes, and, as cool as a cumber, said, 'Hi, you've been watching us for days. Why don't you ask my girlfriend out? What's wrong with you?'

I could not help but laugh. This girl had gumption, and above the noise shouted in her ear, 'I'm sorry, it's not your girlfriend I fancy, it's you.'

She smiled, took my hand and dragged me to their table. This was the beginning of a new relationship.

*   *   *

Three weeks later, I received a phone call from Tony in Rabaul, all excited. A pilot had spotted a submarine in shallow water near Three Islands Harbour, New Hanover, and he was holding a photo to prove it. Also, Julian Chow of North Coast Shipping was looking to sell the *MV Michael*. She was built by Halverson in Sydney and had a very slippery carvel hull and was 23 metres overall. She was powered by an economical 8L3 Gardner and capable of a comfortable nine knots.

A submarine, any submarine, was worth at least $100,000 to $150,000 in high-value, non-ferrous metals. I was excited. All of a sudden, my life had a purpose again. But, I was also in love, and the trouble was, she was fond of the finer things in life, and camping and boating were not on the list! I needed to put an extra spin on the 'Adventures in Paradise' story.

A week later, the three of us were seated in a modern Boeing 707 for our flight to Port Moresby and then on to Rabaul. As we taxied down the Kingsford Smith runway, Blondie's tearful words haunted me, 'Simon, you're a pirate, an adventurer, and you always will be an adventurer.'

END

Glossary of Terms

Units

Metric units are used throughout the book with Imperial units in brackets

Knot = I nautical mile per hour or 31 metres per minute (rounded)

1 nautical mile = 1852 metres or 1.15 statute miles (2024 yards)

1 metre = 3.28 ft

Boat Terminology

Stern: the back part of a ship

Amidships: in the middle part of a ship

Beam: the widest part of a vessel from one side to the other

Berth: also commonly referred to as 'bunk', is a bed on a ship

Bilge: the bottom part of a boat from inside

Boom: also 'derrick', a long pole attached to the base of the mast

Bow: the front part of a ship

Bridge: the part of a ship from which it is controlled

Bulwarks: the sides of a ship above the deck

Cabin: a private room on a ship for a passenger or crew

Deck: the outside top part of a ship that you can walk on

Curbing Block: the timber on a jetty that stops things from rolling off

Fender: a piece of rope or a tyre that protects the side of a boat

Galley: the kitchen on a boat

Gunwale: the upper edge of the side of a boat, (like a bumper bar)

Hawsepipe: the hole in the vessel's bow which the anchor chain passes

Helm: a wheel used to steer a ship

Helmsman: a person who steers a ship

Hold: the area in a ship that is used for goods, vehicles, or bags

Hull: the part of a ship or boat that floats on the water

Keel: a long piece of wood or metal along the bottom of a boat

Mast: a tall pole that the sails hang from on or a cargo boom

Masthead: the top of the mast

Nautical mile: A unit of length corresponding approximately to one minute of arc of latitude along any meridian arc. By international agreement, it is 1,852 metres (about 6,076 feet).

Poopdeck: the higher part ship (usually on top of the

bridge)

Portside: the left side of a ship when you are looking forwards

Saloon: a space on a ship where passengers can sit together and talk

Starboard: the right side, as seen looking towards the front of a ship

Topside: on or relating to the deck of a ship

Wheelhouse: a small room where the helm and other controls are

Contact Information

You may contact the author directly at:

Fritz Herscheid
258 Aumuller St
Cairns, Qld 4870

Email: fritzherscheid@gmail.com

Website

Those wishing to leave comments on or engage in discussions about this book and its contents may do so at:

www.salvagepirate.com

Amazon.com

If you purchased *Rabaul and the* Hakkai Maru *Treasure* from *Amazon.com* or have an *Amazon.com* account, please go there and give this book a rating of one to five stars. You may also write a review or leave any comments you feel appropriate. This will be of benefit not only to the author but also to prospective readers.

About the Author

Adventure has always been a constant companion for Fritz Herscheid, and with his roguish charm, he has always attracted people from all walks of life to participate in his adventures.

At the age of nineteen, he completed a five-year apprenticeship in automotive engineering. Later while working in Rabaul, New Guinea, he discovered the excitement and lucrative business of marine salvage.

He studied all aspects of salvage and the use of nitro-glycerine-based explosives and military ordinance, and soon became an expert. Fritz went on to become a qualified small ship's captain and a Commonwealth-certified commercial diver.

Later, as he mellowed with age, a long stint with the Australian Department of Foreign affairs as a commercial adviser to the Pacific region prepared him for his role as a business broker. Brokering was financially rewarding and enabled him to travel the globe diving, researching shipwrecks, and writing stories about his experiences.

His biography, *The Last New Guinea Salvage Pirate*, is a testament to his exploits and many successes. With a lifetime of shipwreck research and deep-diving exploits, and his audacious use of explosives, he is today recognised as one of Australia's great diving legends.

www.ingramcontent.com/pod-product-compliance
Lightning Source LLC
Chambersburg PA
CBHW050304030726
47505CB00003B/569